Praise for *After Darkness*

'... it is hard not to think of another major Australian novel of recent months, Richard Flanagan's superb *The Narrow Road to the Deep North*. While Piper's book rhymes with Flanagan's account of human misery in the prison camps of the Thai-Burma railway, viewed from the perspective of an Australian surgeon, it is a very different work. Piper is less concerned with war as a subject, a dark force at loose in history, than she is with a single individual trapped in those interregnums of reason and virtue.' —Geordie Williamson, *Weekend Australian*

'... [Piper's] mastery of the craft, and willingness to unravel the story at her pace, in a unique way ... She poses important questions, not only about what it means to be Australian, but, more poignantly, what it means to be human, regardless of time, place, or government policy.' —Laurie Steed, *Australian Book Review*

'Piper's calm, polished fictional style makes the factual horrors she reveals the more shocking.' —Alison Broinowski, *Canberra Times*

'[Piper's research] lends credibility to a story that centres on the importance of truly living while alive.' —*Good Reading*

'The biggest theme of the book, however, and the one most relevant to us now, is the conflict every individual faces between what they really believe is right, deep within themselves, and what is "right" according to tradition, promises made to others, or the norms of the day. In this sense, *After Darkness* is anything but a historical novel.' —David Messer, *The Saturday Age*

'Careful, conscientious, conflicted Ibaraki is an achingly sad character whose complexities stay with the reader long after this absorbing novel comes to its plangent conclusion.' —*Adelaide Advertiser*

'... reminds us that there are two sides to every war and that history never ceases to be written.' —Stephen Romei, *The Australian*

Christine Piper's short fiction has been published in *Seizure, SWAMP* and *Things That Are Found in Trees and Other Stories*. She won the 2014 Calibre Prize for an Outstanding Essay and was the 2013 Alice Hayes writing fellow at Ragdale in the United States. Christine has studied creative writing at Macquarie University, the Iowa Writers' Workshop and the University of Technology, Sydney, where she wrote a version of this novel as part of her doctoral degree. She has also worked as a magazine editor and writer for more than a decade. Born in South Korea in 1979 to an Australian father and a Japanese mother, Christine moved to Australia when she was one. She has previously taught English and studied Japanese in Japan, and currently lives in New York with her husband. The winner of *The Australian*/Vogel's Literary Award 2014, *After Darkness* is Christine Piper's first novel. It was also shortlisted for the Readings New Australian Writing Award 2014.

www.christinepiper.com

For Kris

The sun spread on the horizon, bleeding colour like a broken yolk. In the growing light, I watched the details of the landscape emerge. The leaves of the eucalypts became sharply defined. The ochre earth glowed.

The carriage creaked, continuing its gentle sway from side to side as we trundled further inland. I was used to the wide spaces of Broome, but this was a different sort of vastness: acres of sun-bleached pasture and crops that stretched away as far as the eye could see. Here and there, fat-bellied cows and horses pulled at the yellow grass. In the sweep of land before me, not a single person could be seen.

Sweat gathered on my back and the undersides of my thighs, making the seat cling. I reached out to unlatch the window and caught a glimpse of my reflection. Hollow, sleep-starved eyes. Black hair, unkempt and oily. The whisper of stubble on my chin. The last time I had showered was at the camp in Harvey, three days earlier. I hadn't realised the journey to South Australia would take so long. My buttocks were numb from hours of sitting. *Paraesthesia*, I thought, remembering the word from one of my textbooks.

I heard a rustling behind me as someone sifted through his belongings. I knew a few of the men in my carriage—those who'd accompanied me on the journey from Perth. I had met the others that morning at Adelaide central, where we had gathered so early that stars were visible in the sky. Guards surrounded us, rifles strapped to their shoulders, eyes darting to all corners of the terminal. On the deserted platform, we formed a strange group of forty men, united only by our nationality. After bowing and whispering greetings to each other, we fell silent. Judging by the newcomers' deep tans and loose white clothing, I guessed they were from the Pacific Islands. At Harvey Camp, I had met many Japanese from New Caledonia who told me they had moved there decades ago to work in nickel mines.

After we had waited half an hour, a train chugged into view. Japanese faces peered at us through the windows of the carriages. There must have been at least a hundred men inside. The guards corralled us into an empty carriage and then, with a loud hiss and billows of white steam, we set off, leaving the silhouettes of city buildings behind.

As the light grew stronger, I began to relax. Watching the peaceful countryside put me at ease. An old man sat in the seat opposite me. Since our departure, we hadn't exchanged a word. I stole a glance at him as he stared out the window. Wrinkles creased the skin around his eyes like wet paper. One of the soldiers standing at the end of our carriage began whistling a cheerful tune. Two people near me were murmuring. I caught fragments of their conversation. They spoke with an accent I couldn't place.

'. . . soldiers here are much kinder. Did you see one of them offered me a cigarette?'

'Maybe our next camp will be as nice and clean as this train.'

I settled back in my seat, enjoying the breeze on my face. As we turned into a bend, I glimpsed the contours of a wide river, its surface glittering white. Dead trees haunted its edges, their limbs stretching skywards, as if begging for forgiveness.

The train began to slow as we approached the outskirts of a town. Farmland gave way to wide, dusty streets. The river coursed ahead of us, just out of reach. We pulled into a train station, stopping with a jolt at the platform. 'Murray Bridge' the sign read. A woman and small girl were sitting on a bench on the platform facing our carriage. The girl was about three—my niece's age when I'd last seen her—fair-skinned and chubby, with brown curls pulled into bunches on either side of her head. Seeing us, her eyes flashed. She tugged her mother's arm and pointed at us. The woman stared straight ahead. We were at the station less than a minute when the whistle blew. As the train lurched forward, the woman grabbed her daughter's hand and dragged her towards our carriage. She came so close I could see a mole above her lip. She spat. A glob landed on the window in front of my face.

'Bloody Japs!' she said, shaking her fist.

The train groaned as it moved away. The woman became smaller till she was no more than a pale slip, but I could still see her face. Eyes narrowed, mouth tight—her features twisted with hate.

The train reached Barmera at six o'clock that evening. Despite the late hour, the sun beat down, casting everything in a copper light. Dust floated in the air. Aside from the soldiers waiting to escort us to camp, there wasn't a soul around. A wide dirt road stretched ahead of us, framed on either side by swathes of green farmland. In the distance, the slate-grey roof and white walls of a cottage stood out among the greenery; the cottage's open windows were the only sign of habitation.

Four soldiers stood on the platform, plus two on horseback who waited on the track. They wore the same uniform as those who'd guarded us on the train, but everything else about them was different: the way they rested the butts of their rifles on the ground, their craggy faces and easy grins. 'Next stop, Loveday!' one of them yelled, motioning for us to follow the path.

On the train I'd pitied the other men with their scant belongings, but on the three-mile walk to camp, I envied them. As we followed the track, I listened to their conversation. 'How hot will it be in the middle of the day?' one wondered. 'It can't be worse than the ship. At least we have fresh air here,' said another.

The soldiers chatted to each other, and every so often they thrust their hands into the grapevines growing on either side of the path and pulled out bunches of ripe fruit.

Burdened with my luggage, I fell to the back, where the older members of our group were walking. A guard on horseback brought up the rear. I was wondering whether I could abandon one of my suitcases when I heard a cry and a scuffle behind me. One of the men from New Caledonia was on his hands and knees, his head almost touching the ground. I dropped my bags and ran to him. His face was pale and his pupils were dilated, so I coaxed him to lie down.

The guard on horseback called for the others to halt, and a crowd gathered around us. 'Christ, he looks like death,' said the guard.

I pressed my hand to the man's forehead. He was burning.

'How long have you had a fever?' I asked him. He looked at me but said nothing. I asked him again.

'He doesn't speak Japanese, only French,' said someone in the crowd. A slight man with hollow cheeks stepped forward. 'He was on the ship with me.'

'What's the matter with him?'

The man shrugged. 'Probably ill from the ship. They gave us very little to eat—only one meal a day. Even I got sick. We weren't allowed to go on deck. Many died, especially the older ones like him.'

'He's weak,' I told the guard in English. 'I don't think he can walk. Is there something to carry him on—a stretcher?'

'Nah, we've got one at headquarters, but that'll take too long. He doesn't look like he'll last another hour . . . Hey, Jack!'

The guard at the front of the group turned his horse around.

'I have to take this one to hospital. Can't have one cark it already. Can you give us a hand?'

One of the guards and I eased the man up to standing, but we needed the help of several others to get him into the saddle. He was so feeble he could barely sit up, so we broke off vines to wrap around his body and secure him to the guard. They headed towards camp, silhouetted against the darkening sky. We resumed our walk and before long a white glow appeared on the horizon.

'Is that the camp? Loveday?' I asked the guard nearest to me.

'Yep, that's it,' he said. 'It's always lit up like that at night. Bright as daylight.'

I struggled along at the back of the group, stopping to adjust my load from time to time. By the time we reached camp, almost an hour later, my hands were blistered and weeping. We were told to line up outside a concrete building. Then, one by one, we were called by name to enter.

Inside, three men sat behind desks strewn with paper. I approached one of the officers. He looked me up and down, stopping at the sight of my bags. '*Four* bags? Christ, did you bring your entire house?'

'My medical equipment—I thought . . .'

He lifted his eyebrows. 'Occupation?'

'Medical doctor.'

'A doctor? Here or overseas?'

'Both. In Japan I was a doctor, but more recently I was working at a hospital in Broome. Also at the camp in Harvey— they asked me to help. There were not enough doctors.'

'Is that why you got here later than the others from Broome?'

I nodded. 'The military doctor at Harvey, Dr Mackinnon, asked me to stay behind. The camp commander approved the extension.'

The officer turned his attention to the form on his desk. Still writing, he addressed me again. 'I see you're thirty-three. How long have you been here? Your English is good.'

'I came to Australia in 1938. It has been almost four years.'

The man beside me struggled to make himself understood. *Linen factory*, he said over and over in Japanese, referring to his occupation.

'Marital status?'

I was caught off-guard. I opened my mouth but nothing came out.

The officer looked up. 'Well, are you married or not? Got a wife?'

'I—ah . . . Yes, I am married.'

'Where is she? Here?'

'No. She's in Japan. In Tokyo. She's never been to Australia.'

He looked as if he was about to ask something further, but then nodded briskly and returned to his notes. After a while, he paused, tapping one end of his pen on the desk.

'I'm putting you in Camp 14C, where most of the other men from Broome are. But you can't take any of this stuff with you.' He motioned to my open suitcase. 'Scalpels, scissors—it's far too dangerous with some of the other internees. We'll put it in a safety deposit box along with your valuables.'

Before we were allowed to enter the camp, we were subject to a medical examination. Although I knew what to expect—I'd carried out the same procedure on hundreds of new internees at Harvey—I wasn't prepared for the indignity of being probed while naked. The doctor's long, thin fingers prodded me with surprising force while he dictated the condition of my lungs, heart, hair, teeth and genitals to his assistant in a voice louder than seemed necessary. He met my gaze only once, when I mentioned that I was a physician, too. By the time I'd been examined, it was almost midnight and many of the others had already entered camp.

I joined the remainder standing beneath the floodlights outside the entrance to camp. Everything appeared too bright and too crisp. Even the whispers of my companions were amplified in the stillness of the night.

'They're watching us now, aren't they? From that tower?'

The nearest guard tower was twenty feet away, just behind the ring of floodlights. I squinted at the enclosure at the top of the tower. The barrel of a mounted machine gun jutted out against the sky.

'They're always watching us,' another man said. 'When we're eating, sleeping and shitting. They have to. And even if they aren't watching us, they want us to think they are.'

'Will they shoot us?' the first man said.

'Only if we try to escape.'

An officer strode down the incline towards us, his feet kicking up small clouds of dust. 'Ready to enter?' His voice boomed across the landscape. His face was red and shiny, as if he'd just emerged from a hot shower. 'Thirty-two of you are in 14B and the rest are in 14C. All in 14B raise your hand.' There was confusion around me, as many of the men didn't speak English. '14B. Yes?' The guard said more slowly, raising his own hand to demonstrate. 'Right, you lot go first. Tell me your name before you enter the gate. *Your name.*' He pointed at the clipboard he held in one hand, then signalled for the guard standing at the gate to unlock it.

We farewelled the men leaving us. They were mostly Formosans and New Caledonians. Although I'd only been with them a day, I felt a strong kinship with them, having travelled such a long distance together. The old man who'd sat opposite me on the train was among them. He smiled at me before lining up to enter the rectangular wire enclosure. I never found out his name.

After checking off their names, the officer locked the gate after them. 'Say goodbye to freedom,' he said under his breath.

Several minutes passed before it was our turn to enter the gate. We squeezed into the space, which was just larger than an army truck, jostling and bumping each other. A wooden beam cut into the small of my back. I wondered how long we'd be kept like this, but the guard behind us called, 'All in!' and after a few moments a second guard opened the door on the other side. We spilled out onto a dirt road wide enough for four trucks to pass each other. It seemed to go on forever.

'Welcome to Loveday Camp 14,' said the second guard. 'That's the birdcage gate. There's another one like it on the other side. You'll get used to them soon enough.'

We followed him down the road that bisected camp, forming a procession of forty-odd men.

'This is called Broadway, because of all the bright lights,' the guard said, indicating the road. A wire fence ran along both sides. He pointed to a door built into the fence on our left. 'That's the entrance to 14B. They're your neighbours. The entrance to your compound's at the other end.'

He began to whistle. Although the melody was cheerful, hearing it in that empty space filled me with sorrow.

'Hey, look over there,' the man beside me whispered.

To our right, thirty feet away, a figure stood on the other side of the fence. An Occidental man in a light-coloured shirt and pants stared at us with dispassion, the way one would watch cars passing on the street. Although he probably meant no harm, his ghostly appearance perturbed me and I dared not look again.

We passed a juncture where the road intersected a narrower track about fifteen feet wide that marked the start of the two other compounds.

'This small road that cuts across the middle is what we call the Race. And this is your camp, 14C,' the guard said, indicating the fence on his left. 'But we haven't made it to the entrance yet.'

The low line of buildings beyond the fence appeared bleak in the unnatural light. The guard stopped whistling as we neared the end of the road. 'Anyone there?' he called into the space on the other side of the internal fence.

'Yes,' a voice responded from some distance away. Footsteps moved towards us. The guard unlocked the gate to the compound and we filed inside. Three men stood before us.

'Welcome to Camp 14C,' said the tallest of the men. The skin at his jaw was pulled tight. His round, wire-rimmed glasses reflected the glare of the floodlights. I self-consciously touched a hand to my head at the sight of his slick, neatly parted hair and unwrinkled clothes. 'My name is Mori. I'm the mayor of this compound. Together with my colleagues I am responsible for maintaining order and ensuring all internees are treated fairly.' He used the formal language of a native Tokyoite—words I hadn't heard for years. 'This is my deputy, Mr Yamada.' He gestured to the man next to him, who had a broad, suntanned face and close-cropped grey hair. Mr Yamada nodded and smiled. 'And the secretary, Mr Hoshi.' The third man bowed deeply, his paunch pressing against the waistband of his trousers. Sweat shone on his balding pate. 'If there's anything you need, please come to us.

'Usually we'd take you on a tour immediately after your arrival, but as it's very late we'll show you your tent and the latrines and ablutions block tonight, and the rest of camp tomorrow. Your group is being spread across eight tents. Could the men from Menaro come with me? The men from Batavia follow Mr Hoshi. And the one late arrival from Harvey Camp—from Broome, yes?' I nodded. 'Please follow Mr Yamada.'

Mr Yamada stepped forward and greeted me. 'You're Ibaraki-sensei, from Broome? Harada told me all about you. Here, let me take one of your bags. The tent's this way.' Before

I had a chance to protest he took one of the suitcases out of my hand.

'Harada? Harada Yasutaro's here?' I asked, relieved to know I had a friend among the camp population. Harada was the vice-president of Broome's Japanese Association. When we'd said goodbye at Harvey Camp, I wasn't sure whether we'd see each other again.

'Yes, but he's in a different row of tents. I'll show you tomorrow. We were going to put you with him and some of the divers from Broome, but when we found out you were a doctor . . .' Yamada smiled. 'We thought you might prefer to stay in my tent. You'll like everyone in there. It's a shame you didn't arrive two weeks ago with all the others. We appointed the executive committee last week. We could have done with another educated man such as you.'

We walked along the lines of tents, then stopped near the middle of a row.

'This is our tent: row eight, number twelve,' Yamada whispered, so as not to wake the others. 'I've already made your bed. Drop your luggage and change your clothes if you'd like, then I'll show you the latrines. I'll wait for you at the end of the row.'

I set down my suitcases and sorted through my belongings, feeling for my nightclothes and toothbrush. I winced as my blistered hands knocked against something hard. I heard the sigh of breath from inside the tent. A rustle as somebody stirred. I was touched by Yamada's kindness in welcoming me to his tent, especially since I was a stranger to him. I looked up at the heavens and silently said a prayer of thanks. The stars were faint pinpricks beyond the glare of lights.

The next morning I woke early. Light filtered through the canvas opening. It must have been no later than six, but the day was already full of the promise of heat. A warm breeze teased the edges of the tent. A fly circled above me in lazy arcs. My neck and back were damp against the bedsheets. The rise and fall of the breath of the men around me grew louder, filling my ears. I raised my head and sweat trickled down my neck. My six companions slept on, apparently unconcerned by the gathering heat.

In Broome, on Sundays, I would rise at five o'clock and walk for two hours along the shore of the bay, weaving between the pink-red sand and the spiky fringe of grass that skirted it. The sun would burst from the horizon in an orange haze, slowly bringing the sand, the grass and the sea into sharp definition. Those walks always cleared my head and provided me with a calmness with which to begin the week.

I crept to the doorway of the tent and looked out. In the bleak morning light, the landscape appeared completely different to the previous night. Rows and rows of khaki tents stretched away from me. Beyond them, the iron roofs of the mess halls were clustered next to the internal road we'd walked down last night. Stepping out of the tent, I turned to face the outer fence. Between the last line of tents and the perimeter fence was a dusty expanse, littered with pebbles and clumps of stubborn grass. Beyond the barbed-wire fence, dirt, grass and scrub continued in flat eternity.

I walked towards the latrines in the northwest corner of the compound, passing a small galvanised-iron shed with padlocked shutters. Yamada had pointed it out to me last night. 'You can buy cigarettes, razors and other supplies here,' he'd said.

I reached the concrete latrines and ablutions blocks, easily identifiable by their stench. Following the path that hugged the fence, I wandered past two mess halls and a kitchen. The air was alive with the clink of metal pots and bowls as breakfast was being prepared. The rich smell of fried butter greeted me. I looked at my watch. It was just past six. Breakfast wouldn't be served for another hour.

I slipped back in between the rows of tents, catching sight of the men inside, still prostrate on their mattresses, sheets crumpled beside them. I continued until I'd reached the fence that faced the world beyond the camp. From what I'd gathered, our camp formed one section of a roughly circular larger camp that had been divided into quadrants. As well as the Japanese in 14B and 14C, there were Italians and Germans in the other two compounds. A fenced-off divide separated each of the four camps, so although we could see each other, we had limited contact.

The barbed-wire fence stood before me, steel tips dull against the brightening sky. A stretch of cleared land surrounded the camp like a moat. At one spot near the edge of the clearing a stand of tall red gums stood like sentinels. Bark peeled from their trunks like blistered skin.

I'd received a letter from my mother the week before I'd left Harvey. In the months before my arrest she had urged me to return to Japan. But I told her I had to stay in Broome to honour my contract. In truth, the contract had already expired—I wasn't ready to go back to Japan.

'Dear Tomokazu,' my mother's letter had begun. 'Snow has fallen steadily this week. Although the days are getting longer, the ice on the awnings grows heavier each day. Have you been well? I am in good health.'

Mother informed me she saw my sister, Megumi, and her two children almost every day. She'd visited the family graves early in the new year and said everything was in order.

'Your younger brother, Nobuhiro,' began the next sentence, but the rest of the paragraph had been neatly cut from the paper by the censors, forming a rectangle of empty space. The void seemed to have a force of its own, drawing the meaning of the words into it.

The letter ended with: 'Please take good care of yourself. I will write again when I have more time. From, Mother.'

I was anxious to know what had become of my brother, who was in the navy and, when I'd last heard, had been sent to China. Although there were ten years between us, we were close. I often played with him in the fields at the back of our house. He'd planned to study medicine like me, but that changed when the war began. The letter didn't mention my wife. My mother used to see the Sasakis from time to time, but I'd heard nothing of them in the past year.

Trying to calm my mind, I continued walking along the fence. I was surprised to discover a Buddhist altar in the space between the last row of tents and the outside fence. It was a simple structure, no more than shoulder high. It was made from unpainted timber; the roof was cracked and faded from the elements. Two rough-hewn doors splayed open, revealing a miniature scroll with the words 'Eternal Happiness'.

In Japan, I would have lit a stick of incense at such a time. But here, so many miles from home, all I could do was kneel before the altar and close my eyes.

I sensed a movement to my left and saw a figure come to stillness about thirty feet away. As I stared at him, I realised he was half-caste. The eyes were too round and the nose too broad for a Japanese. The young man had a towel folded over his shoulder, soap in one hand—straight-backed and passive-faced, like a soldier on parade. Our eyes met and he nodded almost imperceptibly before continuing on his way.

I stepped into the mess hall and was assaulted by a barrage of voices, clangs and scrapes. The room thrummed with the sound of several hundred men eating breakfast. I longed for the silence of the early morning, when hardly a soul had been awake.

'Meat?' Yamada offered me a tray piled high with thick slices of something dark brown. 'I think it's mutton. Always mutton. Not to my taste, but it keeps me going till lunch.'

The smell of mutton in the morning made me feel weak, but I took a sliver, not wanting to appear ungrateful. Yamada poured me a cup of tea and offered me the first helping of oatmeal, toast, butter and jam. He introduced me to the other people at our table, who were also in our tent. I discovered that three of them had worked with Yamada at a rubber production company in Sumatra. Yamada was the director. He had been sent there from Japan eight years earlier to start up the business. Watanabe, the fifty-something, thick-set man who sat opposite me, was Yamada's deputy. Next to him was the accountant, Ishikawa, and next to Yamada was a man named Maeda, who was the operations manager. At the other end of the table was a dentist who was a few years older than me and also from Sumatra, and an elderly man from Borneo whose name I didn't catch. Yamada leaned towards me.

'We worked hard, but business was tough. Especially after the Dutch froze our assets—those bastards. I'll never forgive them for what they did to us.' As he recalled the Dutch embargo on Japanese trade, his face darkened. For a moment I was worried he would become enraged. I wondered if something had happened on the ship to make him so bitter, but just as quickly, he brightened. 'What about you, sensei? Which university did you go to? Tokyo or Kyoto?'

'Tokyo.'

'Ah, the very best.' He turned to the man on his other side. 'Did you hear? He went to Tokyo.'

In between mouthfuls, I glanced at nearby tables, looking for my friend Harada. Raised voices cut through the din in the hall. I paused, knife and fork raised, trying to make out a conversation behind me. I caught the long, flat vowels of a native English speaker.

'. . . took two pieces—same as everybody else. If you've got a problem with it, why don't you ask that fella over there. Seen *him* take more than his fair share.'

The second speaker's voice was muffled, but the few words I heard were enough to tell me that English was not his first language.

I turned around in my seat. It took me a few moments to locate the men. The first was sitting at a table two rows behind me. He had a tanned complexion typical of many of the divers I'd known in Broome, but there was something distinctly un-Japanese about his person. He had a strong jaw and powerful, sloping shoulders that seemed to dwarf the rest of his body. I sensed he was a living portrait of someone I knew—the photographic ghost-image of a friend.

He leaned forward in his chair, addressing the man opposite him whose face I couldn't see. 'You're telling me I took two *big* pieces? Jesus Christ. Hey, Charlie, would you listen to this?' His companion was similarly broad and muscular, but had fair skin and wavy hair that fell over one eye. I recognised him as the half-caste I'd seen on my morning walk. As I glanced at the others on the table, I noticed several who appeared to be mixed race.

'He reckons I took more than my fair share because I took two *big* pieces. As if counting how many pieces I take isn't enough, they've also got an eye on the size of the meat we take. Next they'll be counting how many pieces of toilet paper we use.'

Charlie shook his head. 'Not worth getting worked up about it, Johnny. Can't win this one.' His voice was flat.

I realised who the first speaker was: Johnny Chang. He'd been a well-known personality in Broome, a young businessman who'd run a noodle shop in Japtown then started up a taxi business, the first of its kind in town. I had a clear mental picture of him standing on the corner of Short Street and Dampier Terrace, one arm draped over the open door of his parked car and the other fanning his face with a folded paper while he chatted to people in the street. He was known to everybody and moved among the Japanese, Chinese, native and even white population with ease. His father was a Chinese immigrant who'd made a modest fortune on the goldfields and moved to Broome to start a restaurant, eventually marrying the Japanese daughter of a laundry owner.

It was strange I hadn't recognised Johnny straight away. Perhaps it was the difference in his attitude; in Broome, he'd always been easygoing, but here it was as if he were another man.

'What right have you got to tell us what to do, anyway? Acting like you own the place, with your so-called mayor who doesn't even follow his own bloody rules.' Johnny's voice filled the crowded hall. 'Yeah, that's right, him . . .' Johnny jabbed a finger towards Mayor Mori, who was sitting a few tables away. 'He gets all sorts of special treatment. Two or three helpings of food, first in line to use the showers, no cleaning duties. Don't think I haven't noticed.'

Mori continued to eat, delicately spearing a piece of mutton with his fork and bringing it to his mouth. His expression was difficult to read.

Yamada hissed to Watanabe across the table, 'That half-caste—what's his name? Chang? The troublemaker. He needs to watch himself. He's an embarrassment to our compound. He's upset many people already.'

I wondered whether I should mention to Yamada my Broome connection to Johnny Chang. But we'd never been intimately acquainted, so I kept quiet.

Yamada turned to me. 'He thinks he's better than everyone else. When I rostered his tent to clean the latrines, he initially refused to do it. Last week he forced his way into the executive meeting when we were in session. Said he'd been waiting to use the recreation tent. We told him the meeting was more important, but even then he wouldn't leave. He has no respect for authority—no respect for our ways. None of them do.' Yamada flicked his hand towards Johnny's table with an expression of disgust.

I was surprised by the news of Johnny's antisocial behaviour. As far as I knew, Johnny had had little trouble with the authorities in Broome. He was friendly with the constables, some of whom he'd known for years.

'You *haafu* fools don't deserve the Japanese blood in you!' said an old man at the mayor's table, speaking in Japanese.

Johnny thumped the table and stood up. 'You bloody racist! I know what you just said. Think I don't know what *haafu* means? You fucking Emperor-worshipping pig—'

Charlie put his hand on Johnny's shoulder, trying to quieten him. It's not worth it, he kept saying, but Johnny shrugged off his friend.'Don't tell me what to do like the rest of these arseholes,' he said.

'Chinese bastard!' someone cried. The remark sparked rage within Johnny. He knocked back his chair and began shouting profanity. I couldn't hear much of what he said because others were calling for him to get out. *'Dete ike!' 'Usero!'* Yamada was one of the loudest, bellowing in my ear. Johnny shoved his table so hard he jolted the people on the other side. I heard gasps. Someone at a nearby table stood up.

'Enough!' I realised it was the mayor who was standing. The room fell silent. 'You go now. Or I report you to Major Locke. You get detention one week.' Mori spoke in clear English.

'You want me to leave? You're a bunch of stinking racists, you know that? I can't get far enough away from you.'

No one said a word as he stormed out of the room, kicking an empty seat at the mayor's table. I heard the sigh of my own breath. My heartbeat filled my ears. But only a few seconds later, the cloud of noise rose again. The screech of cutlery. Shrill voices. The banging of plates.

I looked at the food in front of me. White specks of lard flecked the meat on my plate. The mutton had turned cold.

After breakfast, Yamada led me to my old friend Harada's tent. Inside the tent, figures ducked and weaved as the inhabitants folded bedding, sorted through belongings and swept the ground.

Although I'd rarely socialised with the divers in Broome, when the men saw me, they stopped what they were doing and bowed in greeting. 'Doctor, you made it! I'm so glad to see you,' said one young diver from Wakayama whose name escaped me. I was moved by his warmth. I'd treated him in the hospital once, although I couldn't recall what for. Sister Bernice would know.

'Ibaraki-sensei, is that you?' Harada was crouched next to an open suitcase on the floor. Seeing his face, shiny with perspiration, brought to mind those nights in Broome we'd spent drinking, playing mahjong, faces gleaming above steaming bowls of soup. But when Harada stood up, I was shocked to see how thin he'd become in the few weeks since I'd last seen him.

He walked towards me and gripped my shoulder in an awkward embrace. 'When did you arrive?'

'Just last night,' I said.

'You came from Harvey?'

'Yes. Another military doctor arrived last week, so they sent me here. But look at you; you've lost so much weight.' His collarbones felt like they could snap beneath the pressure of my hand. His skin was hot.

'It's nothing,' he said, pushing away my arm. 'I don't like the food here.'

'Has the doctor seen you?'

'Yes, yes. Me and five hundred other men.'

Behind him, one of the divers who'd been listening to our conversation looked at me and shook his head. I wondered what he meant by that gesture, but I didn't have a chance to find out as someone shouted nearby, a repeated word, taken up by a chorus of people as it was passed from tent to tent. 'Headcount!'

'We have to go,' Harada said. 'Headcount near the fence. Come, I'll show you.' He packed the last of his belongings into his suitcase and closed the lid.

We followed the stream of people walking towards the fence that faced the internal road. The strength of the sun seemed to have doubled in the short time I'd been inside the tent. Even the air was hot, burning my throat whenever I took a breath.

'It's not like Broome, is it?' I said, one hand shielding my eyes.

'No. It's a long way from Broome,' Harada said, gazing at the rows of canvas tents, the wire fence and the flat, dusty expanse beyond. He coughed. 'Think this is hot? It was worse two weeks ago. Forty-three degrees. Even hotter in the tents. Felt like hell on earth.' He gasped between every few words, as if the effort of talking and walking was too much.

When we neared the fence, Harada and I separated to join our respective rows. Yamada beckoned for me to stand in line next to him. I regretted not having had the foresight to bring a hat as many of the men around me had done. We sweltered in the gathering heat as a procession of four army personnel entered the camp from the gate to our right.

'Start the count!' said the officer at the front of the line, and the others peeled away to walk between the rows, counting as they went. The remaining officer stared at each internee in the first row in turn. He was a stout man, with a girth that matched his thick arms and legs. He wore long khaki trousers, a white shirt with the sleeves rolled to his elbows and a khaki peaked hat, whose brim plunged his eyes into shadow. His mouth was a perfectly still line. In his right hand he held a riding crop.

The officers who'd been counting reassembled at the front and compared numbers.

'All present?' the head officer asked.

'All present, sir,' they replied.

The head officer stepped forward and addressed us. 'It has come to my attention that some of you are not observing protocol regarding cleanliness. Belongings in tents must be neat at all times, and beds must be made each day. Failure to do so will result in severe reprimand, and repeat offenders will be detained with a view to punishment. To facilitate this, from this time forward we will conduct surprise inspections of tents and other areas.'

Yamada groaned. 'Just what we need. Major Locke going through our belongings.'

I squinted against the glare, praying the major would stop speaking and we could go back to our tents. He droned on and on. I noticed some of the men around me slump, blinking in incomprehension. Even I, who had a good grasp of English, had trouble following his speech. I wondered why there was no interpreter. My nostrils felt as if they were on fire.

Several rows behind me, I heard a thud. I turned around, but couldn't see past the other men. I heard urgent whispers.

'. . . imperative that you observe these rules as—' Major Locke broke off. 'Silence down the back! What's going on?' He turned to the young officer next to him. 'McCubbin, see what's the matter, will you?'

McCubbin jogged to the back of the group. I saw a flash of blond hair as he passed. A moment later he called back, 'Someone's collapsed, sir. Must be the heat.'

Yamada turned to me. 'Sensei, you should go.'

I pushed my way through the lines until I saw a circle of backs surrounding someone on the ground.

'I am a doctor. Can I help?'

When the men stepped back to make room for me I recognised the man on the ground.

'Harada!' I dropped to his side. 'Harada, it's me, Ibaraki. Can you hear me?'

His body was covered in sweat. His eyes were half-closed. I pulled up his lids and his eyeballs rolled.

I checked Harada's pulse. It was racing. The young officer gave me a canteen of water and I pressed it to Harada's lips.

'Heat exhaustion?' McCubbin asked, crouching beside me.

'I don't think so. He's sweating too much. I think it's something else. He should go to hospital.'

'I'll get a stretcher.'

I asked some of the men to shelter Harada from the sun while we waited for the officer to return. Harada drifted in and out of consciousness, sometimes opening his eyes to look at me. Each time his head lolled to one side I checked his pulse again.

At last the young officer appeared with a stretcher and another guard. The three of us eased Harada onto the canvas. He looked small, his feet not even reaching the end of the stretcher. McCubbin and the guard hoisted him up, and we walked slowly to the exit. Major Locke had resumed his talk about cleanliness.

'Hang on, he's not coming with us, is he?' the guard said to the officer, nodding at me.

'Please, I'm a doctor.' My throat tightened at the thought of leaving Harada in his precarious state. 'This man is very ill. If we delay any longer he might die. If something should happen on the way, I can help.'

McCubbin's face clouded. He looked back at Major Locke, who was still talking. 'Well, okay, then. I'll have to be on guard. Here, you take this end.'

I took the ends of the stretcher from him, careful not to jolt Harada. We crab-walked to the gate and onto Broadway. After shuffling along the internal road for several minutes, lurching beneath our load, we finally passed through the birdcage gate and emerged onto the track towards headquarters. My palms became slippery as the handles of the stretcher scraped against the blisters on my hands. I winced at the pain.

Despite my best efforts to keep a quick pace, I slowed under the load. McCubbin offered to take my end again. I tried to hide my injuries, but blood stained the handles.

'Christ—is that from you?' McCubbin stared at the crimson streaks.

'Yesterday, when I carried my suitcases from the station . . .'

'Geez, I wish you'd told me. I wouldn't have made you carry him.' He shook his head.

We passed a camp on our right, smaller than Camp 14. It was prettier, too, with shrubs and saplings shading the huts. A couple of Italians who were crouched by a garden near the fence, lifted their heads and watched us walk by. We continued in silence for a few minutes more, then the scattered buildings of headquarters came into view: a large concrete edifice that cast a long shadow on the earth, and several white-painted iron buildings skirted by flowerbeds. The hospital was one such structure, with a peaked roof and windows on all four sides.

Inside, standing screens divided the room into two wards: the beds nearest the door contained two ailing Australians, one asleep with a towel on his head and the other with a bandaged foot resting on a pillow. I assumed they were military personnel. From the beds beyond the screens, occasional coughs punctuated the silence.

The medical officer who had examined me the previous day stood at the foot of one of the Australians' beds. He wore a khaki shirt and shorts beneath his white coat. He looked up from his clipboard. 'Another one? What is it, the heat?'

'His pulse is very fast,' I said. 'He has a fever too. I do not think it is the heat.'

The physician glanced at me. 'You're the doctor I saw yesterday, aren't you?'

I nodded.

'Bring the patient into the internees' ward, then.' He indicated the back of the room. 'You too, doctor. You can help with the diagnosis.'

There were only two Caucasians among the ten or so patients in the internees' ward; the rest were Japanese. They stared dully as we manoeuvred Harada onto an empty bed.

The doctor checked Harada's pulse, temperature and eyes.

'Well, he definitely has a fever. How long's he been like this?' he asked.

'Almost half an hour,' I said.

'Has he had any water?'

'Yes, a little. A few mouthfuls.'

'What's his name?'

'Harada. Tsuguo. Or just Harada.'

25

'Harada? Can you hear me, Harada? Can you open your eyes?'
Harada turned his head away.

The doctor put his stethoscope to Harada's chest. 'Has he been coughing?' he asked.

'I was with him for only a few minutes, but I think so, yes.'

He continued to examine Harada, checking his glands and kidneys. After a minute he folded his stethoscope and returned it to his coat pocket.

'You're right, it's not the heat. This patient has TB. I'm surprised we didn't detect it when he first arrived. Of course, we've had hundreds of new internees in the past few weeks.'

Fever, chills, shortness of breath. I often saw cases of tuberculosis in Broome. Why hadn't I thought of that? My failure to detect the disease had probably allowed it to spread and worsen.

'George!' the doctor called out. Moments later the assistant who'd been present at my medical examination entered the room.

'Can you grab this internee's file?' The doctor turned to me. 'What was his name?'

'Harada. Tsuguo Harada,' I said.

'H-A-R-A-D-A?' the doctor asked.

'That's right. From 14C.'

'And what's your name?'

'Ibaraki. Tomokazu Ibaraki.'

'Dr Ibraki,' he said, mispronouncing it. 'I'm Dr Ashton. We could do with another doctor at camp. We just opened an infirmary in 14B. You'd also have to help the orderlies—handing out meals, that sort of thing. You wouldn't be paid much, but it beats sitting around doing nothing. I'm sure Major Locke will appreciate your language skills, too, as there's such a scarcity of Japanese-speaking personnel. So how does that sound?' He held out his hand. When I hesitated, he glanced down. His expression changed. 'Good Lord. Whatever happened to your hands?'

After Harada was given nourishment and allowed to rest, his condition became stable. In the afternoon, he was moved to the tuberculosis ward of the infirmary. I visited him the next day. The complex hugged the eastern corner of 14B, a stone's throw from the duty guard camp. As I approached, I could see the guards and officers through the fence arriving from headquarters in trucks or on horseback along the dusty road.

The three galvanised-iron buildings of the infirmary stood side by side, perhaps the largest structures in our camp. An enclosed walkway ran through the middle of the buildings, connecting them, and it was through this I entered, eventually finding my way along the dim corridor and past the other wards to where Harada was kept.

The TB ward was at the back of the complex and had a heavy curtain covering the doorway. Inside, the shutters were closed against the wind. A dozen patients occupied the room, the sigh of their breaths and gentle rise and fall of their chests the only signs they were alive. Harada lay in a bed close to the door, and when I stood beside him, his eyes fluttered open and he gave a brief smile.

'Feeling better?' I asked.

'As good as an old man can.' His voice was raspy and he paused to catch his breath.

Not wanting to tire him, I returned to my compound. I decided I would apply to work at the infirmary. I'd be able to monitor Harada, and I could think of no better use of my time at camp.

I mentioned the idea to Yamada after lunch, the midday sun bearing down on us as we walked back to our tent. With little shade at camp, there was no escape from the heat.

'Is that part of the voluntary paid labour scheme, where the Australian government pays you a shilling a day?' Yamada asked.

'I think so.' I mopped my brow with a handkerchief.

'We discussed it at the executive meeting last week. Some of the New Caledonians expressed interest in working in the vegetable gardens. While we don't oppose it, we don't want to work for the enemy just for pocket money. You can see how that presents a problem, can't you?'

I blinked. Yamada's expression was serious.

'But we also know boredom could lead to unrest in camp,' he continued, 'so we've approved the scheme, with the suggestion participants commit small acts of sabotage from time to time.'

'Acts of sabotage?'

'Pulling out plants, planting seedlings upside down, that sort of thing. Not so much that it's obvious, but a few disruptions here and there. But in your case, that would be impossible.' He laughed. 'Imagine! Deliberately making patients ill. No, your employment at the infirmary is for the good of the camp, so I'm sure Mori would find no problem in you working there. What's the matter, Doctor? Are you all right?'

At the mention of ill patients, I had suddenly felt weak. I pressed my fingertips to my eyelids. I saw blackened limbs and rotting flesh.

'Just the sun,' I said. 'I think I'm all right.'

At the start of my first shift, one of the orderlies greeted me inside the entrance to the infirmary. Stepping in from the sunlight, I took a moment to adjust to the gloom. A fan circled overhead, blowing air onto my face.

'Sensei, it's an honour to have you join our team,' the young man said, bowing deeply. His long, thin fingers fretted the sides of his trousers. His name was Shiobara and he was from Saitama prefecture, he told me, although he'd been a clerk at a lacquer factory in the Dutch East Indies the previous six years. I followed him along the walkway into the first building. Two wards of about sixty feet in length opened up on either side.

'These are the general internee wards—for fever, malaria, non-contagious infections and the like,' Shiobara explained.

A small desk and chair stood at the entrance of each ward. A stocky young man sat at one of the desks, cheek resting on his hand, eyes shut. His lids flew open when he heard us. He stood up and bowed several times, apologising for his sleepiness.

'This is Matsuda, from tent twenty-one,' Shiobara said. 'He's been working long hours. We all have.'

Light streamed through the open windows. About twenty beds lined the walls, more than half of which were occupied. The clean, spartan room, the metal beds and white sheets— even the patients who watched us in silence—in some ways felt like home. I couldn't help but think back to my first few months in Broome, when my senses were keen to the strangeness around me and everything appeared brighter, sharper and crisper, as if a veil had lifted.

We continued along the walkway, crossing into the middle building. An office and storage space opened up on one side. Among the cabinets, shelves crammed with books and odds and ends, chairs, pillows and piles of blankets was a space for the orderlies: an area big enough for a few mattresses, three chairs and a low table. This was where I would spend much of my time, and where I'd sleep if I was on the night shift. Although it wasn't much to look at, the evidence of an abandoned *go* game on the table gave it a homely feel.

Shiobara led me into the final building. The light dimmed. A curtain of thick white cloth covered the entrance to each ward.

'You already know the TB ward,' Shiobara said, nodding to his right. 'And this is the ward for pneumonia and other respiratory illnesses. The orderlies for these wards don't have to sit in the room due to the risk of infection.'

I followed Shiobara outside to a small one-room building near the entrance gate. The heavy aroma of frying fat reached me, and when we stepped into the dark room I heard it sizzle and pop. The dull thwack of a blade on wood stopped. Once my eyes adjusted, I saw a stout Occidental man in a white apron staring at me.

'This is Francesco, the hospital cook,' Shiobara said. 'He used to work in a restaurant. He makes all the meals for the patients, and for us, too.'

The cook looked at me and shrugged, then returned to chopping onions. Shiobara showed me where the trays, dishes and utensils were kept and where to wash them. As breakfast was about to be served, he demonstrated how to portion meals and loaves of bread. Two other orderlies entered the room, both from the Dutch East Indies. Together we carried the trays to our waiting charges.

Soon afterwards, Shiobara left me to return to camp. He'd worked the night shift and had hardly slept. I continued alone in my allocated ward for the rest of the day, asking the other orderlies for help from time to time. The work wasn't difficult but it required stamina—all day I shuttled meals, cleaned dishes, mopped the floor and changed bedpans, so that by the end of my shift my legs trembled with exhaustion. It brought to mind my hospital internship in Japan, where I'd spent much of my time cleaning up after the patients. Despite everything I had been through in the previous eight years, it seemed I had returned to the point at which I'd begun.

When I was young, I only ever wanted to be a doctor. I was singularly devoted to the profession. From my early teens, I kept a notebook with observations of symptoms displayed by ailing family members, to practise for the future. 'Temporary blindness in one eye. Pain in temples. Loss of balance,' read the entry on 17 July 1925, describing my father's sudden, mysterious illness a few weeks before he died.

In many ways, it was fortunate I was so inclined towards medicine, for my father was a doctor, and his father before him—as the eldest son, I was destined to follow their path. My younger brother might have been allowed to explore other careers, but never me. As a boy, I often came home with tailless lizards, five-legged beetles and other injured creatures with the hope of restoring their health. I recall finding a bulbul by the side of the road whose wing had been crushed and leg half-torn from its body. I picked it up and carried it home, feeling it shivering in the palm of my hand, its heart beating through its chest. Hours later, it died at the entrance to our house—my mother wouldn't let me take it inside—and I cried, thinking if only I were older and a doctor like my father, I could have saved it.

It was years before I realised that the ambitions of my childhood wouldn't eventuate—at least not in the way I'd imagined. It wasn't until sometime after I finished my studies and began interning at Tokyo Imperial University Hospital that it dawned on me how incapable I was—how incapable we all were. Medicine was not the noble, enlightened profession I'd envisaged. Patients still died; there was no secret cure. Greater men might be able to achieve more, but not me.

Around this time I received a letter from my former microbiology professor at Tokyo Imperial University. He informed me that a medical research unit was opening within the Army Medical College. The deputy head of the new unit, Major Kimura, was a former student of his, and was looking for diligent junior researchers.

'I know you want to practise medicine like your father, but research offers greater rewards for those at the top,' the professor wrote. 'In time, someone as focused as you could open up entirely new areas. This could be your opportunity to make a difference.'

In the subsequent weeks, his words stayed with me as I spent each day performing menial tasks at the whim of the doctors. If the letter had arrived a year later, when my internship was over and I had already accepted a position at a hospital, things might have turned out differently. But at that time, filled with the utter hopelessness of my work, I was desperate to do something else.

Major Kimura's office was located within the Army Medical College compound in Shinjuku. I walked there from the station, following a road that grew more isolated and leafier the further I went along it, until I saw the cluster of buildings at the top of a small rise. Following the instructions I had been given, I walked through the gate and followed the path to the back of the complex. Several handsome brick buildings surrounded by lush evergreens and hedges rose up on either side, giving me the impression that I was at an elite college in Europe. Now and then, I glimpsed a silhouette through a window but, aside from that, I saw few other people. I assumed that classes were in session and everyone was hard at work. I turned a corner and saw someone in military uniform striding ahead of me. But after a few more steps, he was gone.

I walked downhill for a few minutes, until I saw the guard booth at a fork in the path. I showed my letter from Kimura confirming the appointment, and after the guard checked his schedule, he directed me to a two-storey building at the end of the narrower walkway. The building was different to the others at the college: it was designed in the modern style, with a thick concrete exterior and a line of gleaming glass windows along all sides. The foyer was dimly lit, and carpeted with grey pile that gave way slightly with each step. Glass cabinets displayed photos of various army personnel, ministers and members of the imperial family. The receptionist told me to take a seat. I settled into one of the armchairs, the stiff leather sighing beneath me. After several minutes, I was directed to the second floor.

I had pictured Major Kimura as a version of my micro-biology professor: dishevelled with wild, unkempt hair. But he was nothing like that. He had a compact, well-defined frame.

I know that he was in his late forties, but he had the air of someone much older than that. From his carefully combed hair to the sheen of the buttons on his uniform, no detail was out of place. Despite his academic standing, I realised I had been wrong to imagine him to be like one of my other professors; he was every inch the military man.

Before I had finished bowing and introducing myself, Kimura called me forward and gestured to the chair on the other side of his desk. He held my documents in front of him in one hand, and with the other flicked through the layers. The stiff paper crackled, and I was embarrassed by their cheap quality.

'So, Ibaraki Tomokazu. Top in your class in anatomy and physiology . . . ah, and microbiology, too, I see. Good.'

He took the bundle in both hands, tapped the bottom edge once on the table and then laid the papers flat. He arranged his hands in a loose clasp on top of the pile. His fingernails were neatly kept: thin white crescents atop perfectly uniform pink ovals. I tried not to stare at them.

'Professor Endo says you were one of his best students. Coming from him, I know that is no small honour. You certainly have impressive academic results—they alone are reason enough for me to employ you.'

'Thank you, sir.'

'If I were merely looking to take you on as another junior doctor at the hospital, there would be no question—I would give you the job. But I am recruiting for a new research division, one that demands certain qualities in an employee. And these qualities I cannot determine from papers alone.' He tapped the bundle with the tips of his fingers. 'First, I want to know whether you will be a loyal employee; and, second, whether you will exercise discretion. Discretion, Ibaraki—do you understand?'

'Yes, sir, of course.'

'And how do you suggest I determine that from our meeting here?'

I lifted my eyes. His gaze was hollow. I opened my mouth, ready to declare my loyalty and discretion, but thought better of it. They would merely be words, and I felt that that was precisely what Kimura didn't want. After a few seconds, Kimura sighed and leaned back in his chair, turning his eyes towards the ceiling. It appeared my silence had disappointed him.

'How old are you, Ibaraki?' he asked. 'Twenty-four, twenty-five?'

'Twenty-six, sir.'

'Twenty-six?' he said sharply, his gaze snapping back to me.

'My father died when I was seventeen. I had to help my family.'

Kimura's lips twitched, but his expression did not change. 'So, you are twenty-six. I ask myself: what does a twenty-six-year-old know about loyalty and discretion? For most young men, not much. Maybe he is loyal to his family, maybe he has seen his father go to war, seen him come back changed. But discretion? Few at that age have had the chance to understand it—truly understand it, as it's not just about keeping a secret from one's friends. Discretion takes time to show itself. How will a person conduct himself in ten, twenty years' time? That's what I need to know. But for me, it is almost impossible to judge.'

The interview was not going well. I had hardly said anything, but I felt he had already formed an opinion of me from my appearance and from the papers on his desk, and I was powerless to change it. I thought about pointing out my loyalty to Endo in pursuing a career he had introduced me to, and somehow alluding to the discretion I had had to exercise in the wake of my father's death, when my family had suffered financially. But then I realised he was right—there was no use trying to prove myself. To attempt to prove I was discreet would itself be an act of indiscretion.

Kimura leaned forward. 'Ibaraki, why do you want to work for me?'

I straightened in the chair. I had prepared an answer to this question. It was my chance to redeem myself in his eyes.

'Since I was in my first year of university I have wanted to work for the Army Medical Hospital. Not only is it at the forefront of scientific developments, it would be an honour to serve His Imperial Majesty—'

He shook his head. 'No, no—you are telling me why you want to work for the army, not why you want to work for me.'

I was stumped. I had not thought of an answer as to why I wanted to work under Kimura personally. Flustered, I tried to frame a credible response. 'Well, because it is my dream to work under such an accomplished leader as you—to learn from your scientific rigour, and to follow your example.'

'Yes, that is what I thought.' His voice was soft. His hands, which had been clasped before him, now spread out flat on my papers in a gesture of finality. 'That will be all. If I offer you the position, you will hear from me within a month. If you don't receive a letter, you'll know you haven't been given the job.'

I was crestfallen. My answer hadn't pleased him. I tried to hide my disappointment as I thanked him for his time and said that it had been an honour to meet him. All the while,

I was worried about what I would say to my mother. I got up to leave.

'Wait.'

I stopped at the doorway and turned.

He was looking at one of my documents, frowning. 'Your father was Ibaraki Shuichiro? The surgeon at Tokyo Hospital?'

I nodded.

'I knew him. I worked for him when I was an intern. Why didn't you mention he was your father?' A change had come over his face. The hard expression of seconds before had opened with curiosity.

'I'm sorry, sir, I didn't want to be indiscreet.'

He looked thoughtful. His lips were pressed together, as if they held the germ of an idea. 'Well, then, as I said, you will hear from me within a month if I decide to offer you a position.' He dismissed me with a nod of his head.

Loveday
1942

The kerosene lamp coated everything in a dirty yellow light. The aluminium plates, bowls and saucepans took on a dark sheen. Even the men who washed, chopped and stirred around me appeared almost black. Pale light crept through the open door and shutters but was too weak to reach the bench tops where we prepared breakfast. We jostled for space in the cramped kitchen. Between the chatter of the men, the burble of boiling water and the rhythmic thump of knives against wood, I caught snatches of a song. The voice of one of the old divers at the stove threaded through the din as he alternately hummed and sang an old folk tune. 'No need to work through the night . . . Thinking of my home town, I talk to my loved ones in my dreams.' He ladled beaten egg into the frying pan. It hissed, sending up a cloud of steam.

Our row of tents was rostered to prepare breakfast for everyone in the compound once a week. I'd never been much of a cook—in Broome I had only ever prepared simple meals of rice, soup and grilled fish—so I set the tables, served the food and helped with the washing-up.

Men crowded around the sink in the kitchen, so I went outside to wash three porridge-encrusted saucepans in the standing troughs next to the bins. Grey light filtered through the blanket of clouds overhead. My mind was still foggy with sleep. I plunged the saucepans into the water and began scrubbing them with a brush.

'It's Dr Ibaraki, right?'

Johnny Chang stood before me, a towel slung over his shoulder and his hands in the pockets of his shorts. He smiled. Although I'd seen him a few times from a distance, we hadn't yet met face to face.

'Yes. Johnny, hello.' I wiped my hands on my apron.

'Didn't expect to see you here—a doctor rounded up with everyone else. And doing the washing-up, no less.'

I shrugged. 'Well, I'm Japanese, just like everyone here. No special treatment.'

'Yeah, well, I'm not like everyone else here—I'm only half-Japanese, and they still collared me. Got a raw deal, if you ask me. What tent are you in? I'm surprised they didn't put you in with me. There aren't that many of us from Broome.'

'I only got here a week ago. They put me where there was space. I'm in row eight, tent twelve, with some of the men from the Dutch East Indies—Sumatra, mainly.'

'Yeah? You should come to our tent sometime. There are a few of us Aussies. Come and play a game of cards or something.'

'Perhaps. If I have the time.' I glanced over my shoulder to see if anyone was watching us. 'If you don't mind, I'm on breakfast duty. I have to finish cleaning before headcount.'

He snorted and looked away. 'Yeah, I know all about that. They've got us cleaning almost every day. Kitchen, crap house, tents—'

Johnny's attitude struck a nerve. 'Everyone has to help out, Johnny. This is not a holiday, you know.'

His features clouded. 'You think I don't know that? I'm more than happy to do my fair share. But they've got the boys in our tent doing everything—all the shit jobs that they don't want to do. Just because we're not like them. Because we don't kiss their arse, worship their god, bow to their emperor. Tell me something: is your guy helping you out with the work?'

'My guy?'

'Your tent leader, what's his name—friends with the mayor?'

'Yamada?'

'Yeah, him. Is he doing any of the breakfast duties with you today?'

'No. But he is busy with other things. He is organising the canteen—'

'That's what I'm saying. He and Mori make the rules, but only rules that suit them. This camp's run like a dictatorship, not a democracy. And it's guys like me who suffer.'

I struggled to keep my voice low. 'I think you are being unreasonable. It is hard on everyone here. We are all trying to do our best and fit in.'

He threw up his hands. 'Well, if this is how you want to fit in, you can count me out. I don't want to keep you from your precious cleaning.'

He turned and stalked away, his footsteps flinging stones against the metal drums of the refrigerator. As I stared at him, my hands wet and my fingernails coated with porridge,

I wondered why someone who'd run a restaurant in Broome was so averse to doing chores.

I stood in the doorway and squinted at the sky. It was almost seven o'clock, but the sun seemed unwilling to make way for the evening. I'd already eaten dinner at the infirmary, but I was impatient to return to camp as the entertainment committee was staging their first play—*Matsukaze*, a famous Noh drama. With the major's permission, a low stage had been built, and a young man from the Dutch East Indies who'd had some acting experience in Japan had been chosen to play the lead.

The gate creaked. Matsuda appeared in the doorway, carrying his pillow and blanket for the night shift. I ushered him inside, keen to take him through what needed to be done so that I could hurry back to camp.

The sky was pastel by the time I reached 14C, with not a single cloud in view. I heard laughter and chanting, but not the restrained chanting that usually accompanies a Noh play.

'Banzai! Banzai! Banzai!' someone cried.

Inside the mess hall, a throng surrounded the stage. At first glance, I was reminded of summer parties during my university years, when my friends and I would join the other students and young couples who danced and drank next to the Tama River. But this was not the same. A dozen men in the middle of the crowd clapped and sang 'Kimigayo', the national anthem.

'What's happening?' I asked someone near the edge of the crowd.

'You haven't heard? We got Australia again. Blasted all their planes. Dozens, they say.' He beamed.

'Darwin again?'

Darwin had been bombed a few days before my arrival at Loveday, while I was en route from Perth to Adelaide.

'Not Darwin. Somewhere else up there. I forget the name.'

A chill passed through me. 'How did you find out?'

'The Germans in compound D told the men in the gardening party as they were walking past their fence. We think they have a secret radio. They were the first to know about Singapore, too. You should ask the mayor, he just made an announcement about it.'

Mayor Mori was standing beside the stage, clapping in time to the song. Secretary Hoshi stood next to him. I made my way towards them, weaving through the crowd. The clapping and the chanting rang in my ears. Faces turned towards me with hard expressions, grinning wildly.

A hand touched my elbow. 'Sensei, where have you been?' Shadows danced across Yamada's face.

'At the infirmary. I just finished my shift. What's going on?'

'Didn't you hear?' He grinned. 'We attacked Broome this morning. Destroyed all their aircraft.'

The blood drained from my face.

'What's the matter? Aren't you happy?'

I touched a hand to my cheek. My skin felt like rubber, not a part of me. 'Sorry. I'm just surprised. I didn't think they would get that far.'

'Where's your fighting spirit, hey?' Yamada's grip on my elbow tightened. 'Aren't you glad we got the bastards who arrested you? Do you want to stay in here forever?'

I forced a smile. 'Of course not. Long live the Emperor!'

'That's more like it. I know you're not all posture and politeness like they say.' He winked. 'A month more and it could be all over. These Australian fools with their fat bellies and their rusty guns could soon be our prisoners, and they'll be begging us for mercy.'

'Were there any civilian deaths?' I tried to keep my voice steady.

'Too early to tell. We'll have to check the newspapers for the rest of this week. The mayor has already talked to the cleaning committee.'

Although our compound was supplied with newspapers each week, all the articles relating to the war were cut out by the censors. While cleaning the guards' barracks one day, one of the internees from our camp noticed the guards kept copies of old newspapers in a pile near the latrines. From then on, whenever a cleaning group was sent to the barracks, they always returned with sheets of newspaper with articles about the war hidden in their clothing.

Mori stepped onto the stage. The chanting stopped.

'Today's victory reminds us of the strength and skill of our great nation. So too does the artistry of our people. We're lucky to have among us many talented artists, who have been practising for weeks to bring you tonight's production of *Matsukaze*. Let us continue the high spirits by giving them your full attention.'

I searched for the others from Broome. I couldn't see Johnny, nor any of the other Australian-born men. Harada was still in the infirmary. I glimpsed one of the divers from Harada's tent, a young man they called Shinpo. Turned away from the stage, his face held the light that spilled from outside. Our eyes met. He looked away, as if acknowledging me would give his feelings shape.

Yamada called out to me, touching the empty chair beside him. I yearned to be someplace else, away from his constant gaze.

The flute's thin, haunting melody snaked around the room, silencing the chatter. The travelling priest appeared, his wooden mask adorned with tufts of dry grass.

My thoughts were with all my friends in Broome—Sister Bernice, Dr Wallace, Constable McNally, Sam Male, the McDaniels, and even laundry owners such as Ang Pok. Surely they would have been evacuated? The uncertainty made me feel sick.

At this time of year, Broome would be steamy, a constant heaviness in the air. If it had been before the war, the town would be thrumming with activity. Some of the divers would have just returned, either disembarking at the port or coming overland from elsewhere in Australia. Japtown would be bustling with old friends reuniting and ships' crew buying supplies to finish repairs. But now, with the war under way, no doubt the area was almost deserted, with only the Chinese businesses open. Perhaps even they had left, too.

I thought of Sister Bernice in her white habit, her head bent in prayer, the dark line of her lashes forming two perfect crescents.

The percussionist tapped out a pattern on his drum, the *tsuzumi* sounding its distinctive twang. The ghosts of the two sisters appeared, wearing masks that bore the suggestion of eyes, brows and lips in thin black brushstrokes. The figures glided in their long white robes, skirting the shore, circling each other as they lamented their lost love.

I tilted my head to the side, away from Yamada and from the light coming into the mess hall. The outline of the shapes on the stage blurred, merging into one another and becoming diffuse patches of light. I was glad for the pocket of darkness that hid my tears.

Broome

1938

'That's Broome there, three miles southeast.'

I looked to where the deckhand was pointing. A pink spur of land crested with green rose out of the milky blue water. My pulse quickened in my throat. For days, I had been aching to disembark. Ever since we'd set sail from Singapore and navigated the tropical waters of Java, the air thick with humidity, I'd dreamed about stepping off the undulating deck onto the islands we passed. As we had travelled further south, we left the archipelago and all around us there was nothing but sea, only increasing my yearning to set foot on land. But now that I'd reached my destination, the prospect of alighting in this alien place—what would be my *home*—sent a wave of panic through me.

The ship turned into the bay, revealing a curve of rich red sand that bled into the azure sea. The strange clash of colours was like nothing I'd ever seen, beautiful and unsettling in equal measures. As we neared the shore, I could make out the township. It looked tiny: a couple of dozen buildings, many as dilapidated as some of the shacks we'd seen in the provincial villages in Java. The jetty snaked half a mile out from the shore, the tops of its wooden stilts exposed to the sun. A two-carriage train sat at the end. I heard the clang of the anchor being lowered when we were still more than a hundred yards from the jetty.

'Are we stopping here?' I asked the crewman.

'Low tide soon. Captain thinks it's too dangerous to get any closer. Passengers getting off here will be sent over in a lifeboat.'

I bade farewell to the people I'd befriended on the trip—two brothers from Singapore and a gentleman from Ceylon—and joined the eight others disembarking in Broome. We squeezed onto one boat, our luggage stacked next to our feet between the benches. One of the crewmen started the motor and we puttered towards the jetty.

As we navigated the rolling sea, my trepidation grew. What would the hospital be like? Who would my friends be? Soon, we were close enough to see the crowd standing at the end of the jetty. Many were dressed all in white, evidently the colour of choice in the tropics. The Asiatics wore white collarless shirts and darker slacks, while the Britisher men were dressed in ivory linen suits, and the women wore pale dresses that skimmed their ankles. I spied two men among the crowd who were distinctly Asiatic in their colouring and stature yet dressed well enough to blend in with the Britishers. I decided one of them must be Kanemori, the president of the Japanese Association, with whom I'd been corresponding in previous months. He had offered me the position at the Japanese hospital, arranged my transport, and would pay my salary. As we drew closer, the people's heads loomed and receded from view as the boat surged and dipped on the waves.

We reached the end of the jetty. After lashing the boat to a pylon, two of the crew climbed the ladder, then helped the women up. Our luggage followed, passed from man to man up the ladder, until there was nothing left at our feet. When I finally stepped onto the wooden planks, most of the crowd had dispersed—only the two Asiatic men and a handful of others were left.

'Ibaraki-sensei?' The thinner man approached me. He was wearing a neat white suit and a white hat. His outfit, coupled with his moustache, gave him the air of a movie star. He appeared to be in his mid-forties. 'I'm Kanemori. It's an honour to meet you.'

He bowed deeply and introduced me to his deputy. Harada was a decade or so older than Kanemori, darker and more heavy-set, like many from the southern prefectures of Japan. He had a broad, tanned face and an easy smile, and after our introduction he immediately picked up some of my bags and loaded them onto the waiting steam train.

'Before we go into town, you have to register at the Customs Office,' Harada said. 'Come, we'll take you.'

As we walked along the jetty, the pleasant vista forced me to revise my initial hesitation over arriving in Broome. The blue water sparkled all around us and the land ahead swelled with lush greenery.

'What's over there?' I pointed to a huddle of tents and rickety sheds at the top of the beach.

'Crew camp,' Harada said. 'That's where the lugger crews live during the pearling season. It just started for the year.'

The pink mud of the bay was dotted with the wooden skeletons of boats—pearling luggers still under repair, Harada explained. At the end of the jetty we turned onto the dirt road, passing several stately houses. They were built on foot-high cinder blocks, with sloping galvanised-iron roofs and pretty latticed verandahs.

'These are the European quarters,' Kanemori told me. 'We live further down the road in Japtown, where there's much more to see.'

The Customs Office was a low building a short stroll away. Inside, two Asiatic men who'd been on the boat with me were occupying the two available counters. A third man who'd been waiting on the jetty was running between them, trying to translate for both men at the same time. I thought they were speaking Malay, but I couldn't be sure.

After a few minutes, a counter became free and Kanemori stepped forward. 'This is the new doctor for the Japanese hospital,' he said, pointing at me. 'Name is Ibaraki.'

The white-haired customs official ignored Kanemori and waved me over. 'Speak English, do you?'

'A little.'

'Well, there's a start. Passport and letter of employment.'

The skin of his neck pleated as he looked down at the documents I handed to him. 'Says here you're married. Why didn't you bring your wife?'

Perspiration prickled my forehead. I could tell the truth—why not? Separation was common among westerners, or so I'd heard.

'She did not want to travel to Australia,' I said. Not the complete truth, but also not a lie.

'So you won't see her for two years?'

'No. I think not.'

He looked at me evenly. 'Got any children?'

I shook my head.

He turned back to the documents and made some notes, then asked me about my plans when my contract ended.

'I hope to return to Japan to practise.'

'At the same place you were before?'

'No, not there.' My voice must have been sharp, for the official's head snapped up. I hurried to explain myself. 'I plan to work at the hospital where I interned. My father worked there also. I eventually want to specialise in surgery.'

The official's brows bunched low over his eyes as he fixed me with a stare. My heart hammered in my chest as I waited, but he asked no further questions. He picked up a stamp and brought it down onto my passport with a resolute thump. I felt a brief rush of air.

The little train chugged through the streets of Broome barely faster than walking pace. But I was glad for the view from the open carriage and the cool air on my face. The trees shivered in our wake, glistening in the sun. As Kanemori and Harada pointed out places of interest such as the courthouse and the post office, I began to relax. Broome was a civilised place, after all.

The train lurched around a bend. The wide streets and well-maintained buildings of the European quarter gave way to cramped lanes and ramshackle structures made from a patchwork of iron sheets. In this part of town, people were everywhere—men chatting on the dusty verandahs, children playing on the street, a lone woman sweeping the entrance to her shop.

'This is Japtown,' Harada said, a smile on his face.

I nodded, trying to hide my dismay. It was certainly a poor cousin to the vibrant Japtown of Singapore.

'The hospital's that way.' Kanemori indicated a wide street that forked from the one we were on, seeming to lead nowhere. 'But we'll go through Japtown first.'

We turned another corner, and Kanemori pointed out the headquarters of the Japanese Association, set back from the street on a small hill. Although the two-storey structure had seen better days, it was one of Japtown's more handsome buildings, with white galvanised-iron walls and a wide verandah, skirted by a neat green hedge.

We looped around the block and I glimpsed a sign for Sun Pictures cinema and the long shady verandah of a hotel. Just before we rejoined the original track, the train jolted to a stop. As we disembarked, I peered down a tiny lane that burrowed between buildings. Clouds of steam issued from an opening in a wall. I heard the clang of metal pots and pans, the hiss of frying food and, beneath the clamour, the swooning melody of a Chinese love song playing on a gramophone. As my eyes adjusted to the darkness, I noticed a figure leaning against the wall—a broad-shouldered young man with a dark crown of hair. He appeared to be watching me.

'This way, sensei,' Kanemori called. I turned and followed him.

The Japanese hospital was a short walk from Japtown, past a row of houses and a large vacant lot. Away from the coast, the air was still and thick with humidity; sweat beaded my forehead and chest. The hospital was the last building on the street, next to the dusty expanse of the aerodrome and the racing track. It resembled the houses I'd seen in the European quarter, with a sloping iron roof that was tinted orange from the dirt and a white lattice screen enclosing a wraparound verandah.

Outside, the sun bathed the building in pristine light, but once we were inside I saw that dampness clung to everything. Paint flaked off the ceilings and walls, and dark spots of mould clung to crevices.

Kanemori scratched his head in embarrassment. 'I'm sorry about the state of the hospital,' he said. 'The last physician, Dr Abe, left five months ago, and the place has been empty since then. We decided to close it down during the wet, when most of the divers leave town.' He paused and brought his face close to a wall, extending a finger to touch a dark spot. 'The rain just ended, which is why everything here is so damp. We had a particularly bad wet season this year.'

We passed through a small anteroom into a larger space with three small windows that opened onto the verandah. It was very dim. Harada unlatched one of the windows, letting light in. The floor and walls were made of a dark wood unfamiliar to me. Two cabinets sat at the entrance, and eight single beds filled the rest of the space, jammed so closely together there was no room to move between them. A counter with a sink lined one wall. It was referred to as 'the hospital', but the ward was barely larger than an office and had only basic equipment. I would be the only doctor in attendance.

'The beds are on the verandah for most of the year,' Harada said, perhaps noticing my apprehension. 'Everyone here sleeps on the verandah, if they can—with a mosquito net, of course. Much better than being cooped up inside during summer. You'll want to sleep out there, too.'

My living quarters were on the other side of the anteroom at the back of the property: a bedroom that was half the size of the ward yet equally dank, and a small kitchen with a sink and an icebox. Harada explained that ice could be delivered each day for a fee. 'But I usually eat in town,' he said. 'Yat Son's the place to go. You should try their delicious long soup.'

Over the following week, I started to get the hospital in order. As well as cleaning the hospital from floor to ceiling, I had to check all the equipment and buy new supplies. Kanemori brought a young nun from the nearby convent to meet me. She was dressed from head to toe in white, save for her black-stockinged legs. I pitied her her outfit in the unrelenting heat.

'Sister Bernice will be your nurse at the hospital,' Kanemori explained. 'The Sisters of St John of God have helped us a great deal in the past.'

'Doctor,' she said, dipping her head towards me. There was a sharp line where the stiff edge of her white habit met her hair. When our eyes met I was struck by her clear gaze.

Kanemori also brought two young Japanese lugger crew to help, and together we scrubbed the walls, sanded back the paint and added another coat where needed, and sponged the mattresses with a peroxide solution and put them outside in the sun to dry. The Japanese hospital was once more as bright and airy as the landscape outside.

Sister Bernice and I reached an understanding from very early on that we would not engage in idle conversation as part of our working relationship. She took to the work quickly, so that after the first few months of her training there was hardly any need for us to talk at length. Aside from our morning greetings, brief discussions about the progress of a patient, and my thanks to her at the end of each day, most days would pass with only minimal verbal exchange. To many this might seem strange, but for me it was a relief to be able to work unencumbered, and also because in those early days I was not as confident speaking English as I later became.

I do not mean to give the impression that Sister Bernice was unapproachable or that her manner was cold, for she in fact displayed warmth and kind-heartedness in so many ways. She brought me a cup of black tea every morning, even though on many occasions I told her it was not necessary. In winter, when I sat in the anteroom and the afternoon sun shone through the window into my eyes, she was quick to draw the curtain. And although she was always quiet around me, she readily conversed with patients in her care, her soft voice putting them at ease, sometimes lifting into laughter.

The more I think it over, the more it seems that whenever it was just the two of us in the hospital, Sister Bernice took great care to modify her behaviour to suit me, and for that I am grateful. Indeed, it is one of the greatest services an assistant can give. Sister Bernice wasn't reticent by nature—her conversations with the patients were proof of that—but if I didn't have a patient to attend to, I spent my time consulting books and journals while she busied herself in other ways. In her first month she spent a lot of time cleaning and reordering the files until, one afternoon, I asked, 'Would you like a book to read? I have several in English in my room.'

She stopped polishing the instruments. A fan whirred behind her and lifted the edge of her habit. 'A book? I didn't think it right to read while at work. I didn't think it was professional.'

'Professional? Please, do not worry about that. You may read when you are not with patients. Shall I bring some of my novels?'

'Thank you, Doctor, but that isn't necessary. I have my own.'

The next day, I left a few of my English books on the counter anyway—a leather-bound collection of the poems of Blake that I'd studied during university, an unread copy of *David Copperfield*, and *Robinson Crusoe*, of which I'd only read the first chapter—and I was pleased to catch sight of Sister Bernice a few days later with her head bent over the latter title. I often saw her reading in a chair near the entrance to the ward, but on the rare day when the temperature was cool she'd sit on the window ledge at the opposite end of the room. If I turned my head while at my desk in the anteroom I could see her there, the sunlight pouring over her. The first time I saw her like that, I gasped and Sister Bernice looked up. In an instant, I knew my mind had played a trick.

The association caused me great anguish at the time, but it doesn't shame me to admit it now: seeing Sister Bernice on the window ledge, her habit catching the light, made me think of my wife, Kayoko, on our wedding day. The *wataboshi* plumed over the back of her head in a circle of white. The smooth silk crumpled around her elaborate hairstyle. On the morning of our wedding I had been so nervous I hadn't stopped to take in the beauty of my bride. It wasn't until the *san-san-kudo* ceremony that I finally had my chance. Kayoko took the sake cup from me, sipping the customary three times. A soft shadow from the *wataboshi* fell across her eyes and nose, framing her lips, and on the final sip she lifted her eyes. Her red lips framed within that triangle of light, her eyes lifting to mine—oh, what a glorious sight!

Tokyo
1934

Kayoko was the daughter of one of my father's old school friends from Kanagawa. Apparently I had met her several times when I was a child, although I had difficulty recalling her. My mother mentioned her over dinner one night.

'I visited the Sasakis today,' she said. 'We had lunch together. Their daughter plays the *koto* very well. Her name is Kayoko. Do you remember her?'

We were eating mackerel and vegetables braised in vinegar. I paused, a flake of fish between my chopsticks. Nobuhiro looked at me and smirked. At sixteen, he was the youngest in our family and never missed a thing. I had been his age when our father died, and I moved from my place at the side of the table to the head. Now, Mother faced me at the opposite end, the silver in her black hair gleaming in the light. I shook my head.

'No? You don't remember playing with her on the beach? Maybe you were too young,' she said. 'She is very talented, in any case.'

She lifted her soup bowl to her mouth and a puff of steam rose up. Despite her casual tone, my mother's intentions were clear. A knot formed in my chest, but I knew it would be futile to protest. I was twenty-six and no longer a student. Many of my friends had already married, as well as my sister Megumi, younger than me by two years.

I brought the fish to my mouth and chewed. After a few seconds, I forced myself to swallow.

About two weeks later, on a Sunday morning, my mother and I boarded a train bound for Shonandai, a seaside town about an hour away. Mother was wearing a formal kimono of falling yellow and white leaves against an orange background and a red *obi* accented with gold. I had never seen it before and realised it must be a new purchase, along with the silk chrysanthemum she wore in her hair. The depression was finally over, and silk was widely available again—I recalled my mother mentioning that the kimono shops in Tokyo had new stock for the first time in years. I was surprised she had bought a new one, as we had little money to spare—my intern's wage amounted to very little, and Nobu was still at home.

My mother and I got off at Yamato to change to a local line. While we waited on the platform I noticed a poster on the wall of the stationmaster's office. *Sun of a New Nation*, it read, featuring two smiling farmers: a Chinese holding a sickle and a Japanese with his angled tilling fork. It was typical of the posters one saw in provincial towns. The government was encouraging Japanese to emigrate to Manchukuo, and farmers were given land if they did so. I'd heard reports on the radio about the Imperial Army and the success of the new colony.

Our train came, and we travelled a few stops before alighting and walking the short distance to the Sasakis' house. My mother stopped outside their front door to straighten my hair and tie before announcing our arrival. Mr Sasaki opened the door, and my hazy memory of him sharpened at the sight of his smiling face. He was much greyer and smaller than I remembered, but I recognised him as the kind 'uncle' who used to piggyback me when I visited their house. Mrs Sasaki appeared beside him and bowed deeply.

'Ah, Tomo-kun. Look how big you've become!' Mr Sasaki said, and ushered us into the living room.

The Sasakis had lived in the same family home for almost thirty years. It was spacious and immaculate, yet showed signs of wear: the wooden floorboards dipped in certain places. But it was a distinguished home, far nicer than ours. Mr Sasaki owned a small accounting practice, and business had been steady.

In the living room, we had a view out to the foothills of Mount Fuji. Mrs Sasaki had not entered the room with us—I could hear her preparing tea elsewhere in the house. I had not seen Kayoko yet, and began to wonder whether we would meet on this occasion. Perhaps the Sasakis wanted to vet me first before introducing me to their daughter.

'So your mother tells me you're interning at Tokyo Hospital. That must be exciting.' Mr Sasaki leaned back on one outstretched arm as he sat on the floor cushion.

'Yes, I've been there for ten months now. It's difficult, of course, but rewarding.'

'What are your plans for next year?'

'I'm not certain yet. I'm still waiting to hear back from inter-views—' I glanced at my mother to see if it was appropriate to mention it, but she didn't return my look '—but I hope to stay in hospitals, or otherwise go into research.'

'Research? You mean back at university?'

'Somewhere more specialised than that, but yes, like a university.'

'One of Tomokazu's university professors recommended him for a research position,' my mother explained. 'He has always enjoyed research.'

I heard footsteps and the sound of a tray being placed on the floor outside the room. The sliding door moved back. I had expected to see Mrs Sasaki, but instead a young woman wearing a mauve kimono appeared. She brought her forehead down to the tatami before entering the room, then stood up and carried in a tray of tea. I looked away, suddenly stricken with shyness.

'Tomokazu, this is my daughter, Kayoko. You met when you were children. Perhaps you remember her?'

I was relieved I didn't recognise her, as it allowed me to see her in a fresh light. She had a long, oval face, eyes that were a little too close together and shapely brows. She was not breathtakingly beautiful, but her skin was smooth and she had a pleasing countenance. She smiled as she served the tea, no doubt aware we were all looking at her.

'Yes, I do remember Kayoko—I think we played together on the beach. Wasn't that here at Shonandai?' I said, feigning recollection to avoid offence.

She laughed—a breathy sound that seemed at odds with her well-defined features.

Mrs Sasaki entered the room, bringing a tray of sweets and dried fruit. She and Kayoko joined us at the table, with Kayoko sitting directly to my right.

My mother asked Kayoko about herself, and through their conversation I learned that she had completed secondary school at one of the most prestigious schools in the area. After she had graduated, she had done a bookkeeping course in order to help her father at his practice. While questions and answers were batted back and forth, I found myself unable to look at her, perhaps because I was aware of how closely we were being watched.

My mother turned to me. 'Don't you want to hear her play, Tomo?'

I looked at her blankly.

'The *koto*,' she prompted.

'Oh. Yes, of course.'

'Kayoko, would you mind?' Mr Sasaki said.

Kayoko rose and left the room. She came back carrying a long object wrapped in black cloth. She set it on the tatami and untied the string. The cloth fell away to reveal the wooden instrument shaped like an elongated washing board, with white strings and bridges evenly spaced along its surface. Kayoko fastened the picks to her fingers, and gently plucked the strings several times to tune it. I could watch her comfortably now, without others' gaze on me. She kneeled at one end of the instrument, bowed, and then leaned over the strings, spreading her arms along their length. As the fingers of her right hand plucked the strings, those on her left compressed them. The tune was lilting and mournful, and reminded me of the songs my mother sang to me as a child—songs of loss and lament. Just as I closed my eyes in recollection, the rhythm quickened. The melody pulsed, fluid and staccato at the same time, compelling me to look. I was surprised at the vigour with which she commanded the instrument, the strength she poured into her playing. Her arms jerked to and fro, her fingers snapped the strings. I could see her clearly now. Her talent and passion were apparent, and her girlish laugh that had bothered me before quickly faded away. When she played the last note, I completely forgot the unease I'd felt in her presence a few minutes earlier, and burst into applause.

Major Kimura offered me the position, much to my surprise. My mother was particularly pleased, and wasted no time in telling family and friends of my achievement. I finished my hospital internship at the start of the new year and immediately began at the research unit, which was called the Epidemic Prevention Laboratory.

The research room was located in the basement of the building in Shinjuku where I had had my interview. On my first day, a man named Shimada greeted me in the foyer. He was tall and thin, with a prominent Adam's apple that moved up and down as he talked. I wasn't certain of his age; he looked young but had the sort of mannered effeminacy more typical of someone at least a decade older than me. He said he had been a junior professor of microbiology at Tokyo University before being engaged by the Army Medical College on this project.

He led me past the reception desk and down a flight of stairs to the basement. We entered a brightly lit passageway with doors and other corridors leading from it. As we navigated the maze, Shimada pointed out the bathroom facilities and the tearoom, then showed me to the locker room. 'Before you go into the laboratory, you must come here and change into the uniform first,' Shimada said, holding up a white coat and cotton trousers. 'They are laundered and disinfected after every shift so outside pollutants don't interfere with our experiments.'

Shimada and I removed our slippers and changed into the uniform before returning to the corridor. A door opened ahead of us, and a tall man emerged, one hand hooked inside the pocket of his coat. Shimada greeted him, then turned to me. 'This is the laboratory for the senior researchers. You'll be working with them on bacterial growth. There's another laboratory on the other side of the building that mainly deals with specimen analysis. I can show you later.' He stopped outside a heavy metal door with a thick rubber seal. 'And this is the laboratory where you'll be working.' The door opened onto a small corridor with a disinfectant bath in a large metal tray on the floor. There was a similar rubber-sealed metal door at the end of the corridor. Following Shimada's lead, I walked through the bath, dried my feet on a towel and put on a new pair of slippers. Then I walked behind Shimada into the laboratory. I was accustomed to following procedures to maintain hygiene, but I had never before encountered such stringent methods.

The room was larger than I had expected, with a central workspace and wide benches that ran along two of the walls. Half a dozen shiny microscopes were lined up along the benches, with stools positioned neatly beneath them. At the far end of the room was a glass cabinet containing dozens of flasks, test tubes, funnels and Bunsen burners. There were charts—both hand-drawn and typed—pinned up around the room, and various other equipment, some of which I recognised, but others I had never seen before. Two men were already in the room: one was bent over a microscope and the other was at the sink. They looked up when we entered, but quickly went back to their tasks.

I later found out their names: Nomura and Ota. They were researchers who'd started in the laboratory about a year earlier. Although we were of a similar age, they kept to themselves. In the first few months, the little information I gleaned about them was that Nomura had been in the year below Shimada at Tokyo Imperial University and Ota had studied medicine at Kyoto Imperial University. Even when we were in the tearoom together they said very little, and after several early failed attempts at conversation with them, I gave in and learned to appreciate the silence. I wondered if Nomura and Ota's reticence was what Kimura had meant when he'd talked about 'discretion'.

My duties were simple at the start: I grew bacteria for the senior researchers to use in developing vaccines. Although I was familiar with culturing bacteria from my student days, the equipment at the laboratory was new to me. First, I had to prepare the agar solution in a huge boiler, then sterilise the medium in autoclaves. After distributing the solution into cultivation trays and moving them into cooling chambers, I inoculated each one using a sterilised loop. I finally shifted the trays into incubators, which had apparently been designed by the head of our unit, Lieutenant Colonel Ishii Shiro. I grew various types of bacteria, including those that cause typhus, botulism and anthrax. Due to their virulence, I was required to wear rubber gloves and a mask at all times. 'One wrong touch and you could die,' Shimada had said. My greatest challenge was keeping up with the demand. As the months passed, the researchers requested greater amounts of bacteria, so I was often forced to work late into the night. The cultivation was on a scale I'd never seen before.

About six months into my role, we hired a new junior, a twenty-three-year-old named Yamamoto Daisuke, who had graduated from Kyoto. Yamamoto's mother was a cousin of Kimura's, and his family ties had helped get him the job straight out of university. We got along well—Yamamoto was affable and efficient, and he also thought Nomura and Ota were strange. Like me, he had played baseball at university, and we spent much of our time in the tearoom discussing the players in the American league. There was another reason why Yamamoto's arrival was a welcome change: he took on my role of growing the bacteria, and I was given more senior responsibilities, including analysing samples from infected animals. I was grateful for the opportunity to exercise more intellectual rigour, and I also hoped the new role meant my working hours would be curtailed. Since my visit to the Sasakis', I had begun to think seriously about finding a wife, so I was eager for more free time.

Loveday
1942

I n early April the weather finally started to cool. For the first time since my arrival I woke in the morning not covered in sweat. When I walked to the toilets, the ground was damp with dew. The landscape beyond the fence looked like a scene from a picture book: a bright sky dotted with fluffy clouds above a sweep of yellow-green grass and orange dirt. On the rare days I had off from the infirmary, I sat in the sun on a log near the perimeter fence to read the newspapers. I had found only one brief article about the Broome attack in the papers smuggled from the guards' barracks. It said that Japanese planes had targeted the military craft in the aerodrome and the bay; there were an unspecified number of casualties, all thought to be military personnel. I was relieved that none of the townspeople were harmed.

At night we relaxed in our tents, sharing cups of sake that had been secretly brewed beneath the ablutions block. The men from the Dutch East Indies recalled the hardship of their arrest and subsequent voyage to Australia, when they were at the mercy of the cruel guards. They saw a man being beaten after he asked for extra food for his wife and child. One of Yamada's colleagues at the rubber company died on the ship after contracting dysentery. 'They took all our medicine and wouldn't return any, even though many of us were sick. After Kobayashi died, I wanted to perform basic funeral rites, but they wouldn't let me. They threw him over the side over ship, just like that. I thought I was in hell.' Yamada turned to me, eyes shining. 'It's the only time in my life I wanted to die.' It was a side of Yamada I'd never seen before. I was touched he spoke so openly even though we hadn't known each other long.

Although I enjoyed the mild autumn weather, I was mindful of the effect on the patients at the infirmary. Even though I wasn't in charge of the TB ward, I always monitored it during my shifts. Harada's condition had improved and he now had the strength to sit up in bed. But he still had a persistent cough, which worried me.

The cooler weather at least softened the blow of living in close quarters. New internees continued to arrive, sometimes just a dozen or so, at other times more than a hundred. Internees were also transferred to other camps—often for no obvious reason other than to satisfy the whims of military administration, which were a mystery to us. More and more tents were added to the rows that stretched across the dusty flank of our compound. When there was no more space for new tents, we were told to increase the number of people per tent from six to eight. This triggered complaints about the cramped conditions, but we were told that nothing could be done until permanent huts were built. The materials were said to be arriving soon. As I was the seventh member of our tent, we received only one new person: Hayashi, one of

Yamada's acquaintances from Sumatra, who'd agreed to shift from another tent so that three new internees could move into his former tent.

One of the new internees was a young half-caste who immediately fell in with Johnny's crowd. Tall, thin and pale, he was easy to identify among the gang, with his distinctly Asiatic eyes in contrast to his prominent nose and forehead. He would have been considered handsome if not for his weak mouth, which seemed to swallow itself in one thin, expressionless line.

At headcount one morning, Major Locke announced there would be a film screening later that week.

'The Red Cross has kindly donated a projector to the Loveday internment group, and this Sunday night a representative from the Kraft Walker company in Adelaide will play a reel for the enjoyment of the internees in 14C. I'm told the films will be educational in nature. Mr Mackenzie will be travelling all the way from Adelaide to do this on his own time. I trust you'll make him feel welcome and treat him with the respect he deserves. It should be an enjoyable evening, and if all goes well Mr Mackenzie may be kind enough to make the trip again.'

The film screening became the talk of our compound. One old New Caledonian who'd spent most of his life in the mines hadn't even heard of films, and we had a difficult time trying to explain to him what they were. 'Moving pictures,' was how it was best described by someone in his tent.

I'd been fortunate enough to see a few movies at the local cinema in Broome, where the sea was known to creep in during king tides and lap at the audience's feet. I was delighted by the vaulted iron roof that ended abruptly, open to the stars. Throughout the movie, I was aware of the chatter of my countrymen, the soft beat of wind as the Britisher women in the row behind me fanned themselves, and the laughter of the native Aborigines from the back and sides of the space.

A few days later, Mr Mackenzie of the Kraft Walker company arrived at camp as the sun hovered on the horizon. He wore shorts and knee-length socks over his gangly legs. His cheeks were deep red and balled when he smiled. I had been asked to translate during his visit, so I joined Mayor Mori, Yamada, Mr Mackenzie, Major Locke and two other officers on a tour of our compound. We pointed out the kitchens, the canteen and the shadehouse we'd recently built for the craftsmen. Mr Mackenzie picked up a half-woven basket.

'It's made from grapevines,' I said. 'One of the men from Okinawa made it the way he would in his village.'

'How remarkable,' he said, bringing it close to his face to inspect the tight weave.

Major Locke stepped forward. 'They've also got some lovely gardens and a shrine. Why don't you show Mr Mackenzie that?'

So we led the group between the tents to the outer fence, where the earth was dark inside the vegetable plot. Further along, a thicket of bamboo had been planted to create a windbreak. On the other side of it, a line of grass and flowers created a border, opening into a stone-edged path that led to the altar. The grounds had greatly improved since my arrival, due to the efforts of a dozen keen gardeners. The altar was now painted and raised on a mud-brick platform inlaid with hundreds of stones.

Mr Mackenzie gasped. 'The Japanese made all this?'

'Yes, and in only two months,' Major Locke said.

I'd heard rumours Locke was a schoolteacher before he became head of our camp, and one could see it in his stringent manner and the way he admonished us for not cleaning our tents properly, as if we were schoolboys. So Locke's pride in our work took me by surprise.

'The gardeners collected the plants and materials from the area around camp when they were working outside the fence,' I said.

Mr Mackenzie gestured to the path leading to the altar. 'May I?'

'Of course,' I said.

He walked up to the altar and bent over to inspect the painted roof and the intricate woodwork beneath the eaves. 'Well, I'll be.' He straightened up and turned to take in the entire sweep of the garden. 'Just wonderful. Never seen anything like it. And to think you did this in two months, with what you found near camp? Most Australians could learn something from what you've done here.'

The sky was tinted lavender as we wandered back to the entrance. Two white sheets were tied to the fence to create a screen, their edges flapping in the breeze. A few hundred internees were already sitting on blankets that fanned out around the screen in a rough semicircle, hemmed in on one side by the fence and on the other by a row of seats directly opposite the screen. Voices rang out.

Secretary Hoshi rushed towards us, his face red. 'I tried to get them out of the seats, but they wouldn't move!'

I looked towards where he had come from. Five silhouettes occupied the seats reserved for Mr Mackenzie, the army personnel and the camp executive. I didn't need to see their faces to know who they were: Johnny and his gang.

Mori's expression turned stony. 'Yamada, get rid of them— *quickly.*' He turned to me. 'Stall the group so they don't see what's happening. We can't have them knowing about the trouble with the *haafu*. They're an embarrassment to us all.'

'What's going on?' said the officer closest to us.

I took a deep breath. 'Before we start the film, there's something else we wanted to show you . . . The vegetable plot. We've planted some tomatoes, pumpkins and celery.'

'But that's back near the shrine,' the major said. 'We've already seen that.'

'Yes, but there are some other plants Mr Mackenzie might be interested in—'

A squall of voices sounded from the direction of the seats.

Locke swung his head. 'What in the devil is going on? Perry, see what's wrong, will you?'

Lieutenant Perry dashed towards the commotion, his long legs scissoring.

'So, shall we go to the vegetable garden?' I prompted.

'No, no. We've already been there,' Locke said.

Mr Mackenzie smiled. 'I don't mind.'

'It's getting dark,' Locke said. 'Mr Mackenzie needs to set up the projector soon. You'll have to show him the vegetable plot another time.'

I hung my head as we walked towards the seats. Johnny was sitting with four others near the projector. I recognised the stout bodies of Charlie Khan and his younger brother Ernie; the half-Thai pair from Perth were Johnny's constant companions. To their right was Ken Takahashi, a teenager born and raised in the Dutch East Indies by

Japanese parents. The new *haafu*, whose name I didn't yet know, sat next to Ken. He slouched in his seat, eyes darting between Yamada and Hoshi, who stood silently in front of them. Yamada clenched his jaw, a line of shadow appearing along his cheek.

'Johnny Chang,' Major Locke said. 'Should've known. What's the problem this time?'

'No problem, no problem,' Hoshi said, waving his hands in front of him as if he was shooing away a fly.

'They won't get up,' Perry said. 'These are the seats for Mr Mackenzie, us and the mayor's party, and they won't get up.'

'Oh, no need to worry about me,' Mr Mackenzie said. 'I can stand up. I'll be at the projector most of the time.'

'No!' Mori's voice was shrill. Everyone turned to him. 'You are our guest. You must sit. We have seat for you.'

'Settle down,' Johnny said, standing up. 'I'm more than happy to give up my seat for *him*.' He walked towards Mr Mackenzie, hand extended. 'Johnny Chang. Nice to meet you. I want to thank you for coming all this way. If only there were more people here at camp like you, being locked up would almost be pleasant. Please, take my seat.'

Mr Mackenzie shook Johnny's hand and laughed. 'Why, thank you. Australian, are you?'

'Australian born and bred. Lived in Broome all my twenty-seven years.'

Mr Mackenzie's features clouded. 'Then why . . . ?' He glanced at Locke.

'Then why am I in here?' Johnny said. 'Good question. I'm an Australian citizen, just like you. Only my mother's Japanese. But I was arrested—'

'Now's not the time, Johnny,' Locke said. 'Everyone's waiting for Mr Mackenzie to start the film. If you want to air your grievances, you have Dr Morel of the Red Cross for that.'

Johnny drew his lips in tight. He muttered something about injustice.

Major Locke took Mr Mackenzie by the arm and led him to the projector. 'A lot of these half-breeds are upset about their internment. But we didn't make the decision, we just have to uphold the law. It's not up to us to decide who's a security risk and who's not . . .'

Johnny's behaviour had almost ruined the evening. Mori and Yamada would not let him off lightly for the disgrace he had caused. I took a few steps towards him, about to say something in reproach, but then I realised an argument was just what Johnny wanted. Instead, seeing one of the carpenters standing nearby with a gift for Mr Mackenzie, I moved towards Mori to get his attention.

We approached Mr Mackenzie as he was bending over the projector. I cleared my throat. 'Mr Mackenzie, the Japanese of 14C would like to thank you for coming such a long way. We are grateful for the kindness of Australians such as you. As a token of our appreciation, we would like to present you with this gift.'

Mori stepped forward. He held out the wooden box and bowed deeply. Mr Mackenzie accepted the box and opened the lid. He took out a carved wooden chess piece, the cross-topped shape of a king.

'A chess set. An entire chess set. Goodness, I'm touched.' He brought a finger to the corner of his eye. 'Did you make this?' he asked Mori.

'Mr Sawada here did most of the work.' I motioned for Sawada to join us.

'Thank you, thank you,' Mr Mackenzie said, shaking Sawada's hand. 'What a wonderful present. I'll show it to everyone in the office. And my children will be delighted.'

Sawada smiled sheepishly and asked me to translate for him.

'He says it's only small. If he had had more time, he would have made you something bigger.'

'No, no. This is perfect. I can't believe how intricate the pieces are. I'll cherish it.'

'People from the Red Cross have visited us in the past, but you're the first outsider to come,' I said. 'It means a lot that an Australian would do this for us.'

Mr Mackenzie nodded. 'I wish I could do more. It doesn't seem fair you lot are locked up in here, just for being Japanese.'

As Mr Mackenzie returned to setting up the projector, we looked for a place to sit. The *haafu* had shifted along the row so that Major Locke and the two officers could sit next to Mr Mackenzie. There were two empty seats at the other end.

'I'm not sitting next to *them*,' Mori hissed. 'We'll sit on the ground. I don't want a fuss. The formalities are over, anyhow.'

Some internees made space for us on a blanket, and with a whirr and a flash of light, the film finally started. Some of the internees cheered. A kangaroo appeared on the screen, silently scratching through undergrowth, the slender feet of a joey poking from her pouch. There was hardly a sound except for the flap of the sheets as they caught in the wind and the occasional gasps and laughter from the audience.

I looked back at the row of seats. Johnny's arms were crossed in front of his chest. In the flickering light reflected from the screen, I saw his narrow eyes and the hard line of his mouth.

The new internee appeared small beside him. His shoulders were drawn inwards, his hands pressed together and tucked between his legs. He watched the screen with such concentration I doubted he was enjoying the experience at all. I pitied him for having been swept up in Johnny's trouble so soon.

Darkness crowded the corners of the orderlies' room as I sat on a chair. Grey light shone through the window; the sky was the colour of steel. The weather had put me in a sombre mood. I was thinking of Tokyo, of the cold empty mornings of my last weeks there before I had left for Australia.

Shiobara walked into the room. 'Excuse me, Doctor, would you mind coming to my ward? There's a new patient with an injury.'

The recently arrived half-caste who'd been sitting with Johnny the night of the film screening was at the front of the ward, holding his forearm as if he were cradling a child. I inspected the young man's wound. A purple-red bruise spread from his forearm to his bicep. A gash furrowed his elbow, the flesh around it red and swollen and crusted with purulent exudate.

'What happened?'

He shook his head slightly. 'They just . . . attacked me.'

'Who?'

'These four men. I was sitting in the mess hall trying to write a letter, and they came and told me to leave. They spoke in Japanese, so I didn't know what they were saying at first and I didn't move, and they just started yelling at me and grabbed me. One of them hit me with a tent pole. That's how I got this.' He nodded at the wound on his arm.

I was surprised by what he said. Our camp was populous but everyone seemed to get along well. Mayor Mori saw to it that everything ran smoothly. I wondered if the altercation had anything to do with the stand-off at the film night. I'd heard several people complaining about the behaviour of the *haafu* that evening. I thought about pointing out the importance of maintaining face, but a lecture was not what he had come to me for.

'When did it happen?' I asked.

'Yesterday, after lunch. They were yelling something about a meeting, then they started attacking me. I thought I could leave the cut, but it blew up. Now I can hardly move my arm.'

I took my time inspecting him. Building rapport with a patient had never been something at which I excelled. In Broome I had always relied on Sister Bernice. She only needed to speak a few words in her low voice to put a patient at ease.

'It's badly bruised, but it's not broken,' I said. 'The wound is infected. I need to clean and dress it.'

I turned away to get the iodine and gauze. Someone shifted in their bed and coughed. Outside, the high-pitched squeal of a train could be heard—it must have been the cargo train bringing supplies from Barmera.

'I'm sorry,' I said, turning back to my patient, 'I do not know your name.'

'Stanley Suzuki,' he said. 'But you can call me Stan.'

'Are you new to camp?'

'Yeah. Got here last week from the camp in Liverpool. I thought it would be better here, but . . .' His face contorted. At first I thought he was wincing in pain, but as he began to draw noisy, stuttering breaths, I realised he was crying.

Head bent, he massaged his brow with one hand. 'Sorry,' he said. 'Been a tough year. I've been transferred all around the place. I shouldn't even be in here. I was in the AIF, you know? Did eight months in the survey branch before I was kicked out because I'm Japanese, even though I've lived here since I was six months old. First that, then they lock me up in Liverpool, and now this. Everything . . . it's all gone to hell.' His shoulders trembled.

I began disinfecting the wound. Stan flinched when I touched him. His skin was hot, like the *kaichu kairo* pocket warmers I sometimes used in Japan. I unrolled the length of bandage and slowly wound it around his arm, careful not to knock the gauze.

'Don't worry, you will fit in here soon,' I said. 'I know from my own experience. It was difficult to meet people at first, but now I have many friends. You will, too.'

'It's different for you. You're Japanese.' He pressed his palm into his eyes.

'Did you report the attack to someone?'

'Just the guard at the gate. He said I should file a report with an officer.'

'Why don't you say something to Mayor Mori? He could give a warning. He'd want to know about this anyway. Or maybe Yamada can help. He's the leader of my row.'

'Yamada?' Stan's head jerked up. The skin around his eyes was pink and swollen. 'That's the name of one of the guys who attacked me. Johnny said so. I recognised him from the film night. He was one of the men who were standing in front of us when we were in the seats.'

I let go of his arm. 'Not Yamada Denkichi.'

'I don't know his full name. Short guy, grey hair. The one who stood right in front of us. You were there, weren't you?'

'Yamada Denkichi is a very good friend. He would never do something like that. He was the one who introduced me to everyone when I first arrived here. You must be mistaken.'

He shook his head. 'No, it's him. The same Yamada. About fifty, tanned. Johnny said he'd had run-ins with him before. Said he was the worst of them.'

All at once it became clear: this was part of Johnny's plan to create havoc at camp. Due to jealousy or some personal vendetta, Johnny wanted to bring down the leaders of our compound, and he had somehow convinced Stan that Yamada was to blame for his attack. For all I knew, Stan might have inflicted the wound on himself.

'"The worst?" Johnny told you that? I'm sorry, but I refuse to believe Yamada would attack another man. It is Johnny Chang you should be careful of. Do not let him influence you.'

Stan stared at me without blinking. I heard the whistle of his breath through his nose. I grew uncomfortable under his gaze and reached for his arm to finish bandaging it. He finally spoke. 'I'm not lying. I know you don't believe me, but I'm not.' His voice quavered.

Although I sympathised with him, I said nothing. I hoped he would recover from the setback and find some better friends at camp. In silence, I wound the remaining length of bandage around his forearm and tied a knot at the end.

Broome
1938

Something was calling me from the darkness—a pattern that roused me from slumber. I raised my head from the pillow, and the sound condensed. A *tap tap tap* on my door.

'Hey, Doctor! You home?'

I heaved myself from bed and shuffled to the entrance. A young man I vaguely recognised stood on the other side of the door. Was he Japanese, Malay, Chinese? It was difficult to judge from his broad shoulders, his nut-brown skin and the sharp angles of his face.

'There's been a fight at the Roebuck.' His Australian accent caught me by surprise. 'Some Japs and Malays got stuck into each other. One got his face cut up. McNally and I brought him here in my car. The other one's walking over with the inspector and Rooney. Can we bring the first one in?'

'Yes, of course.' I touched a hand to my rumpled nightshirt. 'Bring him into the ward. I will be there in a moment.'

I hurried to the closet and changed into a smock then entered the ward. I washed my hands and cleared a space around one of the beds.

Constable McNally and the young man who'd knocked on my door shuffled in, swearing under their breath as they carried the patient by his arms and legs. He slumped in their grip, insensate as they manoeuvred him onto the bed. I paled at the sight of his injuries. He was coated in blood, still bleeding from the cuts on his face and his neck. I could hardly make out his eyes through the swelling on his face. Panic filled me.

I turned to the young man. 'Could you go to the St John of God convent and ask for Sister Bernice? I'll need her help.'

'At this hour?'

'Please.'

I tried to calm my racing mind, praying my training would come back to me. In the two months I'd worked in Broome I'd performed only a few minor operations, such as resetting broken bones, sewing cuts and removing abscesses. The biggest emergency had been a diver with caisson disease, and treatment required little skill on my part. There was an old decompression chamber on the grounds of Dr Wallace's practice. He mainly treated the Britisher community, while I mainly treated the Japanese as I was paid by the Japanese association, but we worked together when required. We placed the diver inside it for twenty-four hours before checking on him, keeping him in there until his symptoms disappeared.

I asked Constable McNally to assist me until the sister's arrival. McNally held the patient down while I swabbed his cuts with a mixture of alcohol and iodine. As soon as I touched him, the patient screamed, his mouth wide open, back arching in pain, as if a current ran through him. When he settled again, I stemmed the bleeding on his neck with wadding.

The distant hum of voices cut through the stillness of the night. Footfalls on the verandah steps. The creak of floorboards. And then Inspector Cowie and Constable Rooney appeared, gripping the shirt of a young man. I smelled alcohol on his breath when I inspected him. One side of his face was swollen, but I recognised him as one of the divers who often hung around the boarding houses in Japtown. He cradled his right arm to his chest.

I addressed him in Japanese. 'Your arm. Show me.'

He turned his hand towards me. His knuckles were cut and grazed. Blood pooled in a deep laceration on his palm, but his wrist was unaffected. I directed him to a bed against the wall then went to the kitchen to fetch some ice.

Inspector Cowie was hovering near the doorway, his face creased with concern. 'The other one—the Malay kid—he doesn't look good. Shouldn't you start stitching him up?'

'I—I'm waiting for the sister. I need an assistant.'

'What if she doesn't come?'

I blinked. If she didn't come, who would help me? I'd have to ask one of the constables. But they wouldn't have the sister's grace, nor would they be able to calm the patient like she could. I nodded, gave the ice to the Japanese diver, then started assembling instruments for the operation. My hands trembled as I thought of the last operation I'd been involved in in Japan, and its disastrous outcome.

I was about to begin the procedure when I heard the rumble of a car along the road. Two doors slammed, then Sister Bernice walked into the hospital, her habit as smooth and neat as if it had just been pressed. I exhaled with relief.

'I came as soon as I could,' she said, moving towards the sink to wash her hands.

'The cuts are non-arterial, but he is still losing blood,' I said. 'We should operate at once. Are you ready?'

'Ready.' Her brow furrowed in concentration.

McNally crossed to the other side of the room to assist Cowie in questioning the Japanese diver.

Sister Bernice shifted to the other side of the table to hold down the patient's arm. I threaded the needle then dipped it in alcohol.

'The neck first,' I said, and Sister Bernice removed the wadding, then guided the patient's face to expose his neck. Bright red blood spurted from the wound. I brought the needle close and then stopped. My hand was trembling. My mind was a jumble of images. A swollen node. Black dots on a child's belly. I was unable to go on.

'Hold his arm,' Sister Bernice said. Then, without a word, she took the needle from me, leaned forward until her face was inches from the patient's, pursed her lips and in one movement pierced the skin and brought the needle through it. The patient wailed, a sharp sound like the cry of a child. He sobbed in a language I didn't understand, writhing under my grip.

'Shhh, I know it hurts, but it will be over soon. Shhh,' Sister Bernice said.

Anguish contorted the young man's face but he was quieter as she continued to sew. She tied a knot and cut the thread. Hearing the patient cry out had unlocked something within me. I blinked, now fully aware of the situation.

'Thank you, Sister. I will do the next.'

She nodded and gave me the needle, then stood behind the patient, placing her palms on either side of his head. She continued to whisper to him as I tended to his remaining cuts. I took a deep breath and drove the needle through his skin. He grimaced but didn't utter a sound, soothed by her voice.

My unease had entirely disappeared by the time I treated the diver. The cut on his palm required stitches and his sprained wrist needed a sling—both relatively simple procedures, but they took longer than expected on account of his agitation.

'How dare he?' he said in Japanese, leaning forward until he almost toppled off the bed. Liquor laced his breath. 'She's my girl. How dare he!'

I assumed he was referring to a girl at one of the boarding houses. Although no one else in the room could understand him, I was embarrassed by his behaviour and frustrated by his constant movement, so I rather tersely told him to be quiet.

He snapped, 'You? What do you know about love?'

I looked up. His stare cut to the deepest part of me. I didn't address him again.

When I'd finished treating both patients, the constables walked the diver back into town to the police station. Before the inspector left, he thanked the sister and me, then turned to the young man with the car. 'Johnny, you've been a big help. With the patrol car in for repairs, I don't know what we would have done without you. If you can't get those bloodstains off the seat, let me know. We might be able to reimburse you.'

Johnny batted his hand in front of his face. 'The seat will be fine. If there's a stain it'll add character. But next time one of your boys stops me for speeding, how about we call it even, eh?' He winked.

The inspector laughed. 'Yes, well, we'll see . . .'

The Malay patient's condition was still critical, so I set up a bed in the anteroom for myself. Johnny offered to take Sister Bernice home. She insisted on cleaning and putting away all the equipment and supplies before she left, even though I told her she needn't do so.

When I followed them outside and saw Johnny's brown Dodge Tourer I realised who he was: he had a taxi business in Broome. I'd often seen him driving down Carnarvon Street or ferrying passengers from the jetty. His family ran the popular Yat Son noodle shop in Japtown.

He turned to me before he reached his car. 'I'm Johnny, by the way,' he said, holding out his hand.

'Tomokazu Ibaraki. Pleased to meet you.'

'You're new here, aren't you?' he said. 'I remember the old doctor—he came with his wife and two kids. But it's just you now, right?'

'Yes, that is right.'

'This kind of thing doesn't usually happen—tonight's fight, I mean. We haven't had trouble like this for years, maybe because numbers are down. During lay-up there's sometimes a spat. Some divers think they can treat the others like dirt. But they're not all like that.'

'Is that what happened tonight, with the Japanese diver and the Malay?'

'I'm not sure. Someone said they were fighting over a girl. But everyone usually gets on with each other—Japs, Malays, Chinese, blacks and whites.' He placed one hand on his chest. 'I'm proof of that.'

Darkness blanketed the landscape, but the first cries of the dawn chorus sounded from the dunes. A kookaburra's stuttering call broke out. I moved to the other side of the car and opened the door for Sister Bernice.

'Are you sure you'll be all right?' she asked. 'I can come in tomorrow if you'd like.'

I never asked her to come in on the weekends, and certainly not on a Sunday.

'No, thank you, Sister. That's quite all right. You were remarkable tonight. I could not have done it without you.'

'You trained me well.'

I hesitated. 'About the operation . . . I do not know what happened to me at the start. It has been a long—'

'There's no need to explain. These things happen. You finished the job all the same.'

'Yes, well, thank you. Now, please go home and rest.'

She turned around and climbed into the car. As they drove away, she smiled and gave me a brief wave. I remained in the street for a minute after they had left, listening to the chortle of a magpie. I thought I could make out the distant roar of the sea. I was tired, but my body felt strangely light.

August was the month of the Bon festival in Japan. Honouring the spirits of the dead was the last thing I expected to do in Broome, but I soon discovered it had considerable cultural importance in town. President Kanemori was the first to tell me about it. 'It's going to be big this year—it coincides with the full moon, so we're going to release the lanterns in the bay.'

The festivities took place in a small clearing near Roebuck Bay, right next to Town Beach. On one side, mangroves clung to the shore in a sticky embrace and, on the other, waves crashed against the rocky outcrop that protected the beach. I arrived just after sunset, in time to see the sky turn from pink to mauve to blue, and in the gathering darkness I wandered through the crowd. A young man with an iron griddle was selling *taiyaki*. Next to him, a group of divers squatted on the ground, taking bites of the fish-shaped cakes. Young girls in kimonos seemed to be everywhere, the full-blood and half-caste daughters of laundrymen and divers. Until that night I hadn't realised how many beautiful Japanese girls there were in town.

I stopped to chat to Harada. President Kanemori nodded at me, but he was talking to Captain McDaniels and his wife. I moved away from them, towards the edge of the bay, hoping to catch the moonrise. In the darkness I could barely make out the muddy flats of the bay.

As I waited at the water's edge, people gathered around me. After a few minutes, a blot of colour appeared on the horizon, a rust-coloured stain above the water. Another minute or two passed, and the stain grew larger and brighter. A little girl standing near me cried, 'Look, Mama, I think I see it!' A sliver of orange peeped above the horizon. 'Yes, that's it!' someone else cried, and people began to jostle each other to have the best view. We watched the orange light grow in size until it was a semicircle that cast long shadows across the bay.

The moon grew fuller and paler, shedding its colour as it climbed the sky. Soon it was a perfect white sphere. I stayed there for a long time, looking out at the sea, the stars and the sky, while those around me gradually peeled away. The shadows on the exposed mudflats, which resembled a rickety staircase, gradually diminished, until the moon was high in the sky, casting a cold distant light.

I wandered back to the clearing to watch the *toronagashi* on Town Beach. A number of people were already standing on the shore. Some held paper lanterns in their hands. I turned my head, and saw Sister Bernice in a group of St John of God nuns, standing on the edge of the wharf that overlooked the beach. Although I'd grown accustomed to seeing her every day, now it was as if I saw her for the first time. Our eyes met. She raised her hand in greeting. I smiled and bowed. She beckoned me over.

'Dr Ibaraki,' she said. 'We were just wondering if we could find someone to explain the significance of the lanterns, and then I saw you.'

She introduced me to the other nuns. Two of them were about Sister Bernice's age, while the other two were older.

'Did you come by yourself?' one of the younger nuns asked, studying me with her pale eyes.

Perhaps sensing my discomfort, Sister Bernice spoke before I could answer. 'The lanterns—could you tell us what they mean?'

'They represent the spirits of the dead. At this time every year our ancestors return to visit us. To guide them back to the other place, we release lanterns on water. It is especially important for those who died in the past year.'

'Are you going to release any lanterns this year?' the young nun asked.

'Sarah!' Sister Bernice scolded.

I laughed. 'No. Fortunately, I do not need to release any this year. I did that long ago.'

Sister Bernice's gaze lingered on me.

'Look—there's the first one now,' I said, pointing to a light on the shore.

'Can we go closer?' Sister Sarah asked.

The two older nuns stayed on the wharf while I escorted Bernice, Sarah and the third young nun, Agnes, along the beach. We watched the line of people taking it in turns to release their lanterns into the ocean, fragile ships aglow with candlelight. Some were swallowed by darkness soon after they left the shore, their candle extinguished early by poor design or a strong gust of wind; but most made it past the point of land still alight and drifted far away until they were tiny pinpricks of light. After a while, bobbing lanterns blanketed the ocean as far as the eye could see.

Sister Bernice and I stood a little way behind the other nuns, discussing lanterns that caught our eye. She liked ones of unusual shape or colour; I preferred small, sturdy ones that were sure to go far. I explained to her how I had made them as a boy: with bamboo and string and old sliding-screen paper.

'They were terrible,' I said. 'They always sank or tilted. One even caught on fire. But each year I became better at making them, until finally, the year of my father's death, I made one that lasted the journey from the top of the river to the bend.'

She nodded. 'It's a lovely tradition. I wish I had done something like that when my parents died.'

'Oh?' I knew she had family in Geraldton, so I had presumed her parents were alive.

'A car accident. When I was young. My mother's sister's family brought me up.'

'I'm sorry.' And because I did not know what else to say, I looked out to sea.

We said nothing further as we watched the surface of the water dance with light. Standing in silence by the shore, I felt closer to Bernice than I ever had before.

Loveday
1942

At camp, I emerged from the darkness of the kitchen into the glare of the midday sun. My hands were wet and numb, as I had just finished lunchtime dishwashing duty. I sensed movement to my right. The bobbing habit of a nun. But it was only someone's laundry—a white shirt flapping in the breeze.

As I walked towards my tent, I heard a cheer coming from the quadrangle. I moved closer and a knot of figures unbraided and scattered. Someone in the middle of the group stepped forward and laughter erupted. It was Ebina, one of the men from Batavia who was also an orderly at the infirmary. His arm circled the air. Thirty feet away someone swung a bat, then dropped it to the ground with a hollow clunk.

'Ganbare, ganbare!' one of the men called, and the batter began to run.

The first baseman was on the ground, scrambling on hands and knees to grasp the ball. He jumped up and ran back to his base a second before the batter reached it. The baseman raised his arms and cheered.

The batter doubled over, laughing. 'I'm too old for this. I can hardly breathe!' he said, his chest heaving.

'Well, you're in better shape than this ball. Look—it's already falling apart,' the baseman said. A bundle filled his hand. 'At this rate, we'll need a new one for every play.'

'Ibaraki-sensei,' Ebina called, waving me over. 'Want to join the game?'

I shook my head. Although baseball had been one of my favourite pastimes as a youth, it had been a decade since I had picked up a bat. At university, I had sometimes played catch with the other students on the grassy slope near the medical wing. If the weather was good, we walked across to Ueno Onshi Park to hit a few balls. The sun on our faces, the smell of the leather mitt—the simple joys of those days. Once we started our internships, however, we no longer had time to play. By the time I was married and working full-time, I rarely thought about baseball.

'I'll just watch,' I said. 'It's been a long time since I played.'

'It's been a long time for us, too. Can't you tell? We can't even remember how far the pitch is from the home plate.'

'Well, in the major league it's sixty feet away . . . But obviously you wouldn't need to replicate that here.'

Ebina's face creased into a smile. 'So you do know how to play! Come on, sensei, why don't you have a go? We're a few people short of a team. We could use someone who knows what they're doing.'

I shifted uneasily on my feet.

'It's just for fun,' the first baseman said. 'Here, look at our ball. We're not going to get very far with it anyway.'

He threw it to me and I caught it. It was surprisingly heavy. Wound strips of fabric formed a misshapen sphere, much like a dense ball of string. The ragged fabric ends peeled off like dead skin.

'There's a stone at the core. We got the roundest one we could find. Then we covered it in fabric strips taken from some of the kitchen cleaning rags—and one of Ebina's old shirts.' The baseman smirked.

'Here, let me show you,' Ebina said, taking the ball from me. He hurled it at the ground. I expected it to land with a thud, but it bounced once, twice, before landing several feet away. 'It's not perfect, but it's the best we have. And there's only one—we don't even have enough material to make a second one! And here, look at our bat . . .' He gestured to the catcher, who came trotting towards me, holding out the bat for me to inspect. It was a crudely hewn piece of pale grey wood that tapered at one end. The surface had been lightly sanded but was full of bumps.

'It's a branch that one of the men dragged in from the vegetable gardens,' Ebina said. 'We asked one of the carpenters to make us a better one, but he hasn't found the right type of wood yet.'

Seeing them playing baseball together reminded me of the divers in Broome, who were always so at ease in each other's company. When I walked through Japtown on my way to a meeting of the Japanese Association, I would see them crouching in laneways and conversing, or leaning against the verandahs of the buildings on the main street, passing a cigarette between them. I'd glimpse them through the windows of the Roebuck, glasses in hands, faces red. They were my countrymen, but the way they conducted themselves was almost alien to me. To be a diver was never to be alone.

'Why not have a hit?' Ebina urged.

'No. I won't be any good.'

'Come on, sensei. Just one ball,' said the catcher, still holding out the bat. A few others voiced their support.

'Oh, all right, then. But I warn you, I haven't played in years.'

The men clapped and cheered as I walked up to the plate and aligned my body. Ebina gathered himself on the pitcher's mound. 'Ready?'

I nodded.

The ball came towards me much slower than I expected. It was slightly wide, and although I was tempted to reach out and tap it, I refrained from doing so, knowing that the hit would be weak. Restraint, after all, is the secret of any good batter. It hurtled past my shoulder, turning slowly. I wondered if Ebina had meant to give me a slow ball. But as he wound up for the second pitch, the concentration was clear on his face. The second ball came surer, faster, and I steeled myself for a hit. I swung hard, but too soon, and connected with the ball at the end of my swing, so that there was little force to propel it. The ball bounced once, then landed in a fielder's cupped hands. I had only taken a few steps away from the plate when he threw the ball to first base. I laughed as the baseman stretched out his arms. In less than a minute, I was out.

I finished my shift at the infirmary at seven o'clock and began the long walk back to the compound. When I'd first started at the infirmary, the sun set right in front of me, the horizon ablaze with orange and red, wispy pink clouds streaking the sky. I paced myself on these walks, enjoying the spectacle that seemed to have been staged just for me. It made me think of the time I'd first stepped off the ship in Broome as a twenty-nine-year-old, overwhelmed by the hugeness of the sky. Even during the wet, when dark clouds hung low week after week, I never grew accustomed to its size.

But the days were becoming shorter, and now only a thin line of orange could be seen above the horizon. The rest of the sky was the colour of ink.

Sometimes I looked across the road to 14A and saw the Italians leaning against the fence or standing in the quadrangle. They would wave and yell, 'Medico! Medico!' at me as I went by. But as I walked towards the gate tonight, there was not a soul in sight. The guard let me back into camp. I was aching for a shower. My shift had not been particularly difficult, but I was tired. The weeks were catching up with me.

I hadn't taken more than a dozen steps away from the gate when a figure appeared from behind the nearest row of tents. I recognised the rolling gait before I saw his face.

'Hey, Doc.'

'Johnny. What do you want?' I hadn't seen him since the film night and was immediately on my guard.

'I've been trying to get a hold of you all week. I was beginning to think you were avoiding me. Look, I know we probably haven't got off to the best start here, but I wanted to ask you a favour.'

'A *favour?*'

He took a deep breath. 'It's about the baseball. We want to play too. The Australians deserve a go, just like everyone else.'

'I don't understand. Why can't you make your own team?'

'Don't you think I've tried? I've got six other blokes who want to play, but no one else wants to join our team or play against us. I swear the mayor has told everyone to steer clear of us. Has he?'

I shook my head. 'Johnny, not this again.'

'What? We're outcasts in here. Can't you see that?'

The half-castes and Australian-born had formed a clique, sleeping in tents a little way from the others, eating at a separate table and doing different chores. Even when they worked outside the camp grounds, they didn't have to wear the maroon uniforms that everyone else wore. They spent their time chatting to the guards and officers, which didn't help their reputation in camp. If they were outcasts, they were outcasts of their own making.

'All I want you to do is make a suggestion to Mori. Convince him to start a baseball competition that gets every tent involved—a big, inter-compound competition. First the different teams in each compound play each other, then the winning team plays the winner of 14B. Mori won't listen to us, but you're a doctor; he respects you.'

I shook my head. 'I am not sure I could convince him,' I said, thinking of my failure to delay Major Locke and Mr Mackenzie on the night of the film.

'Just *try*. Come on, what harm can it do?'

'You forgot Major Locke—he will have to approve the competition. He will have final say.'

'Locke will love it. The commander's been going on about internee morale and sports and this and that. The baseball comp will fit right into that. Plus, I can sweet talk McCubbin and some of the other officers. They're bored out of their brains here, too. The comp will give them something to look forward to.'

I hesitated. Although I took issue with Johnny's attitude, it was a good idea. But I didn't want to be seen as his ally. Wind stirred the trees, making them whisper to each other.

'I can try,' I said. 'But I cannot promise anything. I might have more luck approaching Yamada first.'

Johnny curled his lip in disgust. 'Not that bastard. Not after what he did to Stan.'

I bristled at the slur. 'If you want my help, stop spreading lies about Yamada. He is the deputy mayor and a good man. You must treat him with respect.'

Johnny's eyes flashed. 'Lies? What lies? Yamada kicked Stan out of the mess hall and hit him with a steel pole, and now Stan's so hard up he can't work. Yamada's a thug. People like that don't deserve my respect.'

'Yamada would never hit Stan. I would not be surprised if someone in your group said it was Yamada, just to hurt him. If you don't change your attitude, you cannot expect my help in the baseball competition.'

Johnny stared at me. 'Christ almighty, what's *wrong* with you?'

A gust of wind lifted a layer of loose dirt and blew it between us. I held my hand to my mouth and coughed, but Johnny didn't move. The directness of his gaze put me on edge. When he finally spoke again, his voice was strange.

'You know, I used to like you in Broome. Some of the divers didn't. They thought you were odd. The way you didn't talk to them in hospital, letting the nun do all the talking—they thought you acted all high and mighty. Even Captain McDaniels thought you were odd. What was the word he used? Aloof. I heard him say it to Mrs Dunn once when she asked why you didn't come to all the parties like the previous doctor. But I thought you were a decent bloke. You were quiet and you didn't stick your nose into anyone else's business. But now I see you're just a coward—like the rest of the Japs here.'

In the corridors of my family home, I followed a woman with long, dark hair. It was my mother, in her silver *obi* that flashed in the light. Then she was Kayoko, in her colourful wedding kimono patterned with swooping cranes. I strained to see her face behind the curtain of dark hair. The hall stretched before me, impossibly long. At the end was a door leading to the storage room of the laboratory where I worked.

Don't go there, I called. *Kayo, wait!*

But she couldn't hear me. I tried to run ahead, but I didn't get far. Helpless, I watched as she put her hand on the doorknob. And then—

'Sensei? Sensei! Are you awake?'

A hand shook my shoulder with startling firmness. I blinked. A black shape loomed above me beneath the canvas roof of the tent. For a moment I thought it was Kayoko, her hair in a loose bun.

'Yamada-san—is that you?' I asked.

Yamada's hair formed unkempt peaks at the top of his head. 'An officer wants you. There's a problem at the infirmary. Can you go with him now?'

I shivered. Cold wind pierced the heavy woollen fabric of my coat. Officer McCubbin buried his hands in opposite armpits as he walked, his rifle bumping against his back.

'This Suzuki fella, we think he tried to kill himself. Tried to cut his wrist with glass,' he said.

I caught my breath. 'Suzuki? Not Stanley Suzuki? Stan?'

'Yeah, that's him. Know him, do you?'

'He came to see me at the infirmary the other day.' I was stunned. Stan had been upset when I'd seen him, but I hadn't detected any deeper malaise.

'Yeah? What for?'

'He'd hurt his arm. A minor injury.'

'Yeah, well, he's a bloody mess now. Someone from his tent found him in the ablutions block, so he grabbed me and we carried him to the hospital at HQ.'

Images floated up from somewhere deep. A bloodstain on wet clothes.

'What is his condition?'

'Hard to say. I think he'll survive, but I can't be sure.'

'Is he conscious?'

'Yeah, but a bit out of it. When we picked him up he was telling us to stop. The commander's worried because it's the third suicide attempt by a Japanese since January. Any more and the authorities will be asking why.'

'Three?'

'There was a New Caledonian in 14B who bit off his tongue, the New Caledonian in this camp, and now Suzuki.'

'The New Caledonian in this camp?'

'Yeah, the one who actually died. You don't remember? He ate a packet of rat poison from the kitchen. Someone found him the next morning. This was back in February, I think.'

'It must have been before I arrived.'

I was unfamiliar with the nuances of treating a suicidal patient. Although suicide was common in Japan, failed attempts were rarely treated in hospital. It was usually a private affair.

'Powell, the medical assistant, is looking after Stan because Dr Ashton is out of town,' McCubbin said. 'Then I remembered you were a doctor. From Broome, is that right?' He peered at me. One of his eyes wobbled outwards. A triangle of sand-coloured hair was visible on his forehead beneath the peak of his military cap. He was younger than most of the other officers, some of whom were veterans of the First World War.

'I worked at a Japanese hospital in Broome for several years, until I was interned.'

'There was a Japanese hospital in Broome? Just for the Japanese?'

'Not just for the Japanese—we treated others, of course: Malays, Manilamen, the local Aborigines and sometimes the Britishers.'

'They brought you all the way out from Japan to work in Broome? Christ, you must be good.'

'To be honest, the salary was only modest. But I was still young, with little experience. And I wanted a change.'

He nodded. 'Now *there's* something I can relate to,' he said. 'Wanting a change. That's why I joined the army when I was eighteen. I grew up in Victoria. A town called Charlton. Couldn't wait to get out, see the world, do my bit for my country. I was posted in Egypt for a few months, that's how I got this bung eye.' He pointed at his lazy eye, and pulled his scarf aside to reveal a purple-red scar that ran from his nose to his cheekbone.

McCubbin continued talking about his injury, and the horrific wounds he saw while a patient at a hospital in Cairo. I nodded but didn't say anything. I was anxious to get to the infirmary as soon as possible.

The wind lulled, and the silence amplified the sound of our footsteps. Our strides were out of rhythm; his long, loping gait kept a steady pace against my staccato steps. Here and there stubborn weeds were growing; they held drops of dew that shone like glass beads under the floodlights.

Before long, we reached the birdcage gate, then continued along the road to HQ.

Inside the army hospital, Johnny was leaning over Stan's bed, but when he saw me he stood up. We locked eyes. Lieutenant Powell, the medical assistant, touched his fingers to Stan's neck to take his pulse. Then he stepped back to allow me to inspect the patient.

Stan's eyes were closed. He cradled his right wrist to his chest, the elbow still bandaged from his prior wound. The front of his shirt was splattered with blood.

'Stan,' I whispered.

His eyelids flickered open. He stared at me with glassy eyes, then turned his head aside.

I gently lifted his arm and eased away the blood-soaked wad of gauze. A shard of glass was lodged in his wrist. Blood caked the edge of the wound at one end, forming a bridge between skin and glass; at the other end, bright red blood bubbled. I quickly replaced the gauze.

'What do you think?' Powell asked.

If I had been at the hospital in Broome, I would have made preparations for surgery straight away. But at camp, I wasn't sure.

'He has severed a peripheral artery. It is deep, but a clot has started to form. If I try to remove the glass, he could lose a lot more blood. I think it is too dangerous to operate here. He should go to the hospital in Barmera. In the meantime, I'll dress the wound.'

Johnny snorted. 'Some doctor you are . . .'

'Pardon?'

'That's all you're doing, dressing the wound? Stan could die in the next few minutes and all you want to do is slap a bandage on him? Oh, but I forgot: you're the reason he's in here.'

McCubbin had been standing near the entrance to the ward so quietly I'd almost forgotten he was there. He stepped towards us now. 'Cut it out, Johnny. We don't need another scene from you.'

'What? It's true,' Johnny said. 'Stan was different after he went to the infirmary. Said the doc thought he was lying about what happened in the mess hall. After that he didn't want to talk to anyone. And then tonight he goes missing and turns up on the floor of the shower block with his wrist cut up.'

The air in the ward was heavy. I opened my mouth, then closed it. I glanced at Stan, but he was still turned away from me.

McCubbin checked his watch. 'How about we quit fighting and take him into town. I'll get a truck from HQ. Sound okay?'

I nodded, glad for the suggestion. Lieutenant Powell and I began to dress Stan's wound. All the while, I was aware of Johnny's presence nearby, like a shadow that fell over me. Hours later—long after we had moved Stan into the truck and I had returned to camp—I lay awake in bed, unable to forget what Johnny had said.

The materials to build sleeping huts finally arrived, and not a moment too soon. The temperature had dipped sharply in recent weeks. At night, once the sun sank below the horizon, we huddled in our tents with the canvas closed, playing *hanafuda* and *shogi* until it was time to sleep. In the morning, frost coated the tent ropes in lines of crystal beads.

Building the fifteen huts required a major camp reshuffle. Although there were several dozen trained carpenters and shipbuilders in the population, dozens more men were needed to complete the task. Able-bodied men were asked to work at the rate of a shilling a day, to be paid for from the profits of the canteen. At the infirmary, I was sorry to lose Shiobara to the hut-building project. He had been an attentive orderly. Hayashi, Yamada's friend from Sumatra who'd moved into our tent, agreed to start working at the infirmary in his place.

Although training Hayashi kept me busy during the long shifts, whenever I was cutting the hard loaves of bread or washing the patients' dishes, I found myself thinking of Stan. The operation had been successful, we'd heard, and he was recovering in hospital. The news brought me great relief, and I felt vindicated in my decision to send him to Barmera, where he was no doubt receiving very good care. But I couldn't shake the feeling I was to blame for Stan's attempt to take his life. As much as I tried to convince myself no one could have known the extent of his despair, the incident continued to weigh on me. There was no one I could turn to for advice. My closest friend at camp, Harada, was far too ill to listen to my troubles.

Lying in bed at night, I turned over the possibilities in my mind. *Could* Yamada have been the one who hurt Stan? It seemed ridiculous. I felt it more likely that in his compromised mental state Stan had misidentified Yamada, or perhaps he'd even deliberately hurt himself and somehow convinced himself that it was Yamada's doing. His recent self-harm certainly attested to that possibility. I could raise the topic with Yamada, but the thought of doing that made me uncomfortable. If only there was a way to ask him indirectly. Then I remembered the executive meeting the next day—it was held in the mess hall every Wednesday after lunch. I had attended the meeting in my first week to familiarise myself with the executive members and the running of the camp, but since I had started working at the infirmary I'd had no time to attend. Stan's attempted suicide would surely be discussed; then I could see Yamada's reaction for myself, and hopefully clear up any doubts I had, once and for all.

I finally drifted into sleep. I dreamed I was searching for oysters on the ocean floor. My gloved fingers were clumsy as I felt for the shells among the sand and reeds. I felt a tug on my line, the signal for me to surface, but I pushed on. I kept seeing something before me, a glimmer of white, but no matter how much I sifted and scraped away the sand, I couldn't find the shell.

The following afternoon I stepped into the mess hall, momentarily blind in the darkened space. The air was sweet with the scent of curry, the lingering remains of lunch. I heard a voice ahead, speaking in a monotone. As my eyes adjusted to the gloom, I saw the head of the news committee, Nishino, standing at the back of the hall, reading from a piece of paper in his hand. Tables and chairs were arranged in rows around him, occupied by about two dozen people.

'. . . Australian–American forces in the Coral Sea. The Japanese side, led by Commander Inoue, invaded and occupied Tulagi before launching an airstrike against Allied forces.'

News of a battle in waters northeast of Australia near New Guinea had circulated earlier in the week, so everyone listened intently. I was hoping to slip in unnoticed, as it was not my custom to attend the weekly committee meetings, but as I moved away from the door, my shadow danced across the floor. Yamada's head snapped up; he saw me. He sat with Mori and Hoshi at the front of the room. Mori's hands were clasped on the table before him, head down as he listened. Secretary Hoshi scribbled notes.

'Total Japanese losses included one aircraft carrier, one destroyer, three warships, plus several more damaged. One article noted Japan lacks the facilities to build new warships, so every loss is worth double. Reports on Saturday stated that after five days of action, the battle temporarily ceased on Friday, with Japan retreating. They're expected to return soon in greater strength, with the aim to take either Australia, New Caledonia or the Solomon Islands.'

There was silence as Nishino finished and looked up from his notes. I was surprised by the news of Japan's losses: prior to this, Japan had seemed unstoppable, with victories in the Philippines, Singapore, Burma and Broome coming one after the other.

'Are you sure you translated that correctly—Japan *retreated?*' Mori asked.

'Yes, sir. The reports stated Japan was repulsed.'

Mori frowned. He whispered in Hoshi's ear.

'Well, how many ships did *they* lose? Why didn't you include that?' Yamada asked, leaning forward in his seat.

'None of the articles specified the number of Australian or American losses. Only that they were comparatively light

. . . Although a recent report from Tokyo said bad weather prevented a Japanese victory.'

'That's a lie!' Old Imagawa, the leader of row eleven, thumped his fist on the table. 'We wiped out their fleet, just like in Java. One of my men said the Germans heard it on the radio. Japan would never retreat—we fight until death!'

Nishino ducked his head. He studied the notes in his hand, as if rereading them would provide a different meaning.

Mori spoke up. 'Yes, the Australian newspapers must be lying. They can't be trusted. I recommend you don't post these translations on the board in the recreation hut. It will only cause confusion and distress.'

Nishino looked alarmed. 'But people will ask us where they are. There's always a line of people waiting to read them on a Wednesday afternoon. What will I say?'

'Tell them the enemy is writing lies that aren't worth reading. Tell them the newspapers can't be trusted. All those in favour of withholding translations this week?'

Two-thirds of the room raised their hands. Nishino sat down and stared at the table with troubled eyes. I pitied him, although I wasn't surprised at the response in the room. Had it been me, I would have avoided translating the articles in question. It is better to be discreet and present a partial truth than risk conflict.

Discussion moved to the progress of the building of the huts. The project leader explained they were already behind schedule. Not all fifteen buildings would be completed by early June, as planned. A lengthy discussion followed about how we'd cope in tents in winter, the possibility of increasing labour numbers to speed up construction, who'd be moved into completed huts first and the logistics of shifting them.

It took up so much time that I wondered whether we'd cover anything else. I looked at my watch: forty minutes had passed. But before long the conversation dwindled and Mori looked up.

'We don't have much time, but is there any other news?' he asked.

At the back of the group, Umino, the leader of row two, raised his head. 'We haven't yet talked about the attempted suicide by one of my members.'

'Ah, yes. The half-caste, Suzuki,' Mori said. 'Please describe the incident for our records.'

'Actually, I noticed Dr Ibaraki in the room. Maybe he could explain, since he was at the hospital that night.'

Put on the spot like that, I was stunned. Everyone looked at me, including Yamada. Then he smiled, his eyes full of curiosity. Seeing him like that, I was reminded of how kind he could be, and it put me at ease.

'Yes, of course. I was woken in the middle of the night, maybe one or two o'clock. An officer asked me to come to the hospital at HQ to tend to a critical patient, as Dr Ashton was away. Upon my arrival I found Suzuki weak yet conscious, suffering considerable blood loss. He'd been found in the ablutions block, having cut his wrist with glass. Luckily, the piece of glass in his wrist stemmed some of the blood flow. I deemed it too risky to perform the operation at HQ, so the officer took Suzuki to Barmera hospital, where they operated on him.'

'How is his condition now? Stable?' Mori asked.

'Yes, stable, I believe. But Dr Ashton or his assistant, Powell, would know best.'

'And in your opinion, it was definitely a suicide attempt?'

'I believe so, yes . . . But he'd also come to the infirmary earlier that week with a badly bruised arm. He said he'd been beaten by a group of men here in the mess hall.' I hadn't intended to bring up the alleged beating in front of Yamada, but it seemed appropriate given the context.

My eyes flicked to Yamada, and I was surprised to discover that his expression had changed. His eyes had narrowed and his lips were puckered in something like a scowl.

'But how is this connected to his suicide attempt?' Mori asked. 'Are you saying you think these men who beat Suzuki tried to kill him, too?' A pause. 'Sensei, did you hear me?'

I had to drag my eyes from Yamada. 'I'm sorry. Do I think the men tried to kill Suzuki? No, not at all. Suzuki admits he cut his wrist. I just wonder if the beating contributed to his despondency and his attempt to take his life. Shouldn't someone investigate?'

'Only if he makes an official complaint. Unfortunately we don't have the resources to look into every dispute we hear about. And with the population increasing, it will only become more difficult. Just to clarify, sensei, did Suzuki appear despondent when you saw him at the infirmary?'

'In hindsight, I suppose there were signs of mild depression, but not enough to cause alarm. He came to see me about his arm, not his mental state.'

'But if what you say is true—that you didn't notice anything particularly unusual about Suzuki's state of mind when he came to see you about his bruised arm—you can hardly draw a link between that and his subsequent suicide attempt, can you? I mean, if a doctor can't detect mental instability, who can?'

I shifted in my seat. Mori's gaze bore down on me, like a light exposing my flaws. The silence expanded.

'Well, he did cry when he saw me at the infirmary,' I said softly.

If Mori heard me, he made no indication of it, bundling together the papers on the table before him. 'Thank you for your concern, Doctor. If Suzuki decides to lodge a complaint, we will look into it more fully. Now, as we're running out of time, I'd like to get on to other matters.'

The meeting moved on to a discussion about a ceremony to mark Navy Memorial Day on the twenty-seventh of June. I was so consumed by the change that had come over Yamada when I'd mentioned Stan's beating that I lost track of time. Was he guilty of hurting Stan, or just angry that I would dare to take an interest in the *haafu*?

It was only when Mori called for any final points to discuss that I remembered Johnny's request. I raised my hand. 'I have a proposal regarding baseball. Do we have time to discuss it now?'

'If it's quick. What do you have in mind?'

'After only a few weeks of practice, we now have three full teams: the team from Batavia and Menado, which I'm a part of; the team from Sumatra and Surabaya; and the New Caledonians and divers from northern Australia. Others at camp are interested in joining. And from what I'm told by the orderlies at the infirmary, B compound have their own baseball teams, too. This made me think: perhaps we could start an inter-camp competition? The winners of our camp could play the winners of B Camp. That way, we could get both camps involved.'

'That's a good idea,' someone murmured.

Yamada nodded.

'I appreciate your enthusiasm, sensei,' Mori said. 'But how will we ever convince Major Locke to allow us to move between camps? He's very averse to risks, as you know.'

'Yes, but I hear Commander Dean encourages sports—anything to counter boredom, which he thinks leads to unrest,' I said. 'We could partner with 14B and take our proposal straight to the commander.'

Mori shook his head. 'No. I don't want to risk angering Major Locke by going straight to the commander. He could make things difficult for us.'

I slumped in my chair. No one said anything for a moment.

'Perhaps we should just start with a competition within our compound,' Yamada said. 'Then, Ibaraki-sensei, through your contacts at the infirmary, tell the interested parties in 14B to start their own competition. With any luck, once Major Locke sees the enthusiasm for the competition, he'll allow the two camps to play each other. And if not, we'll keep it as a competition within our own camps.'

Mori nodded. 'That sounds reasonable. Does anyone have any comments or objections?'

I searched the faces of the men around me.

'Shall we vote? All in favour?'

Almost everyone in the room put up their hand.

'All against?'

There were no hands in the air.

'Good. Motion passed. Ibaraki-sensei, I trust you can take it from here?'

I nodded, glancing at Yamada. He exuded calm benevolence once again. The reversion was so complete that I wondered if his previous expression had just been my eyes playing a trick.

Tokyo
1935

Kayoko and I had our first rendezvous on *setsubun*, the last day of winter. Wanting to avoid the crowds that would flock to the larger shrines and temples for the day's festivities, I suggested a visit to an old temple in Kita Aoyama. It was a charming temple I had stumbled on some months previously, featuring a dramatic double-eaved roof. The grounds were compact yet meticulously manicured, with camphor and zelkova trees in abundance.

I arrived early and waited for Kayoko at the entrance. At my mother's insistence, I had worn a *hakama* over my kimono, an outfit reserved for very special occasions. 'She'll be wearing her best kimono—it would be rude not to do the same. Besides, it's *setsubun*,' Mother had said.

Not used to wearing the sandals that cut between my toes and the heavy silk skirt that swished around my legs as I walked, I was glad for the opportunity to stop walking.

It was a cold, bright day. Sun shone through the canopy of leaves and threw dappled patterns at my feet. I heard the low beat of a drum from somewhere within the temple. People strolled along the stone path in twos or threes and larger family groups. Children ran ahead of their parents, excited by the prospect of tossing beans to ward off evil spirits. In my *hakama*, I felt out of place. Although there were several younger men in kimono, I was the only man of my generation in such formal attire. I fretted about the impression I would make. Would I seem a traditionalist to Kayoko? I cursed myself for listening to my mother.

Before long, Kayoko came towards me. As she neared, she smiled shyly. She wore a kimono of the softest peach, a grey *haori* on top of it and an elaborate cloth *kanzashi* in her hair. I breathed a sigh of relief. She was dressed as formally as I was.

'Kayoko, it's a pleasure to see you,' I said, bowing stiffly.

She murmured a greeting, dipping her head. Neither of us said anything for a moment. She glanced towards the temple. 'Shall we go in?'

As we walked along the path, I inquired after her parents and she asked after my family. She described the snow she had seen from the train to Tokyo. Two military officers passed us. The insignia on their khaki jackets indicated they were captains, and I was reminded there was an elite army training facility nearby. Silence fell between us as we passed under the stone gate and into the grounds of the temple.

'Did you do the *mamemaki* this year?' I asked.

Kayoko laughed. 'Father wanted to, but I told him I was too old to be throwing beans while he danced around like a devil. I must admit he looked rather sad when I said that. Sometimes I think he wants me to remain a child. They both do. They forget I'm already twenty-two, and almost ready for—' her eyes darted towards me '—marriage.'

I remembered Kayoko was the Sasakis' only child. Perhaps that was why they had often invited our family to outings to the beach, to give Kayoko someone to play with. As she talked about her family, I began to relax. Her *koto* performance had suggested a serious personality, but she was much more amiable than that. I had a hazy memory of the tomboy who used to run along the shore with Nobu and me, even when Megumi preferred to stay with our mother on the dunes.

We reached the area in front of the main hall, where several dozen people had congregated. The space thrummed with activity. On one side of the elevated cloister a taiko drummer was rhythmically striking the wide skin of his drum, while on the other a performer in red and black robes and a devil's mask danced and writhed for show. The crowd in front of the hall threw beans at the devil, calling, 'Out with the devil! In with good fortune!' It was fun for a while, watching the devil's antics and the children screaming in delight, but I sensed Kayoko growing restless, so I suggested we take a walk along the alley at the back of the temple.

The alley was one of the reasons I had suggested this particular temple. About twelve feet wide and lined with various stalls, it provided the perfect setting for our first outing—quiet enough to carry on a conversation, yet providing enough distractions to fill any awkward silences. We wandered past the stalls, savouring the smell of grilled food. *Taiyaki* sizzling on an iron griddle; *yakiniku* skewers, sardines and squid scorched over hot coals. I stopped to buy some squid for me and *taiyaki* for Kayoko.

We were discussing our recollections of our childhood encounters when two girls sauntered past us, making everyone's heads turn. They wore pale, wide-brimmed felt hats and wide-legged trousers—the type favoured by American movie stars. One of the girls had her hair cut short, very short, with a sharp fringe framing her face. Among the dozens of women clad in colourful kimonos, the two modern girls certainly stood out. I had seen this type of western clothing on women in fashionable districts such as Ginza, although the trend seemed to have diminished in recent years. I'd never before seen it worn in an alley behind a temple. Without thinking, I said, 'Those girls should know better than to flaunt themselves like that.'

'Like what?' Kayoko's face was turned towards me, her eyes full of curiosity.

'Well, I mean, the modern style. The way foreign women dress.'

A smile played on her lips. 'Is there something wrong with the modern style? I've worn it myself in the past, you know.'

I blanched, aware of how conservative I must have sounded. 'No, I'm sorry. There's nothing wrong with it. I just thought, in this situation . . . Anyway, it was a silly thing to say. Shall we keep walking?'

'But it's *setsubun*,' she said. 'Surely, today of all days, they can dress up how they want?'

I had forgotten that on *setsubun*, when spirits came close to the living and the world was thrown into disarray, there was a tradition of role reversal. Girls sometimes dressed as men or wore their hair in the style of older women. Still, I couldn't deny that something about the girls bothered me. I was about to say as much when I heard a commotion behind me and someone shrieked.

I turned and craned my neck to look past the small crowd that had gathered a dozen feet away. I heard a scuffle, someone shouting. Then I saw them: the two army officers who'd passed

111

us earlier were confronting the two modern girls. One of the officers, his cap pushed back to reveal his red face, gripped the arm of the girl with the short hair. Her hat was gone, presumably dropped to the ground or snatched away.

'You want to dress like foreign whores, do you?' the officer shouted. 'Well, do you? Answer me!'

The girl's eyes were wide with fear. She stood stiffly in the officer's grip, unable to speak or move. Her friend sobbed behind her, hands over her mouth. Everyone else was quiet. In the lull, the sound of the sizzling meat and distant taiko drumming swelled like a surging heartbeat.

'Are you hypocrites, like the foreigners you admire? You must be, if you call yourself Japanese yet dress like this.' The officer shook the girl's arm. Her body quaked.

Before I could stop her, Kayoko had made her way past me. I called to her to wait, but it was no use. I watched the back of her head, adorned with tortoiseshell combs and silk flowers, move between the people who had stopped to stare. There was nothing I could do but follow. I had almost reached Kayoko when I heard her voice.

'Sir, these girls are just young. They mean no harm. I'm sure their clothes are just play for *setsubun*.'

The officer spun around. He glared at Kayoko, then me. 'The young girls of Japan are our biggest problem. They drink and smoke and dress like the foreigners they idolise—the very same foreigners who mock us from across the seas. These girls shame the Emperor. They're a disgrace to our nation.'

'That may be so,' Kayoko murmured, lowering her gaze.

The officer said nothing for a moment as his eyes roamed over Kayoko. Then he spoke more calmly. 'You look like a respectable young lady. Perhaps you could teach these girls

a thing or two about how Japanese women should behave.'
With Kayoko in her finest kimono, and me in my *hakama*,
we must have looked a very proper couple.

He turned to the girls. 'Next time I see you wearing such
trash, I won't be so kind.' He dropped the girl's arm and,
signalling to his friend, stalked away.

When the officers were out of sight, Kayoko whispered to
the girls, 'Go home quickly, before they come back.'

The girl who was crying nodded. She tugged at her friend's
arm. 'Come, Aya, let's go.'

Still dazed, the short-haired girl stooped to pick up her
hat from the ground. It was crushed and covered in dust.
The girls walked away.

Kayoko's poise during the affray at the temple left a lasting
impression on me. Our bond strengthened in the following
weeks. We met at coffee shops and parks, talking freely
about our views and dreams. She didn't believe husbands and
wives should keep secrets from each other, and she wanted
children—'at least three'—as did I. With each encounter, I felt
surer we'd be happy as husband and wife. I often thought
back to our conversation about the modern girls, how she had
defended them. She was self-assured, yet sensitive to others.

One Sunday, after I'd returned from a trip to Ueno Zoo
with Kayoko, Mother stopped me in the hallway. 'You're not
married yet. It's not right for two unmarried people to spend
so much time together—people will start talking,' she said.
'And besides, if you keep this up, when you do get married
you'll have nothing left to talk about. Your father and I were
engaged for a year and we only saw each other four times

in that period. It made the first year of our marriage all the more enjoyable, being able to learn so many new things about each other.'

I proposed three weeks later. Mother was overjoyed, yet a little surprised—I suspected she hadn't thought I'd warm to the idea of marriage so quickly. We planned a wedding at Kayoko's family home in early autumn, when the surrounding hills would be covered in green and golden leaves.

The ceremony took place at a neighbourhood shrine near Kayoko's home where she'd had her *shichi-go-san* ceremonies as a child. We kneeled inside the sanctuary with the priest before us and our families on either side. Gold-panelled folding screens encircled the room, casting everything in a rich light. I was so nervous that my hands shook as I poured the sake. Kayoko put her hand over mine to steady it. Her *wataboshi* caught the light, framing her face like fire.

Afterwards, we greeted guests at the Sasakis' house. More and more arrived, until a line of people spilled out the front door. With caterers weaving among the visitors, the house, which had seemed like a mansion when I was a boy, suddenly felt small.

Mr Sasaki made a touching speech in honour of his only child, describing Kayoko's many talents and her deep compassion. 'She brought light into our lives almost twenty-three years ago, and continues to do so for each new person she meets.' He also spoke very kindly about me. 'I have known Ibaraki-kun since he was a boy, when our families spent much time together. Whether making sandcastles or pursuing a medical degree, he is steadfast to the very end. Now that he and Kayoko are joined together, I know they will have many happy years ahead.' My mother glowed with pride.

That much I remember. Everything seemed to pass in a blur: drinking endless cups of sake with my friends and colleagues, laughing when someone tripped on a step, white envelopes being pushed into my hand. And, of course, my beautiful bride. As she had walked beside me along the path at the shrine, I had stolen a glance at her face: beneath the bold sweep of her black-lined eyes, her red lips trembled slightly. Despite her outward composure, she had a deep fragility. I vowed to protect her for as long as I was alive.

One day, after I'd been working at the laboratory for almost a year, I was called into Shimada's office. I was nervous at being summoned, but my fears were allayed when Shimada greeted me, smiling.

'Major Kimura and I have been discussing the performance of our technicians. The quality of your work and your commitment to our unit have not gone unnoticed. You have a promising career ahead of you, as long as you maintain your focus.' He handed me a letter.

After leaving Shimada's office, I read it and was thrilled to discover I was to receive a considerable salary raise before my first year was over. In previous months, disaffection had been growing within me, and I'd begun to fear I had chosen the wrong career path, and wonder whether I was better suited to practice rather than research. But the money and Shimada's praise revived my spirits. I approached my job with renewed determination, reminding myself that mundane laboratory work was essential to the advancement of medical knowledge.

With my increased salary, and some help from Kayoko's parents, we were able to buy a small twelve-*tsubo* house in

Setagaya. The house had been occupied by an elderly couple who'd let it fall into disrepair—soot blackened the kitchen walls, the bamboo shutters had rotted off their hinges, and the tatami was so worn in places that its broken fibres pricked our feet—but the foundations were stable and it was well located in a quiet street. It also faced south, so natural light filled the sitting room from morning till sunset. We were fortunate to have our own bathtub, even if mould darkened the cypress slats; we wouldn't need to visit the local bathhouse as many of our neighbours had to—this was one of the main reasons Kayoko had favoured the house.

We moved into our new home early in the new year and started on repairs straight away. There were doors to be measured and mats to be ordered. We bought new shutters and installed latches that stopped them from banging in the wind. We replaced our fence with new bamboo stalks, binding them together with rope. We scrubbed the soot from the kitchen, the mould from the bathtub, and the grime from the floors. Kayoko took to the work with a vigour I'd previously only seen in her when she played the *koto*. She insisted we do everything ourselves. 'It's our first house—it should be just the two of us. We'll feel more proud this way.' She could be sentimental about such things.

We were lucky to enjoy an early start to spring as we set about refurbishing our home. As the ice melted on the eaves, Kayoko and I let our inhibitions fall away. During the first few months of our marriage, when we'd lived in my family home, we'd been too aware of ourselves. Around my mother and my brother, our roles as new husband and new wife came to the fore. Kayoko and my mother prepared meals in the kitchen, although Kayoko always ate last. A pillow of silence surrounded us that took away the words we really wanted to say. But in the new house, with only each other to answer to, we found our more natural state.

When I left for work one morning, she was kneeling in the sitting room, surrounded by rolls of rice paper as white as fresh snow. She trimmed a sheet, cutting it to size to replace the torn and yellowing paper on our sliding doors.

'I'll help you put them in place after I come home tonight,' I said, knowing how difficult it was to do alone.

She looked up. A wisp of hair had escaped from her bun and fallen over one eye. Her lips were pressed together in concentration. She gave a small nod. She was beautiful like that.

It was a long walk to the train station, but I didn't mind. Green buds were unfurling on trees and early *sakura* were in bloom, their pale petals shivering in the breeze. I caught the two-carriage train into town, and squeezed in with the other workers in a jumble of elbows and legs. At the laboratory, I spent the day examining blood samples of mice specimens. Although the pathogen being tested was codenamed in the documents I received from Shimada, I recognised the serotype as that of *Typhimurium*. I thought it was odd we were studying the effects of typhoid fever, as a vaccine was already available, but I was too preoccupied with thinking about what needed to be done at home to give it much thought.

I returned home that night expecting to find the house in disarray, but the door at the end of the hallway glowed white. Even in the dark I could tell that the rice paper on the door had been replaced. I eased it open and stepped into the sitting room. The sliding door that led to the kitchen and the one that opened to the bedroom were also lined with fresh paper. The only sign of the task undertaken that day was a neat pile of paper in the corner of the room. A savoury scent drifted from the kitchen. Miso, *konbu* and meat—some kind of stew. I brought my face close to where the edge of the paper met the wooden frame. A perfectly straight line of white.

'You did this by yourself?' I called out to Kayoko in the kitchen.

A shadow filled the doorframe, the ghostly echo of my wife. Then she appeared before me, face flushed pink from the heat of the kitchen, more beautiful than ever. She held a steaming bowl of pork soup in her hands. Sliced shallots flecked the surface. 'Of course. Why? Didn't think I could?'

'No, I just . . .' I glanced around the room. The new paper in the doors brightened the entire room, despite the frayed tatami underfoot. 'Well, yes, I suppose I am a little surprised. You've done such a good job, I thought someone must have helped you.'

'Never underestimate your wife,' she clucked, and started to move past me towards the table. I caught her waist playfully. 'Don't—the soup!' she cried, but when I pulled her close I could see she was smiling.

We purchased a new set of tatami for the sitting room and our bedroom, and it was delivered in two great stacks that crowded our entrance. I wanted to ask my brother or her father to help install them, but Kayoko refused. 'Just ourselves the first time—remember? For our next home we can get their help.'

So over one weekend the two of us pulled out the old tatami mats, stirring up clouds of dust. Kayoko's strength almost matched mine as we hauled them outside and deposited them in a pile at the back of our house to dry out in the sun. We hoped to sell them to the tatami supplier for a small amount. We swept the floor and opened the windows, allowing the breeze to fill the room. After a few hours, we closed the windows and swept again, then carried the new mats one by one into the room. I was surprised by Kayoko's deftness as we guided them into place, she taking charge and slotting them tightly into the corners. She used a metal length to flatten the edges, just as I had seen the tatami supplier do at my family's house when I was a boy. I wondered where Kayoko had learned to do that. After we had installed the very last mat, she trod barefoot across the edges of each one, arms out, like a *maiko* learning to dance. My talented wife, who never ceased to amaze me, tipped her head back and laughed, then continued her nimble dance.

During the first two weeks of spring, Professor Shimada was scarcely in the laboratory to supervise us. It didn't bother us, as we'd all been at the lab long enough to be able to work independently, and it was a relief to carry out our tasks at a more leisurely pace. When Shimada did come down, his eyes would dart about the room, seemingly without taking anything in. His hands worried the sides of his coat.

One time he entered the lab moments after Yamamoto had broken a beaker. Yamamoto was stooped over, sweeping up the shards of glass.

'You broke another beaker? Idiot! Do you know how hard it is for me to get these supplies? Stupid, stupid boy! You're paying for this out of your own salary.' Shimada looked at the rest of us, his face dark with rage. 'That goes for all of you. From now on, anything you break you have to pay for. I keep an inventory, so anything you break—' He caught his breath. His eyes shifted from face to face. Then he turned and left the room.

I went to Yamamoto, took the dustpan and brush out of his hands and swept up the remaining mess. 'Don't worry about him. He must have something on his mind.'

'Have you noticed how often he's up on the top floor these days?' Nomura said, staring at the closed steel door. 'Something big's happening.'

'A restructure?' I suggested.

'Maybe. I just hope we're not going to lose our jobs.'

Later that week, we were called to a meeting in the training room on the top floor. Poor Yamamoto was convinced it had something to do with him breaking the beaker. Although I did my best to persuade him otherwise, considering Shimada's strange behaviour of late, I wasn't sure.

A dark wooden desk stood at the front of the room. Its heavy base and bevelled edges were distinctly European in style. We gathered in a rough arc around it, with Kimura and Shimada facing us on the other side. The room's empty space yawned behind us, yards of untouched carpet and rows of folding chairs stacked neatly along the walls. Through the windows I saw a thick bank of clouds. The overcast day threw sombre light on the left side of Kimura's face. He stood before us, the span of his uniform echoing the broad planes of his face. Shimada appeared smaller beside him, even though he was actually the taller of the two. He looked down, the skin of his jaw drawn tight.

This wasn't just a restructure, I realised, it was something bigger than that—Shimada couldn't even look at us. I glanced

at Nomura, who held my gaze as if he, too, realised the gravity
of the situation.

'You must be wondering why we called you here today,'
Kimura said, placing a folder on the desk. He drew his hands
behind his back. 'We have exciting news that affects everyone
in this unit. From next week, our primary research focus will
change. Instead of solely engaging in bacteriological development, our attention will shift to specimen analysis. We're
entering a new stage, led by our chief, Lieutenant Colonel Ishii
himself. He personally chose our unit to undertake this new area
of research due to the outstanding diligence of our personnel.'

I sighed with relief. So it was a restructure of sorts, that
was all.

'But with our new responsibilities comes a new set of
concerns. Issues of duty, loyalty and prudence—or what I
call discretion.' Kimura's eyes met mine. I wondered if I had
done something wrong. 'Confidentiality is our number-one
priority. The work we are about to undertake has worldwide
significance, as we are the first country to do this kind of
research—I want you to keep that in mind at all times.

'Neither I nor Shimada has ever doubted your loyalty up
till this point, but the new responsibilities may place certain,
shall we say, *strains* on some of you.' Kimura reached out and
flipped the folder on the desk open. 'That's why it's necessary for you to sign a new confidentiality agreement that
replaces the existing contract. You can't talk about your work
to anybody—not your spouse, your parents, your friends,
your children, not even to each other. To do so would put
the entire unit at risk, indeed the entire army. Your actions
could affect those who serve the Emperor now and in years
to come. Do you understand the importance of this?' He

leaned forward and stared at each of us, as if searching for the smallest glimmer of dissent.

'Yes, sir!' we said. I thought of my brother, Nobuhiro, who had just turned eighteen and wanted nothing more than to serve the Emperor in battle. My discretion would be for his sake.

'Good. Any breach of this agreement will have serious ramifications. Not only will it result in your immediate dismissal, but your medical licence may also be revoked. Professor Shimada, do you have anything to add?'

Shimada drew a deep breath. He unclasped his hands and lifted his eyes. His voice was soft. 'As Major Kimura said, it's a groundbreaking area of research. Although the work will be challenging, the overall benefit to medical science is undeniable. We're asking for your full involvement in this matter. So I urge you all to sign the new agreement. Are there any questions?'

'Could you tell us more about the project?' Ota asked.

'At this stage, no. But if you do not wish to sign the agreement, we may be able to find a role for you elsewhere in the department.'

The room was silent. I don't think any of us wanted to move to another unit; it would surely result in our demotion. Despite the strange situation, I did not even consider not signing the contract. I had been waiting for an opportunity such as this and was delighted we had been chosen for the project. Shimada glanced at us but seemed unable to hold our gaze. I wondered why he still appeared so troubled.

'If there are no further questions,' he went on, 'please take a contract and either return it to me before you leave today or speak to me if you have other plans. I'll be in my office for the rest of the day.'

Broome
1939

Soon after the start of the second pearling season since I'd arrived in Broome, I received an envelope in the mail. In elegant cursive script written on smooth rice paper, I was invited to attend an afternoon garden party at President Kanemori's house to 'celebrate the birthday of His Majesty the Emperor of Japan'. The fluid lines of ink slipped down the page.

'*Tenchosetsu* is celebrated here, too?' I asked Harada when he visited me at the hospital the next day.

'Oh yes, it's a big deal,' he said. 'We host a ceremony at the Japanese Association, and there are parties all over town. I'm surprised you haven't heard about it yet. The Japanese businesses close for the day—even the divers at sea get the day off.'

Over the following two weeks, I heard about *tenchosetsu* almost every day. Some of my patients talked about the parties they were going to attend. Dr Wallace wanted to know if I intended to close the Japanese hospital for the day. Umeda, the shop assistant at Tonan Shokai, urged me to display the Japanese flag at the hospital for the occasion. I agreed to help Harada and Kanemori set up the association headquarters and greet guests.

The holiday took place on a mild late-April day, with a southerly that brought cool relief for the first time that year. As I walked through Japtown that morning, I witnessed the early stirrings of life. Ah Wong emptying a pan of dirty water in an alley. Mrs Tan sweeping the front verandah of her store, her youngest child crouched in the doorway watching her. All the Japanese businesses were shut, their verandah railings or front doors proudly displaying the Japanese flag alongside the Union Jack.

The Japanese Association's headquarters had been rejuvenated since my last visit, with a new coat of paint on the latticed verandah and the hedge at the entrance trimmed. Inside, the assortment of tables and chairs that usually filled the meeting room were gone, save for one long cloth-covered table against a wall and a clutch of seats in one corner. A rug I'd never seen before graced the centre of the floor. Bird-of-paradise stems in white vases flanked the portrait of the Emperor on the mantelpiece. I joined Kanemori, Harada and several others in setting out glassware, jugs of lemonade and chilled tea.

I stood at the entrance to greet guests as they arrived. Most were Japanese Association members—long-time residents of Broome with standing in the community—and their families. The wives and daughters, who so rarely wore kimonos around town, appeared in their finery—autumnal red and yellow silk panels and gold-stitched *obi*. Several of Broome's white population also attended—master pearlers such as Captain Kennedy and Captain McDaniels, Magistrate Reynolds and

Sam Male, the acting honorary consul for Japan. Although I'd had the honour of attending parties hosted by the master pearlers before, I realised that for most of our members, *tenchosetsu* offered one of the few opportunities to mingle with the upper echelons of Broome society.

President Kanemori moved to the front of the room and stood beside the image of the Emperor and the birds of paradise, and it struck me that the spear-shaped orange and blue petals perfectly encapsulated Broome's hostile beauty. He spoke in Japanese first, then in English, about the Emperor's wisdom and strength as a leader, illustrated by how far and wide his loyal subjects had spread, including to places such as Broome.

'His courage and devotion fuel the prosperity of our great nation and Greater East Asia,' Kanemori said, but he omitted this sentence in English. He concluded by inviting everyone to toast 'the continued friendship of Japan and Australia'.

Mr Male also gave a short speech, highlighting the contribution of the Japanese community in Broome and the long-standing respect it had commanded.

The gathering lasted a couple of hours, then guests slowly disappeared, returning home to escape the heat of the day before continuing on to other parties. To my surprise, I was one of the last people left, and there was only just enough time for me to walk home, change out of my suit, bathe and put on a white cotton shirt and trousers before departing for the Kanemoris'.

The president lived near the Japanese hospital in a large house similar in style to the master pearlers' bungalows, with a sloping galvanised-iron roof and timber walls. An open verandah encircled the house, and it was within that shady refuge that at least a dozen people were mingling and lounging in chairs when I arrived. I greeted Mrs Kanemori, who looked smart in her long skirt and silk blouse, a pearl brooch at her throat. Harada, already flushed with alcohol, pushed a drink into my hand; the lime and gin cocktail slipped down my throat easily.

Koepanger waiters weaved between us, bearing trays of crab sandwiches, cold prawns and shucked oysters. A table near the steps to the back garden was laden with plates of chopped mango, pawpaw and stuffed kingfish. I was surprised at the choice of food. I'd eaten at the Kanemoris' several times before and had always enjoyed Mrs Kanemori's traditional cooking—she prepared dishes such as glazed eel on rice, and cold noodles with pork, egg and cucumber, the sort of meals I sorely missed from home. I realised the Kanemoris had catered to the western palate on this occasion, yet none of the white men at the ceremony had come to the party. Indeed, the guests on the verandah were almost entirely Japanese, or at least half-Japanese, save for the Chinese wives of a few of the men.

The crowd on the verandah grew, and I found myself conversing with people I'd only exchanged cursory greetings with before. I talked to the new clerk at the Japanese grocery store, Kato, and his wife, who'd recently arrived from Japan. I discovered that they were expecting their first child.

'And what about you, Doctor?' Mrs Kato asked. 'Do you have any children?'

'No,' I said. 'Unfortunately I don't.' And for once I didn't feel uncomfortable admitting so.

As the sun waned, guests began to spill into the garden at the back of the house, clutching their lukewarm drinks as they gossiped beneath the frangipani tree. Two young girls crouched on the ground inspecting the dirt, their *yukata* hitched up to their knees. Crisp clouds tumbled across the sky, and I thought how fortunate I was to be in Broome. By that stage, I'd had four or five drinks—more than I'd had in a while. But instead of feeling tired, as I usually did when I drank, the alcohol suffused me with a pleasant warmth. I gazed at the garden for quite some time.

When I turned back to the verandah, I realised that many guests had gone. Only the men who had come without their wives remained: Harada, the old tender Minami who had assisted some of the best divers in Broome, some of the laundry owners, and the young taxi driver, Johnny, whom I'd met the night of the fight between the Japanese and the Malay. Johnny knew enough Japanese to socialise with the remaining men. Even Mrs Kanemori was nowhere to be seen. I took the opportunity to slip away.

The sky was pink as I started walking home. Wagtails flitted across the sky. Mid-journey, I turned into Carnarvon Street. In my merry state I had a sudden thirst for one of Ellies' special lemon drinks, which Harada had introduced me to soon after I'd arrived. In large glasses about the length of my head, snowy mounds of shaved ice were topped with a lemon concoction, just sweet enough to temper the citrus tang and the frosty hit of ice. Slurped through long straws, it provided a delicious respite from Broome's heat.

I wandered along Carnarvon Street, my focus on the uneven, pebbly surface. The streetlight flickered on, and I was suddenly conscious of all the young people around the entrance to Sun Pictures, talking and laughing as they strolled in couples and groups. I headed towards the open door and yellow lights of Ellies'. William Ellies himself was behind the counter, green eyes twinkling as he smiled at me. Ellies, as he was always called, was much loved in Broome for his cheerful nature as well as for his refreshing drinks. He knew nearly everyone in town by name, and hearing him say, 'Good evening, Dr Ibaraki. Something to quench your thirst?' in his melodic Ceylonese accent was enough to banish any feelings of isolation. His long brown fingers circled the rim of a glass as he dried it with a cloth. I stared dumbly at the menu on the wall behind his head for a few moments, my mind blank. Then I realised someone was calling me.

'Doctor? *Doctor?*' Sister Bernice stood a few feet away from me, her face aglow in the soft light. She looked like an angel.

'Sister! You're here.'

I instantly regretted saying such a silly thing, but she laughed, her eyes crinkling. 'Yes, I'm here. I came with Sister Agnes to get a lemon drink. Are you doing the same?'

Ah, the lemon drink—that's what I wanted. 'Yes. I was just on my way home from the Kanemoris' . . . Sister Agnes—where is she?' I swung around, trying to catch sight of the sister's stiff white habit among the thin cotton shirts and floral dresses inside the cafe.

'She just left. She's on night duty at Dr Wallace's. I was about to leave too, until I saw you. How was the holiday today?'

'*Tenchosetsu?* Oh, it was wonderful. I did not realise what a big event it is here. At least fifty people came to the ceremony, and President Kanemori and Mr Male spoke. After that, I went to a party at Kanemori's house. There was so much food. I met Mr Kato's wife. Do you know him? The young man who works at Tonan Shokai . . . What is it? Is something wrong?'

Sister Bernice was smiling strangely. 'No, I'm sorry,' she said. 'It's just that I've never seen you so excited before.'

Blood rushed to my face as I realised I'd been babbling—the alcohol had loosened my tongue.

Perhaps sensing my mortification, she hurried to put me at ease. 'No, it's fine, really. I'm glad to hear you had such a good time today. You should take time off more often—you obviously needed a break.'

I nodded and said she was probably right.

'Anyway, I should be going,' she said. 'Sister Cecilia will be wondering where I am.'

'Wait, I'll walk with you.'

'But aren't you going to order something?'

I'd completely forgotten about that. I glanced at Ellies, who lifted his eyebrows and smiled—an expression so serene it revealed nothing.

'Actually, I am not very thirsty. I only came here to stretch my legs. It's such a nice night.'

'Well, in that case . . .' She inclined her head and moved towards the door.

Outside, stars were beginning to emerge. The sky was bruised, a purple blush that leaked into the horizon. Bats crowded the expanse on their nightly migration from the mangroves of Roebuck Bay in search of food. They flew so low I could hear the flap of their wings, could smell their pungent odour.

Sister Bernice and I strolled down Carnarvon Street, away from the crowds outside Sun Pictures. Although we had spent many hours alone together at the hospital, we had rarely interacted socially before. I was relieved when she spoke first.

'When you were growing up in Japan, did you ever think you'd end up in a place like this?'

I laughed. 'Never. I did not even know about Australia until middle school. Even Osaka, where my aunt lived, seemed like a long way then. To think—a Japanese hospital in Australia?' I shook my head.

'When I was a child in Perth, my mother used to take me to Kings Park,' she said. 'I loved watching the boats on the Swan River, and I always imagined they were sailing to Africa, because of a silly book I'd once read. I thought: that's where I'll go, one day.'

I was touched that she would share memories of her mother.

We approached the Roebuck Bay Hotel. Chatter and the bitter scent of cigarettes filled the air. I recognised some of the pearling lugger crewmen leaning against the verandah. Lugger crews were paid their annual wages at the beginning of the year and, according to Kanemori, many drank and gambled away everything in the first few months of the season, which was why Japtown boomed at this time of year. It was always the young ones, especially the Japanese and Malay divers, who fell into that trap. They'd return to their homes in December without a cent in their pockets.

Sister Bernice continued speaking of her childhood in Perth, where she'd roamed the bushland at the back of her family's house and spent summers at the beach. Not wanting to interrupt her, I touched her upper arm and guided her across the road, steering her away from the hotel patrons spilling onto the street. She stopped talking. When I looked to see why, her face was closed. Her right hand covered the place on her arm that I had touched. We walked in silence for a few moments.

'Look,' Sister Bernice said suddenly and walked ahead. She stopped in front of a large boab tree and placed her hand on its bloated trunk, as if feeling for its pulse. She peered up through its sparse canopy of glossy green leaves. 'It still has some fruit.'

I joined her beneath the tree and followed the direction of her gaze. Several brown nuts the size of my fist dangled from the uppermost branches.

'Did you see it flower during the wet?' Sister Bernice asked. 'You must have.'

My first thought was that I'd missed it—I recalled a lush green canopy but little else. But then I remembered something. 'Actually, yes, I think I did. Walking home from the Japanese Association one evening I saw white among the leaves. I thought it was birds.'

Bernice nodded. 'That was the flowers. They open for the first time at night, as if they have a secret. And they don't last long—only one or two days. But they're beautiful and have the most wonderful perfume. I always look out for them. When I first arrived in Broome I wasn't sure if I would stay. The sisters were kind, but everything else about the place—the heat, the humidity, the remoteness—I couldn't stand. But then I was out walking one night and I saw flowers bloom on this tree. I was reminded that God watched over me, even in places as distant as Broome. So I decided to stay.'

I smiled. I looked up through the gnarled branches to an inky patch of sky. For the first time since I'd arrived in Broome, I felt as if a weight had been lifted, releasing me from the past.

Loveday
1942

At the infirmary, I stood in the orderlies' room compiling an inventory of the supply cabinet. I wanted to be sure we had the basics in case a second emergency occurred when Dr Ashton was unavailable.

I glanced up. A tall figure filled the doorway.

'Officer McCubbin,' I said. 'Is anything wrong?'

'I think you better come outside.' He stepped back from the door and gestured down the hallway.

My blood ran cold. 'Stan. Is it Stan Suzuki? Did something go wrong?' Perhaps he'd developed an infection after the operation at Barmera hospital and died. Such occurrences were not uncommon. My actions would be called into question over his death. After all, I had seen him just before he cut himself, and it was my decision to send him to Barmera.

McCubbin shook his head. 'No, Suzuki's fine. It has nothing to do with him. Come outside, and I'll tell you.'

I followed him along the dark corridor. I had the feeling I was in a dream, being led towards something I didn't want to see yet unable to stop it. Outside, the landscape was gilded by the afternoon light. The buildings were the same colour as the houses in Broome just after a storm. The sky yawned. Its emptiness was overpowering. McCubbin squinted against the slanting light. He took off his khaki cap and held it to his chest. His face was tight.

'A telegram arrived for you the other day. The censors . . . they thought you should know. Major Locke approved. He asked me to tell you. Anyway, you can read it for yourself.' He reached into his breast pocket and removed a yellow slip of paper. 'I'm so sorry.'

I took the piece of paper and unfolded it. In blue ink, the typed message read, 'Brother Nobuhiro killed in action in Philippines. Funeral Thursday. Letter follows. Mother.'

I read it again. The typed English letters were so unlike my mother's writing that I initially thought it was a hoax. Someone was playing a trick on me. One of the officers, perhaps McCubbin himself? Someone had underlined the words 'Brother Nobuhiro' and 'Funeral Thursday' in red pencil, and written beneath the message, 'Inform recipient due to proximity of date?' As I stared at the words and the date stamp of 15 May 1942, I realised it must be true. No one would play a trick so cruel.

I jerked my head up. McCubbin was saying something.

'I'm so sorry. I know how you feel. I lost a lot of good mates in Egypt. Not my brother, but still . . . Will you . . . will you be all right?' His eyes searched my face.

'The funeral. It says it's on Thursday. Is that tomorrow?' I was aware of the flatness of my voice.

'Yeah, tomorrow. The telegram came Friday. You can send a reply telegram if you want. The Red Cross covers you for two a year.' I must have given him a strange look, for when he next spoke, his voice was softer. 'Or maybe you need some time alone?'

'Yes. I think I'd like to be alone.'

He nodded. 'Good idea. Take it easy. I'll tell the boys in the infirmary you're not feeling well . . .'

I started walking away before he had finished speaking. I can't remember how I got to the gate to my compound. One moment I was walking westwards with the sun in my eyes, and the next I was standing behind the guard. I heard the clack of the metal as he unlatched the gate.

I followed the path, instinctively heading towards my tent and the main buildings of camp. I heard a loud crack and the cry of voices, and realised a baseball team was practising in the quadrangle. If it was the Australian team, they would surely call out to me when I passed them. I veered off my route and turned towards the perimeter fence. Here, the path was shallow and indistinct. Pebbles and dry leaves that had blown into camp mixed with the loose earth.

My feet knew their destination before my mind was conscious of it. After I had walked a short distance, I realised I was moving towards the Buddhist altar located at the rear of the camp, away from the kitchen and mess hall. Of course. The altar and the garden were the perfect places to find solitude.

When I was almost at the garden, I saw a familiar figure on the path ahead. I stiffened. Ever since the executive meeting, something had changed between Yamada and me. We no longer sat next to each other at mealtimes, or played games inside the tent before we went to bed. I had no proof that he had hurt Stan, but I was wary of him, and I think he sensed that.

'Doctor. I thought you were working at the infirmary today.' Yamada glanced at his watch.

'I was. I finished early. I was just about to visit the altar.'

'The altar?' He looked at the telegram I was still holding in my hand. Without thinking, I held it out to him. As I watched the change come over his face while he read the message, I regretted having given it to him. Nobuhiro's death, so soon after it had happened, should have been something I kept close.

Yamada returned the piece of paper to me. His expression was grave. 'Your brother's death must be hard to bear. But you should be proud. He died fighting for the Emperor. He sacrificed himself to save thousands of others. Because of him, we will continue to grow and prosper as a nation. Try not to think of his death as a loss but as a gift. His spirit will be honoured for his bravery.'

I nodded and thanked him for his words, but after I moved away from him and continued towards the altar, my chest felt hollow. Yamada's platitudes about Nobuhiro's bravery did nothing to quell my distress. My only brother was dead. It would never be anything other than a loss to me.

Someone was working in the garden, his back bent over the bed of flowers planted next to the bamboo thicket. I walked past him and stopped in front of the altar where he couldn't see me. I kneeled and prayed. Images of my youth came to mind—the times I had carried Nobu on my back when he was a boy. I had last seen him six years earlier, when he was about to leave home to begin his military training. He had looked taller and stronger in his uniform, the khaki jacket stretched across his chest. 'Look at you, all grown up,' I had said. I hadn't sent him a single letter while he was posted overseas. Now he was dead. As I kneeled before the altar, praying for his soul, something bothered me. A phrase Yamada had uttered kept repeating in my head. It nagged at me, like a pattern tapped upon my soul. *He sacrificed himself to save thousands of others.*

The next day, I rose before the others in my tent had stirred. I decided to roam the perimeter of the camp, as I had the first morning after my arrival. Although the sun was yet to emerge above the horizon, the sky was turning paler in the growing light. It promised to be a fine late autumn day. Our compound was scheduled to go on an excursion to the river that afternoon—the first outing we'd ever had. Major Locke had announced it at headcount the previous week. 'As a reward for 14C's consistent good behaviour, the commander has granted you a trip to the river,' he'd said. There were murmurs of excitement. 'But before you get ahead of yourselves, there are a few things you should know. The river is a two-and-a-half-mile walk from here. Older or weak internees may not be able to walk this far. We want to avoid any risks, so if there's any doubt, stay behind at camp. Second, we expect all internees to be on their best behaviour. As this is one of the few occasions you'll be allowed out in public, it is imperative you present a good front.' Locke scanned our faces. 'I have spoken favourably of the behaviour of the Japanese at Camp 14C to many members of the community, so it would do me personally a great disservice if *any* of you disappoint me. Is that clear?'

Last night, I had vowed not to go. I was still reeling from the shock of Nobuhiro's death and didn't want my emotions paraded in front of everyone. But as I circled the camp in the gathering light, my feelings changed. If I was left alone at camp without any distractions, I feared my thoughts would turn dark on the day of my brother's funeral. In any case, only Yamada and a few others in my tent knew about my loss, and I hoped they would have the good sense not to question me about it.

At the appointed hour that afternoon, I joined my fellow internees assembling at the gate. It was a sight to behold: hundreds of men formed a sea of red, as we were all dressed in the maroon uniforms we were required to wear outside camp. Although I had seen my colleagues in it dozens of times when they went outside to work in the fields, standing among so many similarly dressed men gave me the queer feeling of being a carbon copy of an internee. My unease was evidently not shared by those around me; the red uniforms seemed to be a source of amusement to many, as the bigger internees struggled to fit into the standard small sizes we had all been issued. Men laughed and gleefully prodded the exposed ankles and bellies of their larger friends.

I heard a voice behind me. 'Dr Ibaraki, there you are! We're over this way.' Hayashi beckoned to me. I followed him along the line of men and found the rest of my group gathered in two neat lines. 'We wondered whether you would come today.'

I pursed my lips. I was sure Hayashi knew about Nobu's death; he and Yamada were good friends, plus he had been working at the infirmary when I'd received the news. Still, Hayashi was not one to gossip. I felt I could trust him. 'I decided there was no use sitting around. And you managed to get a day off from the infirmary?'

Hayashi nodded. The orderlies had recently stopped working at night, as the twelve-hour shifts had proved too much along with our other duties at camp. The army had agreed to roster on one medical assistant at night.

I joined the throng filing out of the camp. As we passed through the birdcage gate and exited on the other side, two soldiers marked off our names on a list. We started walking towards the river in a long line, two abreast, guided by a dozen officers on horseback. We had never left the camp before in such large numbers, and the strangeness of the situation was not lost on the men around me. They chattered like school-children on an excursion. Soon, though, the tread of our many hundred feet stirred up a cloud of red dust that made talking difficult; the conversation ceased as we were forced to cover our mouths and noses with our hands.

The route we took to the river was one I had never followed before. We walked through coarse sun-bleached grass, green low-lying scrub and past the distinctly feminine silhouettes of the genus of eucalyptus tree that was native to the area. 'It's called a mallee tree,' an officer had told me one day when I was working in the vegetable garden. I had wandered a dozen yards from the garden to inspect a tree, trying to pinpoint how it differed from the eucalypts I was used to seeing in Broome. 'See the bulbous root at the base that all the branches are growing from? That's what makes it a mallee. Some of them start off as single-trunk trees, like this one,' the officer gestured to a similar tree that stood tall among its peers, 'but if it's hit by bushfire it grows back from the root with lots of branches, like all the others here. It's a tough tree. Drought, bushfire . . . it'll survive almost anything.' And as I'd listened to the officer's explanation I was struck by the ingenuity of the tree in its ability to regenerate and create a new shape better suited to its environment.

Gazing at the mallee trees as we walked to the river, I once more admired their inconspicuous quality, the grey-green leaves that stirred so gently in the breeze. Taking a wider perspective, I realised that every element of the landscape—from the grass and trees to the pebbly earth—seemed at pains not to outdo the others, and it struck me as a very noble quality indeed.

We turned a corner and something sparkled in the distance. The track opened up to a grassy clearing where straw-coloured spinifex murmured. Beyond it, the river glittered in the sun, so wide and still it resembled a lake. The hollow trunks of dead trees haunted its edges like lost people. At one point where the grassy clearing met the water, the lip of the riverbank had crumbled and ochre earth spilled over the edge. Beneath the deep blue sky, the river formed a grand setting.

'Look at the water here—it's so blue!' someone said. 'Is that a rowboat on the other side?'

I looked to where the man was pointing and realised he was right: at the far side of the river, some two hundred yards away, was a small rowboat containing three people. The two figures at one end of the boat appeared to be women, the neat shapes of their bodies crowned by the pale blur of sunhats. The larger person at the oars must have been a man, and from the frantic reach and pull of his arms I saw he was hastily rowing away from us. We must have been a frightening sight: hundreds of men in red, fanned out along the riverbank. Seeing such a large group of local men would have been daunting enough, let alone several hundred internees.

The officers on horseback had assumed positions at two points about a hundred yards apart, marking the boundaries of where we were allowed to roam. The officers gazed at us, their faces blank like the glassy surface of the water, rifles taut across their backs.

As the others from my tent began spreading blankets on the ground and unpacking sandwiches they had brought from the mess hall, I wandered to the water's edge. The river moved lazily before me, but further downstream the surface was ruffled where it narrowed into a bend. If I closed my eyes I was transported to Broome, where I used to stand on the rocky headland of Town Beach. I had often wondered what it was like for the divers, who had to work alone for hours on end in their subterranean world. Was the silence a comfort or a terror to them?

Immediately after my arrest in Broome the previous year, I had been interned in the town gaol with a group of four divers. Although I had seen these men dozens of times, and had treated one or two at the hospital, I rarely socialised with them, so gaol presented the first opportunity for a conversation. We were some of the last to be arrested, so on 31 December we were still waiting to be transferred to a camp. The officers had been kind enough to share their beer for the New Year's Eve celebration, and the five of us sat in a circle on the cell floor, talking by candlelight.

Our talk turned to the jobs that had lured us from Japan to such a remote location. The other four men all came from small fishing villages on the Wakayama coast.

'And what about sensei?' one of them asked. 'What happened in Japan to make you give up such a prestigious job and take up a position in Broome?'

I was filled with unease, even though there was no way he could have known the reason for my departure. 'It was hardly a prestigious job—I was only a junior doctor,' I said. 'And the offer in Broome came at a time when I had a strong desire to see the world, and I thought the experience of running my own hospital would serve me well. And it has, of course—I'm now an expert in caisson disease . . . and in stitching up drunk divers.'

'And getting *into* fights, too!' someone said, referring to the bruise on my face. I brought a hand to my cheek and winced, thinking of the blow that had knocked me unconscious.

The men around me laughed, except one, a boy of only eighteen, who asked, 'What's caisson disease?'

'It's a condition that afflicts divers when they come up to the surface too quickly, causing joint pain, headaches and dizziness,' I said. 'It is extremely painful, as I'm sure Asano can confirm.'

Asano nodded. Although he was only in his forties, he had stopped diving a few years earlier due to complications arising from decompression sickness. He now only occasionally worked as a tender, monitoring the air supply and safety of the divers who were his friends. He had come to me at the hospital several times about his chronic joint pain.

'I was unlucky—I had it in my very first month of diving,' Asano said. 'I started on a second-rate boat, apprenticed to an arrogant first diver who didn't want to teach me. He never explained what would happen if I didn't spend enough time decompressing on my way up. Unfortunately, I found out the hard way. After a long day of diving, I was too tired and hungry to come up in stages, and rushed up to the surface. I got onto the deck okay, but as soon as I removed my helmet, my head felt like it was about to split apart, my vision blurred and I passed out. When I came to I was thirty feet under and it was pitch dark. I didn't realise I'd been down there for hours and it was already night—that they'd put me down there to help me decompress.'

Asano rubbed his arm and stared at a point somewhere behind us. When he spoke again it was as if he were seeing not the scene before him but the distant shapes of his past. 'Waking up down there was the most frightened I've ever been. I didn't know where I was at first—whether I was underwater, on the boat or on land. I wondered if I was dead. But the air tube was there, I could hear the hiss of it being filtered in. And I began to smell it, too. They were cooking dinner up on the deck, and the scent of fried fish and onions came to me through the tube. When I smelled that, I knew I was alive.'

Now, from my own position at the edge of the river, I thought of Asano waking up in the darkness of the ocean. I considered the slender divide between our perceptions of life and death. And how one life could be valued over another.

Behind me, I heard laughter. I turned to see Hayashi and Yamada doubled over, giggling like prepubescent boys. The contents of Hayashi's sandwich had spilled onto his lap. I narrowed my eyes. Perhaps because I was upset on the day of my brother's funeral, something hardened within me to see them so carefree.

Tuesday was my day off from the infirmary, a chance to relax and catch up on my chores. I wanted to write a letter to my mother regarding Nobuhiro's death, plus I had offered to help Secretary Hoshi with a translation. It was also the day Stan was due to return to camp. I'd found out from Lieutenant Powell that he would be transferred to the infirmary in the morning. 'In a few more weeks, his wrist will be fully healed, but his mental recovery will take longer,' he'd said. 'Just between you and me, he's pretty heartbroken about having to return to camp. I was afraid he'd cut his other wrist, he was that upset. HQ are allowing him a few concessions—privacy, a few books, that sort of thing.' As I sat on my bed with a half-written letter and the documents to translate spread out before me, I couldn't stop thinking about Stan. When the hands on my watch reached eleven-thirty, I pushed aside the papers and headed to the infirmary.

Hayashi sat at the front of the ward. His arms were on the table before him, elbows butterflying open a book. Behind him, beds stretched back in two long rows. Patients lay or sat on their beds, in various states of fitful rest. One man swaddled in blankets lay on his side at the edge of his bed, staring at the floor. Another patient sat upright, turning over his hands while inspecting them as if searching for clues. Although the air was crisp, his shirt was wide open. No one spoke and hardly anyone moved. The scene was like a photograph, preserving the strangeness of the moment.

Hayashi looked up. 'Sensei—I didn't think you were working today.'

'I'm not. I heard Suzuki was back. I wanted to see him.'

'Suzuki? You mean the boy?' Hayashi frowned. He inclined his head towards the back of the room. In one corner, two sheets had been hung from the ceiling to create an enclosure. Through a gap between the edges of the sheets I could see a bed, and the shadows of a rumpled sheet traced the contours of a body. 'I didn't know you were friends with him.'

'He came to the infirmary to see me a few weeks ago. I'd like to check on him, that's all.'

'Well, the officers who brought him back said he needed rest and shouldn't be disturbed. That's why they put up those sheets. For some reason, Suzuki gets special treatment. But I don't mind, as long as you make it quick.'

I nodded. 'I won't be long.'

I made my way to the back of the room, trying not to make eye contact with the patients who watched me pass. A light breeze entered the room, stirring the suspended sheets so that they gently swung back and forth, slightly off-kilter in their timing. As they moved, the triangle of empty space between them widened and narrowed, altering my view of the bed. It was as if I were looking through a kaleidoscope—one moment I could see a sheet that covered a leg, the next an arm and then a fleeting glimpse of a chin.

I stopped just before reaching the suspended sheets. They continued to flutter before me like *noren* on a summer's day. The subtle movement seemed grand in that otherwise still space. There was something very soothing in their motion—ebbing upwards and outwards, never still—yet it also seemed false, a kind of trick, and I felt that if I allowed the sheets to touch me something would change, I would be drawn into that enclosure with its own rules of movement, breath and time.

The breeze died down, and in the lull that followed I was able to see Stan clearly for the first time. He was lying on his back with his head tilted away from me, angled in a manner that accentuated the sharp line of his jaw. In the absence of movement in the air, the kaleidoscopic illusion also disappeared. Framed within the now-still sheets, he appeared inanimate. A rectangle of light from a window fell diagonally across him, illuminating part of his torso and jaw as if he were a statue hewn from two different stones.

A patient coughed behind me, a rasping sound.

I continued to watch, but Stan was so still I could not even detect a rise and fall in his chest. My unease grew. It wasn't unusual for a seemingly stable patient to die suddenly. And he certainly wouldn't be the first to pass away at camp—there had been at least six deaths since I'd arrived, mostly elderly internees. As I recalled those patients and the wretched circumstances of their deaths, I began to tremble with regret. Stan had opened up to me, and I hadn't listened. I was horrified to think my insensitivity could have led to his death.

I lifted my hand to pull aside the sheet and step inside when the slightest of movements stopped me: Stan's lids flickered a fraction. He was watching me from the corner of his eye—and not in a sleep-like reverie, but in a fully lucid state. And although I could barely see the wet glint of his eye, his gaze seemed absent of reproach—and that realisation almost made me weep.

I heard the *whack whack whack* of the hammers long before the builders came into view. As I walked down Broadway, I passed the intersection at the middle of camp. Beyond the fence to my left, I glimpsed the wooden frame of a sleeping hut, its crossbeams hanging like the ribs of a great whale. Builders clung to its roof and sides, hammering, sanding and measuring. Behind them stood a nearly completed hut, its roof and four sides clad with galvanised iron. Only the windows were missing, leaving dark holes like the eyes of an empty soul.

A baseball team was practising in the area near the gate. As I drew closer, I recognised Johnny and the other members of the Australian gang: Charlie, Ernie, Ken, teenage Australian-born half-caste Martin Nishimura, and Australian-born full-blood

Andy Makino. Three other men I didn't recognise were scattered around the diamond. Johnny was at the pitcher's plate. He lifted his head when I entered the compound, and signalled to the others for time out. We hadn't seen each other since he'd approached me about the baseball competition, and we'd argued about Yamada attacking Stan. I now felt ashamed I had so strenuously defended Yamada, and was apprehensive about confronting Johnny again, but he was smiling as he walked towards me. A lock of black hair stuck to his shining forehead.

'Hey, Doc. You got a sec?' He wiped his hands on his trousers. 'I just wanted to thank you for organising the baseball comp. It was you, wasn't it?' Johnny cocked his head to the side. The action reminded me of the young man who used to wait outside the hotels in Japtown, full of energy as he peddled his taxi service to the pearling crews.

'It was your idea. All I did was suggest it at the meeting. I realised it would benefit everybody.' I inclined my head towards the other players. 'So you've already formed a team?'

'Sure have. All the boys are keen for it, plus we found a few Formosan fellows who said they'd have a go. And there's a new Aussie kid who just arrived from Hay camp who's really good. The skinny one over there, Dale.' A tall dark-skinned figure kicked the ground with the toe of his shoe, sending up a small cloud of dust. 'All the camp rejects, I guess.'

I laughed. 'Well, I'm glad you found some fellow "rejects", as you say.'

Johnny pushed his hair off his face, leaving a smear of orange dust on his forehead. 'I also wanted to say I'm sorry to hear about your brother. McCubbin told me. That's really tough. I lost one of my sisters a few years ago, so I know how you feel.'

I nodded. Although I was upset McCubbin had told him, I appreciated Johnny's kind words—especially after Yamada's insensitivity.

We were silent for a few moments, then Johnny's face brightened. 'Did you hear? I might be leaving.'

'Oh?' I tried to maintain an air of nonchalance, but my mind raced with the possible reasons for Johnny's departure. Was he being released? Or being transferred to another camp?

'I just found out my appeal has been scheduled in Melbourne. I'm going down there in July. Could be my ticket out of here. My lawyer says I've got a good chance because I'm Australian-born. I should never have been put in here in the first place.'

My heart sank. It seemed that just as Johnny and I had a chance to make peace, circumstances would take him away. But I smiled and wished him luck.

'Did you hear Stan is back from Barmera hospital?' I said. 'I saw him in the infirmary today. He is still very weak, but he should make a full recovery.'

'Poor guy. He must've been in a state to have done something like that to himself.' Johnny shook his head. 'Being locked up in here will do that to you. If I didn't have my appeal coming up I could wind up that way. I might drop in to see him next week.'

'I'm sure he would like that.'

'Anyway, I should get back to the game. We need all the practice we can get to have any chance of winning against the Batavia team. I heard they're good. But I just wanted to say thanks. You really helped us out.' He held out his hand. His palm was rough against mine.

We parted, but after a few steps I heard him call out to me. 'By the way, some of the guards are letting us use the tennis courts at the duty guard camp. You should join us one day.'

The sun shone through the clouds, making me squint. The *tap tap tap* of the hammers rang out as the builders knocked the structure into place.

'I'd like that,' I said.

Morning light streamed through the open windows of the ward, making everything appear pristine. The patients, many still half asleep, lay in their rumpled sheets with skin scrubbed clean by the trick of the light. In the corner, the sheets suspended from the ceiling glowed like a lantern. I approached the enclosure with trepidation, as I had each day since Stan's arrival. Once again he lay on his back in silent repose, head turned towards the window within his partition. The awning-type shutter swung outwards from a top hinge, revealing a rectangle of sky. I studied Stan for a second or two—just long enough to see the subtle movement of his chest—before creeping back to the entrance of the ward. Hayashi was watching me from the doorway.

'Does he ever get up?' I asked. Whenever I checked on Stan, his face was turned towards the window, drinking in the light that shone through. Even late in the evening, at the end of my shift, he was always in the same position: face angled towards the window, like a flower that bloomed at night.

'Sometimes I think I hear him moving behind there, but it's hard to tell. You should ask Powell. Maybe he gets up at night. Maybe he's like those animals we saw on the documentary film. What was the word? Nocturnal.'

I began visiting Stan's bedside every day to change the dressing on his wrist. A crust had formed over the wound; its edge was still wet when he first arrived, but it dried after a few days. Finally, the skin around the wound contracted, and the dark crust began to flake away. But Stan's disposition remained the same. He stared at the window all day, displaying little inclination to move or speak or even eat. I made feeble attempts at conversation. 'How are you feeling?' I asked. Sometimes he nodded, but mostly he said nothing at all. I offered to get him some books, but he said he didn't feel like reading. I asked him if his family knew of his condition, but he shrugged. If I managed to engage him for a moment, as soon as I finished talking, he always turned back to the window, seeking out the light.

The following week, Johnny appeared at the entrance of the orderlies' room while I was eating lunch. For a moment, I thought it was Hayashi or one of the other orderlies calling me to inspect a patient. Then I noticed the broad shoulders, the shirtsleeves rolled up to his elbows and the dirt caked on his forearms.

'Stan here?' he asked. 'McCubbin said I could see him after I finished my shift in the gardens today.'

'He's in the general ward, in the corner behind the sheets. Here, I'll show you.'

I led him down the corridor to the other building. Before we entered the ward, I turned to him. 'You can go in and see him, but I have to warn you: he is still unwell. He is distracted and he rarely speaks. But a visit from a friend may help.'

We walked past the beds to the end of the ward, and I pulled back one of the hanging sheets. Stan was on his side, staring at the window. It was sunny outside, and the sheets around the bed reflected the light. Framed like that, Stan's slight figure took on a childlike purity.

'Poor bugger,' Johnny said. Then he stepped into the space and moved to the far side of the bed, positioning himself between Stan and the wall. He leaned down. 'Stan, old boy. It's me, Johnny. How've you been? Doing okay?'

Johnny bent down even further, staring into Stan's face. I held my breath.

'Johnny,' Stan murmured. 'I've been worse.'

Johnny broke into a smile. 'Good, mate. I knew you were all right. Charlie, Ernie, Martin—all the boys have been thinking of you.' He lowered his voice to a whisper. 'Mate, I know it's tough being in here, all this shit we have to put up with, but we'll get through it. Before you know it, we'll be home.'

Johnny continued speaking, describing the competition he'd had with the others to determine who could clean the latrines the fastest, and the corners of Stan's mouth twitched into a smile. As I listened, a feeling of shame came over me. My past failings as a doctor became clear—not just with Stan, but also in Broome and in my previous experience in Japan. I had been wrong to leave the kindness of the human touch to Sister Bernice and others. In keeping my silence, I hadn't exercised the very quality that makes us human: our capacity to understand each other.

That afternoon, the sky darkened and the wind picked up, lifting dirt and other particles into the air. Sunlight peeped through the clouds and mingled with the agitated dust, making the world outside opaque. I closed all the windows in my ward. The wind grew stronger until I could hear it howling around the infirmary. Stones struck the galvanised-iron walls and clinked against the windows. I checked each of the patients in the TB ward, as their symptoms could flare up on a windy day. Fortunately, they seemed unaffected by the squall outside.

I went to the orderlies' room to fetch my coat, as the temperature had dipped. Something caught my eye when I glanced through the window. A figure stood in the infirmary grounds near the perimeter fence, about a dozen yards away. I realised it was Stan. Clutching a cloth over his mouth and nose, he gazed through the fence at the sky. Dust whirled around him and the wind teased the edge of his jacket and sifted his hair.

I heard footsteps behind me.

'Is that . . . ?' Hayashi exhaled. 'What's he doing out there?'

'I'll go get him.'

Hayashi gripped my arm. 'No, just leave him. It's the first time he's left his bed. It's what he wants. Just let him be.'

'But he could get sick out there.'

'Not any sicker than he is now.'

And so Hayashi and I watched for the next few minutes as Stan stood alone, staring at the sky. He adjusted his grip on the cloth at his face, switching it to the other hand. The wind tore his jacket open and he hugged it to himself. Other than that, he was motionless, his face lifted towards the heavens. The light grew weaker as the sun disappeared behind a bank of clouds. The sky turned a murky brown. Finally, he turned around and shuffled back inside.

The internees in our compound began moving into completed huts in late May, just as the nights turned bitter. Icy winds cut through our clothing and knifed our skin. When we ate dinner inside the mess hall, our breath unfurled in translucent puffs. In the mornings, icicles clung to the sides of the trough outside the kitchen, and the water that issued from the taps stung our hands and turned them red.

Elderly internees were shifted into the huts first. The order for the remaining spaces was determined by a lottery. Our row of tents was unlucky: we would be one of the last to move. A few people grumbled, but nothing could be done. We huddled close inside the tent and bundled up in extra blankets. Many nights I woke shivering, dreaming of the balmy evenings in Broome.

Although the nights were frigid, the days were sunny and crisp. It was perfect weather for the baseball competition, which was now underway. Our team was knocked out in the first round, losing to the rubber-industry workers from Surabaya. Ebina was disappointed, having cultivated ambitions of making it to the finals, but I was relieved. Although I'd had fun during practice, I didn't enjoy the pressure of competition or being the focus of attention.

I had a shift at the infirmary the day Johnny's team was scheduled to play its first game, but I returned to camp in time to catch the final inning. The match had attracted an enthusiastic crowd. People lined the fence, huddling together so tightly they looked like plates of armour. Every so often there would be a cheer, and a chink in the armour would appear, offering a fleeting glimpse of the pitch.

In the crowd I spotted Nagano, the eldest in my tent. Although in his mid-seventies, Nagano was sprightly and often volunteered to do chores older internees were exempt from. He stood on tiptoe, trying to peer over the heads in front of him.

'Who's winning?' I asked.

'They are,' he said, pointing a gnarled finger at Johnny's team, 'but not for long, I hope.'

The Australian team were standing near the perimeter fence, waiting to bat. Johnny stood with one leg bent up against the fence, smoking a cigarette. Martin and Ernie were stretching. A murmur coursed through the crowd as the next batter approached the plate. I recognised Dale, the new internee Johnny had pointed out to me. His high-bridged nose and wide-set eyes bore little trace of Japanese physiognomy, making him the subject of gossip at camp. 'He isn't even Japanese,' Yamada had declared one night over a cup of sake. 'He's part-Indian but has some distant relatives who are Japanese.'

Dale's limbs were long and ungainly, but when he stepped up to the plate, his legs, torso and arms fell into perfect alignment. The bat seemed light in the unbroken grace of his arms.

The first ball was low as it hurtled towards him. He flinched but didn't take his gaze from the pitcher. The second ball came so fast I didn't see it. Dale swung and I heard a loud crack. Johnny's team exploded, clapping and cheering so loudly it masked the hum of discontent from the crowd.

'The kid's a genius! A genius!' Charlie yelled, his words cutting across the empty space of the pitch.

Nagano tutted. 'What a shame—to lose to these fools.'

Dale jogged lightly onto home base. His teammates flocked to him, ruffling his hair and slapping him on the back. Johnny took his hand and raised it high. He scanned the crowd, grinning. We made eye contact. He waved to me across the field and yelled, 'Did you see?' Although I was mindful of Nagano and the other men watching me, I couldn't help but smile back.

Broome
1940

I n the final months of the year, the atmosphere thickened, becoming so warm and heavy that droplets seemed to hang in mid-air. Grey clouds blanketed the sky, and the sea turned the colour of steel, waves breaking the surface in foam-crested peaks.

Broome's inhabitants always abandoned the town in those last, dying weeks. Kanemori returned to Japan with his family, as he did every year. Only Harada stayed to attempt to protect the Japanese Association building from dampness and tame the dark tangle of vegetation that sprouted during the wet. I'd heard he had a wife and grown children in Japan, although he never spoke of them. He hadn't been back to Japan in more than twenty years. I only found out the reason after I'd known him for almost a year: he had a woman in Broome—an Aboriginal woman, Minnie, whom he'd been with for years. Most of the time, she stayed with him in his house on the edge of Japtown, but some months she went north to be with her people. I met her once, when I was invited for dinner at their home. She was a small woman, about Harada's age, with a heavy brow but a fine nose. She moved sylph-like in the kitchen, barefoot and dark-limbed.

The master pearlers' families headed south to cooler climes, and most of the pearling crew left, returning home by ship or journeying to Singapore in the hope of finding temporary work until the season began again. Only the long-term residents and those lucky enough to find employment maintaining the master pearlers' gardens remained. Fewer birds and insects seemed to crowd the air—they, too, had the good sense to go elsewhere.

In my first year, I had mistakenly decided to stay in town during the wet. Out of some sort of misplaced nostalgia for my boyhood summers in Japan, I ached for the familiar feeling of dampness on my skin. But after experiencing the endless hot, sticky days and sudden downpours, with barely a soul around to share them with, I vowed not to do the same again. At the end of my second year, I took a ship to Perth to escape Broome during the hottest weeks. I stayed at a boarding house on St George's Terrace and spent my days wandering the city's streets. I relished the arrival each day of the 'Fremantle Doctor'—the locals' name for the cool breeze that swept in during the afternoon. From the green heights of Kings Park I watched the Swan River below me, and thought of Sister Bernice looking out at the same view, dreaming of Africa.

This year I planned to go further afield, to the eastern states. I had arranged to stay with some family friends in Melbourne for a few weeks. Time and money permitting, I hoped to make my way to Sydney, too, to see the harbour I had heard so much about. Perhaps the following year I would have the courage to return to Japan.

In my absence, the hospital would be shut for eight weeks, and so Sister Bernice and I began to put everything away. We stripped the beds, stacked the furniture and placed the equipment in the cabinets to gather dust.

One evening as I stood at the cabinet updating the equipment inventory, I reflected on all I had achieved since first arriving in Broome. I had moved to another country, trained an assistant, and more or less gained the trust of the community. Most people—even the master pearlers—knew me by name. Thinking back to the state I had been in when I'd left Japan, I realised how far I'd come.

At eight-thirty, the door creaked behind me. I heard the tread of Sister Bernice's feet.

'Good morning, Doctor,' she said, her voice unusually vibrant.

'Good morning, Sister.'

Sister Bernice always spent Christmas with her relatives in Geraldton, two days south by ship. She was due to depart the following Saturday. Her cousin had joined the army and was about to go to war in Europe, so it would be an extra-special gathering this year. I heard rustling as she rummaged through her bag. Moments later, she was beside me. She placed something on top of the cabinet in front of me: a small package, wrapped in white and tied with a piece of string.

'Merry Christmas,' she said.

My heart sank. 'A present? Oh, you shouldn't have. I wish I'd known . . .'

'Before you go on, I didn't actually buy you anything. It's just something of mine I thought you might like. And Christmas is an Australian tradition, not a Japanese one, so you need never buy me anything. In fact, I'd be appalled if you started buying Christmas gifts because of me. This is just a present I thought of at the last minute.'

'It's very kind of you, Sister. Thank you so much.'

'Aren't you going to open it?'

I remembered the difference in our traditions: westerners liked to open gifts in the presence of the giver. I untied the string and turned the present over in my hands. The wrapping fell away to reveal a book with a faded blue cover.

'Ah, *Middlemarch*,' I said.

'Have you read it?'

'No, I haven't. But I have heard it is very good.'

'It's one of my favourites, although I haven't read it in a few years now. There's a young doctor in the book who arrives in a country town, and it made me think of you. Not that you're anything like Dr Lydgate,' she added quickly. 'I just thought you might like to read it while you're away.'

'Thank you, Sister. I look forward to reading this on the ship. My first Christmas present. I shall always remember it.'

She smiled. I decided I would get her something in the eastern states as an *omiyage* from my travels—that was a Japanese tradition, at least.

'I almost forgot. I meant to return this to you a while ago.' She placed another book on the cabinet. It was my old copy of *Robinson Crusoe*, with its cracked cover featuring a shabby, bearded man and its pages that had turned the colour of cognac over time. 'I took it home with me and forgot to bring it back. I hope you don't mind.'

'Not at all. Did you enjoy it?'

'Yes, I did. Actually . . .' She smoothed the back of her habit with her hand. 'I couldn't help but notice the piece of wood inside the front cover. Is that something from Japan?'

I frowned and picked up the book. Inside the cover, slotted against the spine, was a tag—a wafer-thin piece of wood about the length of my thumb. Inscribed on it was the character *ko*, meaning 'child', along with the numerals 1718. It still had its loop of yellowed string. The knot at the end had left an impression on the page behind it: a small indentation, like a scar.

I snapped the book shut. 'Where did you find this?'

'Inside the front cover, as I said.'

'Well, it shouldn't have been there. I shouldn't have put it there. It was a mistake. You never should have found it.' I walked into the anteroom.

Sister Bernice came in just as I was putting the book and the wooden tag in my desk drawer.

'Yes?' I snapped, irritated she'd seen where I'd put it.

She flinched. 'I'm sorry. I didn't mean to upset you . . . Are you all right?'

'I just . . . I don't like you intruding into my life. Now, if you don't mind, I'm very busy right now.'

She blinked several times. I thought I saw her lower lip tremble, but I couldn't be sure. She nodded slowly, then, without another comment, left the room.

Sister Bernice didn't come to work the next morning. Her absence angered me at first. To fail to show up because of a minor confrontation—she obviously had less mettle than I'd first thought. But as the hours passed and she still did not arrive, I began to see that the blame lay at my feet. I had overreacted when she innocently asked about the tag. She couldn't have known its significance to me.

Throughout the humid morning, patients came and went. One old tender who visited the hospital regularly due to chronic joint pain asked after Sister Bernice. 'She's not feeling well,' I mumbled. He was so concerned he said he'd return with a present for her later.

As the day wore on, I began to believe my own lie and grew worried about her wellbeing. Perhaps she *was* ill—perhaps my outburst had triggered something.

That afternoon, I closed the hospital early and walked to the convent. I stepped onto the latticed verandah and rang the brass bell at the front door. When the Mother Superior appeared, I asked to speak to Sister Bernice.

'Sister Bernice isn't here. She left for Geraldton this morning.'

'Geraldton? Already? I didn't think she was leaving for another few days.' My outburst must have affected her deeply. 'When will she be back?'

'She didn't say—she said it was an emergency. I'm sorry, Doctor, I thought she told you.' Mistaking my dismay for alarm at losing an assistant, she continued, 'I could send someone else to help you. Sister Antonia may be available.'

'No, that's not necessary. I didn't think . . . Anyway, if Sister Bernice contacts you, please give her my regards.'

I became depressed at the thought that my careless behaviour had driven Sister Bernice away. As I stared at the ocean from the ship's deck during the long journey to Melbourne, she consumed my thoughts. What if she never came back? I brooded over that for a long time. Even after my arrival in Melbourne, as I took a tram along Flinders Street and strolled the boardwalk at St Kilda Beach, her abrupt departure continued to play on my mind.

'Tomokazu, is something wrong? You've been quiet all week.' Mr Amano, my uncle's friend, cupped a hand at his brow to shield his eyes from the glare. The sea sparkled behind him. He and his wife had generously opened their home to me and guided me around Melbourne. I had enjoyed my time with them, so I was dismayed to realise that my preoccupation had been so evident.

'I was just thinking about the hospital. I hope no one needs me while I'm away.' I vowed to put the incident with Sister Bernice behind me so I could make the most of the rest of my stay.

But as much as I tried, I couldn't forget. Instead of visiting Sydney, I decided to return to Broome two weeks early. As the ship swung into the bay, my heart swelled at the sight of the milky blue water and the distant pink-red sand. For the first time, I realised that Broome was my home.

The hospital was just as I'd left it, save for the spots of mould inside some of the cupboards and on the walls. I stood in the centre of the ward and looked around me. The bare metal beds with their spring-coil ribs underscored the emptiness of the room. As soon as the weather stabilised, I would dry the mattresses in the sun.

I was relieved to hear from a shopkeeper in Japtown that Sister Bernice had returned from Geraldton. 'She was walking past here the other day,' he said.

The next day, I went to the convent, carrying a present I had purchased on my travels: a teacup and saucer painted with a spray of yellow wattle. My shirt was clinging to my chest by the time I crunched along the convent's gravel path.

I rang the bell, and Sister Bernice herself came to the door, surprise etched on her face.

'Doctor! I thought you weren't returning for at least another week. I would have come to the hospital had I known you were back.' She reached up to tuck a lock of hair beneath her veil. It was a joy to see her again.

'I came back early—I was worried about closing the hospital for so long. But that is not why I am here. I wanted to give you this.' I held out the boxed present, wrapped in brown paper. 'Something from my trip to Melbourne. It is *omiyage*, as we say in Japanese.'

She gingerly took the package, staring at it as if it were something strange. 'Oh, a present. Thank you.'

She held it close to herself without opening it. Her eyes darted away from mine; she seemed unable to hold my gaze. Silence stretched between us.

'How is your family in Geraldton? Mother Superior said there was an emergency. I hope they are well?'

'Yes, thank you. One of the children was sick, but it wasn't as serious as they first thought.'

'And your cousin?'

'Harry left in January. We haven't heard from him yet.' Her reserved manner suggested that my rebuke was still fresh in her mind.

'Sister, before you left, what I said to you at the hospital . . . I didn't mean to—'

'There's no need to say anything, Doctor. It's all in the past now. I think we can forget what happened and move on.' A smile brightened her face.

I exhaled with relief. I wanted nothing more than to put the matter behind us so we could return to our former ways.

Sister Bernice came back to the hospital the following week. Together we scrubbed the mould from the walls and aired the mattresses. When sorting through the patients' files, Sister Bernice was as nimble and efficient as ever. But for all her outward calmness, I sensed something had changed. She still conversed with me and occasionally brought me black tea—although she herself never used the cup I gave her, which pained me—but there was a coolness to her now. She had closed a part of herself to me.

Loveday
1942

S tan's disposition improved each day after Johnny's visit.
When I checked on him inside his enclosure of sheets,
I often found him sitting up, reading a book. Sometimes
he paused to look out of the window, but he was no longer
drawn to it compulsively like before. He began to smile when
he saw me, and responded to my questions about his health.
Eventually, we started to talk while I changed the dressing
on his wrist. I asked him about his family. He told me his
elder sister, Emmy, was interned at Tatura Camp in Victoria.
Their father had died years ago. Their mother was the only
one left at their home in Sydney.

'Ma's at her wit's end with me and Emmy locked up. We're
all she's got. Her health's not good—she has bad asthma.
With the stress of our arrests, I think it's got worse. She's been
writing letters every day—to me, to Emmy, to our friends, and
to the director-general of security to ask for our release. I'm
worried something will happen to her while we're not there.
To make things worse, now that I'm in here, this girl I've been

keen on for a while has finally asked about me. She wants to write to me. Mum told me in her last letter.'

'Why is that bad? Don't you want to hear from this girl?'

He sighed and slumped, jerking his arm. The bandage slipped out of my hand. I scrambled to catch the edge.

'Of course. But she thinks I'm still in the AIF. That's why she wants to write to me. She thinks I'm off fighting the Japs somewhere, like all the other brave men. Instead, I'm locked up as one of them. I can't let her find out I'm in here—I just can't.' His voice quavered and I thought he might cry. I empathised with his unfortunate situation: wanting to tell this girl the truth yet being unable to do so. But I couldn't offer any advice. My handling of my own circumstances had been a failure.

He lifted his head, and I was relieved to see he had regained his composure. 'What about you?' he asked. 'Do you have a wife?'

'Sorry?' I stiffened.

'A wife. Someone special you write to from here.'

'I, ah . . . Yes, I do. I've tried to write to her a number of times, but I'm not sure if she got my letters. The war, you know . . .'

I reached behind me for the scissors. My fingers felt thick as I struggled to knot the end of the bandage. Stan didn't say anything more, but I felt his gaze on me the entire time. When I was done, I excused myself and swiftly left the room.

While on my rounds that afternoon, I stopped into the tuberculosis ward. Harada was sleeping, the hollows on his neck deepening with each breath. Sunlight streamed through the window and touched the corner of his bed. I thought back to our time in Broome and his commitment to Minnie, and I was filled with regret. He could have returned to Japan with President Kanemori, but instead he'd stayed with her. I, on the other hand, had fled Japan and lost all contact with my wife.

I thought about the situation with Kayoko. I had sent her two letters from Broome, telling her of the new life I had begun in Australia, but I never got a reply. After that, I gave up, convinced she never wanted to hear from me again. But perhaps I had stopped writing too quickly. Perhaps I had not written what she wanted to hear. I tried to think of what Harada would have done. Surely he would have fought for her, even at the risk of shaming himself. Honour, duty, pride—Harada would have sacrificed all those things for the woman he loved.

When I checked on Stan the next morning, he was again sitting up in bed, reading. A pile of letters, probably from his mother, was tucked beneath his pillow. The window was open and a breeze stirred the hanging sheets. When I asked him how he was, he didn't reply; he simply extended his arm so that I could change the dressing. I sensed a divide had opened up between us, but I didn't know how to close it. I breathed heavily as I fumbled with the bandages.

'Stan, yesterday, when you asked me about my wife . . .'

His gaze flicked up to mine.

'It is hard for me to talk about it, but my wife and I . . . we are separated. I have not heard from her in years. We had a misunderstanding in Japan. She wanted me to help her, to share her pain, but I had my own problems. I wasn't there for her. I wish I had said more to her before I left. That is my greatest regret. So I urge you to write to this girl you like and share your feelings with her.'

He was quiet for a while. We were just a few inches apart, and I sensed him studying my face. He turned away and spoke into his chest. 'It's not that easy. How am I to write to her from here?'

'Send the letter to your mother. She can pass it on.'

'And have my mother read my sweet nothings to Isabelle? I'd rather not. Besides, how am I going to write with this?' He held up his bandaged wrist. The loose end began to unravel.

I took his arm and pushed it back down onto the bed. 'Let me write it, if you want. Tell me what you want to say to her and I'll write it down.'

He chewed his lip as he thought it over. 'Can you write English? Are you good, I mean?'

I laughed. 'These days, I write in English better than in Japanese. It is not perfect, but I will do my best.'

He eventually agreed to my suggestion. I stepped beyond the sheets to get a chair, passing Hayashi at the front of the ward. He looked at me quizzically, his gaze following me as I pulled a chair into Stan's enclosure. I set it beside his bed.

'A little closer, please—I don't want anyone else to hear,' Stan said.

I moved the chair till it was almost touching his bed. He gave me a pad and a pen and a book to lean on. He inched towards me until he was lying on his side on the edge of his bed. I looked at him, waiting for his cue.

'Dear Isabelle,' he whispered.

'Sorry—her name: how is it spelled?'

'I-S-A-B-E-L-L-E.'

I nodded.

'As you are no doubt aware, my feelings for the past seven years have been sincere, and I believe—no, I trust—' He paused, struggling to find the right word.

'I hope?'

He smiled. 'Yes, "hope"—and I hope you have not regarded my attention towards you unfavourably. Recently, my circumstances have not allowed me to improve our friendship. It is my wish it will one day blossom into something deeper and long lasting.'

I was scribbling frantically to try to keep up. I would have to write it out again neatly later.

'When I left Sydney a few months ago, I was more or less under a cloud, and consequently I have not written to you during my absence. I am sorry to say that I cannot currently meet you in person. However, it would bring me great joy if you would consider a relationship with me in the future.' He paused. 'What do you think, is that okay?'

I took a few moments to read over the lines. Stan shifted, waiting for my response. What would I say if I was writing to my wife? Something true to my feelings. I would talk about our memories, our shared lives.

'It is slightly formal, perhaps. Could you remind her of something you did together in the past?'

He nodded, sucking on his bottom lip as he narrowed his eyes, trying to call up a memory. 'I've known her for a long time. We practically grew up together. She lives on my street. I have so many memories of her. The problem is finding the right one.'

'Think of the happiest memory. The first one that comes to mind.'

He thought. 'I was at the Roxy one night when she came up to me. She would have been nineteen. Said she'd heard I'd joined the AIF and wanted to wish me the best. I was over the moon. We talked a bit—she told me about her job as a typist and about her mother, who'd fallen ill. She seemed to have grown more beautiful since I'd last seen her. I kept looking at her all night. My mates said I was making a fool of myself. They were probably right.' He laughed, breathing out noisily.

'At the end of the night, I wanted to go up to her and ask her out, but I didn't have the guts. Next thing I knew she was leaving—she was at the door and her friend had walked out ahead of her, but Isabelle stopped and looked around. I was praying for her to look at me, and she did—she gave a little nod and a wave goodbye. I should've gone up to her, said something then, but I didn't. I'll always regret that.'

It was quiet in the infirmary. I wondered if the other patients had been listening; if they had, they would've caught only fragments—the odd phrase, further limited by the few English words they knew.

Sitting close to Stan, with a pad of paper and a pen in my hand, made me think of nights at home in Tokyo, going over my English and German medical terminology with my wife.

'*Sensuibyou*,' she had said, holding one of my heavy textbooks close to her chest as she sat on a cushion on the floor.

'*Caissonkrankheit*,' I said. 'Caisson disease.'

The last of the sleeping huts were completed in late June, and we moved into them soon afterwards. The shift brought several changes at camp. Until then, my daily life had been synchronised with the seven other men in my tent: we had slept, eaten and done chores together, under the direction of Yamada, our leader. But my new life in the sleeping hut expanded to include fifty others. The space was almost as cramped as the tents had been, but I welcomed the solid walls and floor to keep out the winter chill. Although I knew some of the men from the infirmary and baseball, many of the others I had only seen in passing in the mess hall or at headcount. I relaxed in the new setting, surrounded by others who were relative outsiders, like me. Yamada was still our leader, but I felt his presence much less than before. Our seats in the mess hall were also altered to reflect the new hut populations, and I no longer sat at the same table as Yamada.

I began to spend much of my time with Ebina and several others in my hut from the baseball team. At night, we played *hanafuda* and talked until the lights went out. Rumours of an internee exchange program had been circulating at camp for months. In recent weeks, the newspaper committee had translated a number of articles that mentioned talks of a prisoner exchange between Australia and Japan. Each country would supply a list of potential prisoners for the exchange, and negotiations would begin until an equal number of names were agreed upon for release. Inside our hut, we warmed our feet against the heater made from an empty milk tin and coal from the boiler, and talked about what we'd do when we were released. Arata, one of the men from Surabaya, said he longed to sleep in, instead of being woken by a bugle call. 'I'd like to wake up next to my wife,' Ebina said.

By this time, the baseball competition was coming to an end. The three Formosans in Johnny's team turned out to be very skilled, having played since high school. Johnny and the other Australians on the team hadn't realised this at first because of the Formosans' limited English. Johnny's team won match after match, and eventually gained a berth in the grand final, much to the chagrin of many, including Yamada. Their opponents would be the team from Borneo. If all went well, the winning team would go on to play the champions from 14B.

A week before the grand final, Johnny, Martin Nishimura and Andy Makino left to go to the Aliens Tribunal in Melbourne. They were due to return just in time to play against Borneo. It would be a fitting farewell if their appeal was successful. On a cold morning in early July, I joined the remaining members of the gang at the gate to see them off. Our breath billowed in the crisp air. Magpies carolled and tumbled across the sky.

'Wish us luck,' Johnny said, his face creased into a grin. 'We might not be around here much longer.' As we watched them filing out of the birdcage gate, I saw that Johnny, Martin and Andy were the youngest of the group going to the tribunal. Most of the dozen or so other men were in their sixties or seventies. They were the older, quieter internees who spoke English well but had little to do with the day-to-day running of camp. They kept to themselves, working in the labour groups if they had the strength, and retiring to bed early at night. Some were married to Australians and even had Australian children. I felt sorry for them—they'd been living in Australia so long that they had little in common with many of the other Japanese.

With Johnny, Martin and Andy gone, my friendship circle dwindled. I saw Charlie, Ernie, Dale and Ken at the mess hall and always stopped to greet them, although the conversation never flowed.

On my day off from the infirmary, I went to buy some soap and a razor blade, and a pen for Stan. As I neared the canteen, I noticed Hayashi at the broad surface of the open counter, talking to the canteen assistant. I was surprised to discover it was Yamada. Although he managed the stocktake for the canteen, Yamada rarely staffed it, saying his time was better spent on other things. When I was about twenty feet away, Yamada noticed me. He said something to Hayashi and they both turned and smiled. Before I reached the canteen, however, Hayashi nodded at me and walked away.

'Ibaraki, I was just talking about you,' Yamada said. 'Hayashi tells me how busy you've been. As well as all the patients in your ward, you're looking after one of his, too?'

I nodded. 'Suzuki.'

'That's the Australian who tried to kill himself, isn't it? How is he?'

'Quite good,' I replied cautiously. Yamada's interest in Stan put me on edge. 'His wrist has almost healed. But his spirit is still weak.'

'When will we be able to welcome him back to camp?'

I hesitated. Stan and I had never discussed his return to camp; I sensed that raising the topic would only set him back. At the same time, I wondered how much longer he'd be allowed to stay in the infirmary. 'Not yet. Maybe in another few weeks.'

'Is that so?' Yamada nodded and looked into the distance, as if deep in thought. 'We'll have to find him a bed in a hut. I'm not sure there's room in ours . . . But we'll deal with that when the time comes. Anyway, what can I get you today?'

I told him what I wanted and he fetched them for me. After I paid, Yamada indicated the clipboard he was holding. 'Well, I'd best keep going with the stocktake. We've almost run out of cigarettes since the baseball competition started. People have been betting with them. We'll be sold out by Sunday's game. I assume you'll be there?'

'Actually, I'm rostered to work at the infirmary that day. But I hope to be back in time for the end of the match.' I didn't want to miss the entire match. If Johnny, Andy and Martin's appeal against their internment was successful, the grand final would probably be the last time I'd see them play. They would only have two or three weeks left at camp before their papers were approved and they were released by headquarters.

'Working on grand final day? *Aramaa*. Why don't you swap shifts with someone? Especially since the competition was your idea. What a good suggestion it has turned out to be—the entire atmosphere at camp has changed. Locke's very pleased—he even bought the compound new balls and bats. Plus your friends in the Australian team are playing, aren't they? You won't want to miss that.'

I said I'd see what I could do. Feeling restless, I spent the rest of the day going through my belongings and rearranging the piles of clothes around my bed.

I slept fitfully that night. Just before dawn, I glimpsed someone's silhouette beside the door. As my eyes adjusted, I realised it was old Fukaya. He stood as quietly as a sentinel, staring at the floor. I had often woken at night to hear him shuffling through the hut as he made his way to the latrines, occasionally stopping on his journey to rest against a wall. But he didn't usually stand there for so long. I crept over to him to see what was wrong.

'Look. It's red,' he said, pointing at the floor.

Dirt spread from beneath the door; it must have blown in during the night. I peered closer. It was much finer than the earth in the gardens, and brighter than the dull reddish-brown earth I was accustomed to at camp. In the pre-dawn light it seemed to shimmer.

'I wonder where it came from. It doesn't look like the dirt at camp.'

Fukaya didn't seem to hear me as he continued to stare at the floor. 'See how it's shaped like a fan? It's like art. It's beautiful,' he said.

As I considered the dirt, I could see it was indeed beautiful. Its symmetry and iridescence suggested a human touch, much like the raked gardens of a Zen temple. Like those gardens, the rust-coloured arc made me think of the transience of life. And how, with just one ill wind, everything could change.

Tokyo
1936

One afternoon early in my second year at the laboratory, Nomura, Ota and I were told to stay back late to accept a shipment from Manchukuo. Yamamoto offered to help too, but Shimada refused.

'This is a job for the more senior researchers,' he said. 'The rest of you, wait outside for the trucks to arrive. I will stay in the laboratory. Major Kimura will also be here—he wants to oversee the arrival of the first shipment. Alert us both when it comes.'

As it was cold outside, Nomura, Ota and I arranged shifts: one person stood outside looking out for the truck, while the other two stayed inside. Every half hour, we rotated.

At around midnight, Ota ran into the foyer. 'The trucks—I think they're here.'

Nomura and I jumped to our feet, and I hurried downstairs to alert Shimada. When I returned, I approached the two army trucks parked outside the entrance. Guards with rifles stood at the back of each truck.

'Can I help unload the cargo?' I asked.

The guard closest to me assessed me with disdain. 'We're under orders to act according to Major Kimura's instructions only. Unless you are him, you can't even touch the crates.'

I slunk back inside. Kimura and Shimada soon arrived, and they directed the army personnel to take the cargo down to the basement and into a storeroom. The two trucks were full of large wooden crates marked 'Fragile'. Nomura, Ota and I helped direct the men carrying the crates down the stairs and into the storeroom. Some crates seemed much heavier than others. I heard the faint clinking of glass from inside them. Throughout the unloading, Nomura and Ota exercised characteristic restraint. Their expressions revealed nothing. I wondered if they already knew what was inside—if they had been privy to a conversation I had not.

The men unloading the crates hardly spoke, but they moved with urgency. The officers beside the trucks whispered their instructions. I wondered why they did so, as the building was not in a residential area.

After forty minutes the last crate was unloaded. Kimura signed a document and saluted the officer in charge of the shipment—the one who had spoken to me with such disdain. When Kimura came back inside, Shimada locked the entrance to the building after him. 'Just temporarily,' he said.

'Come,' Kimura said, and we followed him downstairs.

The storeroom was crammed. Kimura picked up an iron bar lying on the ground and passed it to Shimada. 'You do the honours,' he said.

Shimada went to the closest crate, and worked the bar under the lid, eventually loosening the nails that held it to the frame. He lifted the lid and stepped back so that Kimura could see. I leaned forward. It was full of glass specimen jars of various sizes. From my position I could only see metal lids, some with wooden tags attached to them with string, and glimpses of yellow formalin contained within the jars. But Kimura stood over them and brought his hands together in excitement.

'Ah, here's a good one,' he said. He reached in with two hands and brought out a large jar.

It held a severed head. In the formalin, the flesh was the colour of butter. The scalp was shaved and a section had been cut from the crown, exposing the brain. Several deep incisions ran from the temples to the edge of the cavity. The man's eyes were closed tightly, as if subjected to unbearable pressure, but his mouth was open, the purplish lips forming a slack 'O'. It was as if he had tried to say something, but the final words had been stolen at the moment of death.

When we were finally allowed to go home, I walked out of the building onto the empty streets and breathed deeply. The air had never tasted so sweet. Nomura, Ota and I said nothing to each other as we parted at the gate. I looked at my watch: one-thirty. The last train had left hours ago. I could have slept in the tearoom at work, as I had done before when Shimada needed a large batch of bacteria by the following day, but tonight I wanted to be as far away from the laboratory as possible. I pulled my coat around me and began the long walk home. Cold air stung my face. I tried not to think about what I had seen that night; I trained my thoughts on washing myself clean and soaking in a hot bath when I got home.

I saw almost no one, aside from the occasional drunk curled up in an alley. At one point, I passed a street cleaner in navy overalls. He was bent over, sweeping rubbish into a bamboo basket. When I walked past him, he looked up. One eye was the colour of milk. That pale, unblinking eye seemed to penetrate deep into my soul. A chill passed through me and I quickened my pace.

I was freezing and exhausted by the time I got home. I drew the entry door shut behind me, careful not to wake Kayoko. The table in the living room was clear of bowls. I had been returning home later each night as my responsibilities at work had grown. At first, Kayoko had left dinner on the table for me, but I rarely wanted to eat at that hour and the rice and fried fish became hard by morning, not even good enough to use in rice balls. She began to leave out only simple food—cold miso soup and rice balls. Tonight, for the first time, she had left out nothing at all. It didn't matter, as I wasn't hungry. I went straight to the bathroom and slid the door open, expecting a gush of hot air. But the air inside was cool. My heart sank. I eased the lid of the bathtub open. Empty. I dipped my hand inside, hoping my eyes were playing a trick on me, but no. I put my hand to the furnace, but that too was cold. I forced open the iron hatch to see if I could light a fire, but there were not even a few embers inside. Kayoko must have cleaned it that evening.

I peeled off my clothes and sat on the low stool, my head in my hands. I turned on the tap and filled the bucket with cold water, then poured it over me. I sucked in my breath. The sting was like an electric current. I brought the bar of soap along my arms and legs, then filled the bucket with water again and washed the suds away. I drew another deep breath and shuddered. Behind me, the door scraped on its track. Cool air hit my back.

'What are you doing? You must be freezing.'

Kayoko's voice was high and thin, like a child's. I didn't turn. I couldn't face her, not yet. I needed more time to calm my thoughts before I went to bed.

'The bath. You emptied it. I need to wash myself.' I clenched my teeth to try to contain my feelings.

'I'm sorry. You were so late—I thought you'd stayed at work overnight like you did the other week.'

I shook my head. I prayed she'd leave me alone. As I sat on the stool, holding a bar of soap, silence stretched between us.

'Tomo, are you okay?'

I imagined her expression: lips pressed into a thin line and her big, troubled eyes.

'Yes. Please, just leave me alone.'

I heard her step back and felt cool air again as she closed the door. I hugged my knees to my chest. After a minute, I leaned forward and filled the bucket again.

Ota said he'd seen him in the hallways: a man with a thick moustache and wearing a military uniform bedecked with insignia. I thought little of it, as high-ranking military officers often visited our offices. But a few days later, passing through the foyer, I saw three men standing near the entrance. The one in the middle, facing me, was tall and thin. Perhaps it was his eyeglasses, or the way the light from the entrance threw shadows, but I noticed the angles of his face: the peaked eyebrows that dwarfed his small eyes. I had no doubt he was Lieutenant Colonel Ishii, the head of our organisation.

Ishii Shiro was known as a gifted microbiologist who'd given up a promising medical career to devote his life to research. He and Kimura had studied together at Kyoto

Imperial University medical school and were still good friends. Ishii had started doing research in Manchukuo several years earlier, and I suspected it was Ishii whom Kimura visited when he went abroad.

That afternoon, Kimura visited the laboratory to make an announcement. 'At the end of this week, the head of our unit, Lieutenant Colonel Ishii, will give a lecture on his current research. I'm sure I don't need to point out how fortunate we are to receive him. It will be a wonderful opportunity to learn from a pioneer of modern science. His insight will also help us to analyse the specimens to the best of our abilities.'

On Friday, we walked into the second-floor training room. As some of the first researchers to arrive, we were conspicuous in our white coats. A small group of army officials stopped talking and turned to survey us. Behind them a line of windows offered a glimpse of the tree-lined streets around the station. To the east, out of sight from where I sat, were the extensive grounds of the Imperial Palace. I imagined what these would look like from where we stood: a dark, impenetrable mound encircled by a snaking moat.

On the wall at the front of the training room hung a gilt-framed picture of the Emperor, his kind eyes full of light. Looking at him, my heart swelled with devotion. Beneath the picture stood the desk I had seen on my earlier visit, its surface polished to a high sheen and its brass handles gleaming. The rows of wooden chairs that filled the rest of the room were like statues, not a single one out of place.

'Where should we sit?' Yamamoto whispered.

'At the back, I suppose,' Nomura said. 'Lots of people have been invited.'

Ishii's lecture had been a topic of discussion in the tearoom all week. Nomura had wanted to meet him for years, ever since his senior college classmate who'd studied under Ishii had gushed about his brilliance. 'Apparently he only sleeps a few hours a night; he's always busy thinking up experiments and analysing,' Nomura had said. Ota had pointed out that Ishii had only graduated from Kyoto ten years earlier, and in the past two and a half years had been promoted from major to lieutenant colonel. 'To rise that fast, he must be a genius.'

We took our seats in the back row and watched as more army personnel and researchers trickled in. I recognised many of the faces from the photos in the foyer, although I didn't know their names.

'Isn't that War Minister Sugiyama?' Ota said.

A man in a high-necked jacket decorated with medals stood at the door, flanked by two men in khaki uniforms. People jostled as the seats filled up. Everyone shifted their attention to the front as two men entered the room. We all stood up. Through the gaps I saw Kimura and Ishii. They both stopped, saluted the picture of the Emperor on the wall, then turned towards us and bowed.

Ishii was only a few years older than Kimura, but physically the two men couldn't have been more different. Kimura was short and stocky where Ishii was tall and lean. Kimura's hair was neatly parted, waxed and combed to the side, his uniform spruce, from the pleat in his trouser legs to the shine of his buttons. Ishii's appearance, however, was unorthodox. He had thick, wavy hair about two inches long and wore heavy-rimmed glasses. The top button of his uniform was unfastened—whether it was a genuine mistake or a deliberate gesture of laxness, I didn't know.

Kimura cleared his throat. 'For most of you, Lieutenant Colonel Ishii needs no introduction. He's chairman of the Army Medical College's Immunology Department and was recently promoted to chief of the Kwantung Army's Epidemic Prevention and Water Purification Unit in Manchukuo. His work in the area of water purification and B encephalitis has saved literally thousands of Japanese lives. Today, he'll share the research he's been undertaking in Greater East Asia.' Kimura paused, allowing his eyes to roam the room. 'You've been invited here today as leaders and innovators in your fields, and you are asked to behave accordingly regarding the confidentiality of today's lecture.' Kimura's stern tone brought to mind my interview with him, when he'd questioned my ability to be discreet. 'Without further delay, I invite Lieutenant Colonel Ishii to deliver his lecture.'

Ishii stepped forward and smiled. 'Thank you, Major Kimura. Some of you are already familiar with my research in Manchukuo, but for the sake of those who are new to this area, I'll give a brief summary.' His loud nasal voice commanded attention. He talked with his head slightly tipped back, so that he looked down the length of his nose at the audience. 'In the winter of 1933, thousands of Japanese troops in northern China died from cholera and a fever epidemic prevalent on the China–Russia border, and thousands more died or lost limbs as a result of frostbite. These three afflictions dealt a harsh blow to our expansion, and so, with the support of the Army Medical College, I began developing a treatment for frostbite and a vaccine for cholera and the fever epidemic. In the four years since the Epidemic Prevention Research Group was established, I have expanded its focus to include the bubonic plague as well.

'We've recently completed building a new compound twenty miles from the city of Harbin in northeast Manchukuo. It is the first of its kind: a compound of more than sixty thousand square feet dedicated to epidemic research and prevention. As well as dormitories for workers, there are recreational theatres, swimming pools, bars, restaurants and, of course, laboratories with the most advanced technology in the world. The true purpose of the facility is concealed from the local community through the disguise of a lumber mill. We've even started calling our test subjects *maruta*. It started as a joke, but "logs" has turned out to be a convenient euphemism, so we have persisted with the term.

'Although we are still in the early stages of research, our experiments with logs have proved enormously successful. Take, for example, the fever epidemic. Ticks collected from rats that tested positive to the virus were ground and mixed into a saline solution, which was injected into a group of logs. After nineteen days, most of this group showed mild symptoms of the disease. We took their blood samples and injected them into another uninfected group of logs. This time, after only twelve days, symptoms of infection became apparent. These logs were then dissected, their organs ground and mixed with a saline solution, which was in turn injected into a new group of logs. By repeating this process continuously we were able to successfully isolate a pathogen in a few months. Being able to conduct research in this way has delivered unparalleled knowledge, which we've already passed on to the army to minimise further loss of life.

'Our research into frostbite prevention and treatment has been similarly rewarding. By subjecting logs to repeated exposure to cold air and cold water over weeks, we've ascertained that wet cotton clothing more often results in gangrene, and that the most effective method of treating frostbite is to soak affected areas in a warm bath of thirty-eight degrees.' He turned to his assistant. 'Make sure you circulate those photographs.'

Having seen the specimen jars already, I thought I knew what to expect. The photos reached me first. I leafed through the black and white images: swollen fingers, blistered toes, blackened faces, and grotesque, rotting flesh that shrivelled and puckered to reveal bone. The final photo depicted a child's chubby hands, the tips of the fingers all black.

That evening, after finishing my notes and cleaning my equipment, I decided to leave work earlier than usual. Since the afternoon, pain had gathered and throbbed at my temples. Yamamoto was nowhere to be found, and I hadn't seen Shimada since Ishii's lecture. Nomura and Ota were still hunched over their microscopes, their coats aglow beneath the overhead lights. Without saying anything to them, I slipped away.

As I made my way down the corridor, I heard laughter coming from within Shimada's office. Voices overlapped and merged together. Not wanting to be caught leaving early, I stopped short, but my foot scuffed the floor.

'Who's there?' Shimada called.

'Just me, Ibaraki.'

'Ibaraki? Come here.'

I presented myself in the doorway. Shimada, Kimura, Lieutenant Colonel Ishii and Yamamoto were arranged in the tiny office on an assortment of chairs and stools. An almost-empty bottle of whisky sat on Shimada's desk. They must have been drinking all afternoon, as they were all red-faced—especially Yamamoto, who slumped against the desk, his head lolling on his neck. He smiled at me, blinking slowly like a cat. I was surprised to see him mixing with our superiors, but then I remembered he was a relative of Kimura's and they occasionally socialised together. Seated next to Yamamoto, Kimura seemed to be asleep, nursing an empty cup in his lap. Ishii appeared the most sober. He gazed at me evenly with his long legs stretched before him.

'Aren't you leaving a little early?' Shimada looked at his watch.

As I had already changed out of my laboratory clothes, I couldn't deny that I had intended to go home. 'I'm sorry, sensei. I was trying to find you to ask if I could go home. I have a terrible headache. I'll come in early tomorrow to make up for it.'

Shimada drew himself up. 'A headache? Our soldiers are risking their lives and you have a *headache*?'

I blinked. His expression was severe. A moment later, however, he burst into laughter and the others followed.

'Stop pestering him and give him a drink.' Ishii reached for the bottle. 'No, I've got a better idea. We'll go out. I know a great place just a short ride away. We can take one of your cars, can't we?'

Kimura scowled, his eyes still closed. 'No, not another one of your geisha nights. I've had enough of them.' His words were thick, as if his tongue was swollen.

'Fine then, we'll take mine.' Ishii stood up. 'What are we going to do about your cousin, Kimura? He looks a little queasy.'

Yamamoto jerked his head up, struggling to keep his eyes open.

'Not my cousin . . .' Kimura muttered.

'Ibaraki will take care of him,' Shimada said. 'Yamamoto and Ibaraki are good friends. They sometimes go out together after work. Isn't that right?'

I hesitated, trying to think of how to respond. As if in silent protest, pain shot behind one eye—a pain so intense that I had to close my eyes. I pictured Kayoko beside me as I lay in darkness at home. But I knew I couldn't refuse the invitation. When I opened my eyes, Shimada was on his feet, his coat under one arm while he tidied his desk. Even Kimura was rising from his chair, a surly expression on his face.

Ishii clapped his hands together and turned to me with a look of delight. 'So it's decided. You will come.'

The tea house was in Kagurazaka, an area I had only visited once before, during the day. We turned off the main thoroughfare, and the streets narrowed, feeding into a crisscrossing network of alleys, many only wide enough for two people to pass. They were not like the grimy, rubbish-strewn lanes in other parts of Tokyo. Kagurazaka's alleys were cobblestoned and swept clean; lanterns hung outside the doorways of restaurants and tea houses, emitting a soft light. As we left the car and made our way down one of the narrowest passageways, now and then a door opened, and a hubbub of voices and music spilled onto the street. I was gripped by the feeling that I didn't belong. Although I was from a reasonably well-to-do family, this was a world hitherto unknown to me.

Ishii stopped next to an unmarked dark wooden door. He rapped on the surface. He hardly waited a second before rapping again. 'Aya-chan, it's me, Ishii Shiro. I have a few friends with me.'

The wooden divider slid open. I caught a glimpse of a white face. The girl on the other side said something, too quietly for me to hear. Then the door opened, and we stepped inside. The hallway was so dark I couldn't see anything at first, but from somewhere ahead of us, a girl was singing to the rapid twang of a *shamisen*. The haunting music and that high, lilting voice conjured a world of exquisite refinement. For a moment, my headache subsided, but then I thought of Kayoko playing the *koto*, and with the feeling of guilt, the pain returned. As my eyes adjusted, I noticed that the passageway opened up into a rectangular entrance hall, with gold-coloured *fusuma* panels on all sides. The music emanated from behind one of these panels.

The girl who had answered the door took our coats. Her face was heavily painted white, with pink cheeks and a semicircle of crimson on her bottom lip. She looked to be no more than fourteen.

A slender older woman approached us, moving so smoothly she seemed to glide along the passageway. She wore an indigo kimono and a simple gold *kazari* in her hair, which was pulled back into a heavy bun. 'Lieutenant Colonel Ishii, how delightful you could join us. We are preparing a room for you this instant. So there are five in your party?'

Ishii nodded. 'Are Momotaro and Eriko working tonight?'

'Yes, they are. However, Momotaro is currently with another client. I can send another girl, Teruha. She's very beautiful—'

'If I'd wanted a different girl, I would have asked for one. Send Momotaro. She'll want to come, just ask her. If she can't join us, perhaps I'll take my group elsewhere.'

The mistress's smile faltered for a second, then she bowed deeply. 'Of course, Lieutenant Colonel Ishii. When Momotaro has finished her performance, I will send her to your room. Please, come this way.'

As we passed gold-panelled rooms to our left and right, the sound of laughter and conversation swelled and dimmed like the roar of a passing train. The singing and the *shamisen* grew louder and clearer as we approached the back wall. For a moment, I thought we would be taken to the source of the music, but then we were ushered into an empty room. The grassy smell of tatami greeted us. A long lacquer table graced the centre of the room. Ishii and Kimura sat down on one side, while Shimada, Yamamoto and I sat on the other.

Ishii ordered sake and whisky. 'That will do us to start. And bring the girls, quick!'

As soon as the waitress had pulled the door shut, Ishii made a face. 'The service here is terrible. So slow, and did you see the way the old hag treated me, after all the money I've spent? I should go somewhere else. But they have the prettiest girls. They start them young.'

I knew Nomura and Ota would be bitter when they learned I had been invited to drink with Ishii and Kimura. If they had joined us, they would no doubt have used the opportunity to ingratiate themselves with Ishii—especially Ota. But I was too timid to do such things. Truth be told, Ishii frightened me. He had a reputation for picking on junior workers and forcing them to do the worst jobs. Even Kimura, who was slightly older than Ishii and had once been ranked higher than him, had been bullied into coming out tonight. I hoped the evening would pass quickly and I could return home without humiliation.

The door slid open and a porcelain face appeared.

'Eriko!' Ishii thumped the space next to him at the table to indicate she should join him.

Eriko bowed until her forehead touched the tatami. When she lifted her head, she smiled. She was very beautiful. Her eyes were even and perfectly shaped. Her lips, which were painted crimson, were defined by a deep cleft. Her nose was long and slender—unusual in an Oriental woman. All her features coalesced in symmetrical perfection.

She greeted Kimura and Shimada by name, then introduced herself to Yamamoto and me, before settling herself next to Ishii. Her kimono rustled against the tatami.

'It has been too long, Ishii-sensei. Have you been in Manchukuo all this time?' She had a slightly husky voice, making her seem older than she appeared.

'Aside from a couple of brief visits, yes. The new project has been very demanding.'

'You didn't come to visit me while you were here?' Eriko pouted.

'You'll have to come visit me in Manchukuo next time. I'll give you your own apartment within the compound. There's a cinema there, too.' He tugged at her kimono sleeve.

She playfully swatted away his hand. 'If only I could. You know that's against the rules. As much as I'd like to, I'd be banished from my *okiya* if I ran away with you.'

The waitress appeared with the sake and whisky, and Eriko poured drinks for everyone. She handed me a cup.

Ishii leaned forward and spoke to me. 'I hope you can drink more than Kimura's cousin here. A glass of whisky and he's already asleep.' He nudged Yamamoto beneath the table. Yamamoto jolted upright, murmuring an apology.

Ishii held his cup aloft. 'To His Majesty the Emperor. *Kanpai!*'

We clinked cups and downed the sake. It warmed my chest, but the pain at my temples surged. I winced. Across the table, Ishii was watching me. Heat rushed to my cheeks. I reached across to refill his cup, careful not to let my hands tremble. He said nothing while I poured. Then he lifted the cup and emptied it into his mouth.

'How did you get a position at my laboratory, anyway? I don't recognise your name or your face. Let me guess: a connection to Kimura?'

Before I had a chance to explain, Shimada spoke up. 'Ibaraki's father was a surgeon at Tokyo Hospital. Ibaraki Shuichiro.'

'A surgeon at Tokyo Hospital? Is that so?' Ishii regarded me coolly.

'Yes, that's right,' I said.

'One of the very best,' Kimura said. 'I worked for him when I was an intern.'

Although I was aware of my father's outstanding reputation, hearing Kimura confirm it made me glow with pride.

Ishii took out a cigarette, and Eriko brought out a lighter from one of the folds of her kimono to light it. He leaned back and inhaled deeply, still looking at me as he did so. He tilted his head towards the ceiling and exhaled a plume of grey smoke. It was a showy gesture that demanded an audience. The room fell silent.

'You know, I wanted to be a surgeon when I was younger. It seemed to me to be the noblest of professions. But really, what can one surgeon do? He can only heal patients one at a time. But a medical scientist . . . ah. A scientist can heal the world. When I realised that, I decided to dedicate my life to medical research. As my mentor says: "Great doctors tend their country, good doctors tend people, and lesser doctors heal illnesses." A great doctor, just like a great military commander, knows that sometimes a few lives have to be sacrificed to save thousands of others. When this war is over, great doctors will be remembered. The question is, what type of doctor will you be, Ibaraki-kun?'

It wasn't a question that demanded a response, but over the next few hours as we drank steadily I was concerned Ishii was testing me. Kimura and Yamamoto became so drunk that they fell asleep. As Shimada, Ishii and Eriko continued talking, I became more and more quiet. At about eleven o'clock the geisha Momotaro appeared. She was another porcelain-skinned beauty of tender age, who smiled slyly upon seeing Ishii.

'Ah—she's here!' Ishii exclaimed. 'But she's a bad girl for making me wait.' Eriko got up and Momotaro arranged herself next to Ishii and proceeded to fawn over him, pouring him drinks and speaking to him in soothing tones. Soon afterwards, they disappeared together into the hallway. I took the opportunity to leave.

When I opened the front door to my home, the aroma of simmering broth reached me. My stomach turned. Although I ordinarily enjoyed Kayoko's cooking, I felt ill from the alcohol, my headache and the long day I'd had. I wanted nothing more than to go straight to the bathroom to scrub myself clean. I was surprised to find Kayoko waiting for me at the *kotatsu*, and the table set for two.

'You waited for me? But it's almost midnight.'

'I've hardly seen you all week. I wanted to spend time with you. Come, let's eat.'

She went into the kitchen to serve the meal. A warm bath beckoned, but I knew I couldn't refuse Kayoko after the effort she'd gone to. I removed my jacket and stood at the threshold between the kitchen and sitting area, and smoked a cigarette. I tried to empty my mind of the images I'd seen that day. Rotting flesh. Blackened limbs. I heard the pad of Kayoko's feet and the clack of bowls as she set them down on the table. I smelled soy sauce and mirin. 'You made my favourite?'

The chunks of yellowtail and radish were golden and steaming. Slivers of ginger and green *mitsuba* leaves were scattered on top. Boiled spinach and grated radish were set out in the gold-leaf lacquer bowls we'd been given as a wedding present. Despite my nausea, my mouth began to water. 'What's the special occasion?'

'I'll tell you in a moment.'

I was a little apprehensive, but Kayoko's happy mood suggested something good. Over the first year of our marriage, I'd come to accept my wife's occasionally mysterious ways: every so often she withdrew into herself, avoiding me for hours while she read, practised the *koto* or went outside for a solitary walk. Tonight, however, she was being playful.

'Sit down,' she said. 'Dinner is ready.'

My mind was finally blank. Through the windows I glimpsed the yellow lights of the house next door, like a beacon that aided our safe passage. A silhouette moved across next door's window, a dark shape that separated and merged into the shadows. Sometimes, on the weekends, I saw the elderly couple who were our neighbours. They often walked to the markets together, guiding each other around the holes in the path, and I wondered if Kayoko and I would grow similarly dependent as the decades passed.

Kayoko brushed past me, carrying a tray of bowls. 'Smoking now? *Aramaa*. And I just told you dinner is ready.'

She made a few trips back to the kitchen, bringing more bowls, condiments and utensils.

'Who else is coming to dinner?' I asked. 'This is enough to feed a family of six.'

'No, just us,' she said coyly. 'Come, sit down.'

I eased onto the cushion at the wide end of the table and plunged my feet into the cavity. The coal heater warmed my feet. '*Itadakimasu*,' I said, picking up my rice bowl and scooping a portion of sticky grains into my mouth. My appetite had returned.

'*Itadakimasu*,' Kayoko said softly.

The stew was delicious. Subtly sweet and rich with the flavours of fish, radish and mirin. She must have been preparing it for a long time.

'Soon we'll have to make space for another at the table.' Kayoko spoke into her bowl of soup.

'What do you mean?'

'I went to a doctor today. Tomo, I'm pregnant. We're going to have a child.' Her eyes glistened.

I put down my chopsticks. My spine was tingling. Thoughts crowded my mind. I must have stared at her for a while, because she asked, 'Tomo, what's wrong? Aren't you happy?'

'Yes, of course I am . . . I'm surprised, that's all. I hadn't noticed a change in you.'

'I've had my suspicions for the past three weeks. I was late, and I wasn't feeling well. The doctor confirmed it today.'

'Why didn't you say anything to me earlier?'

'I didn't want to tell you until I was certain. You've been working so hard lately. I didn't want to distract you.'

I reached across the table and touched her hand. 'I'm so happy. A baby. We'll be blessed.'

'I already told Mother. She guessed when I saw her last week. She took me to the doctor today.'

'So it's news, then. I'll tell my mother she'll be a grandmother again. And my sister will be glad her children will have someone new to play with.'

I smiled. But when I thought of our baby, images of blistered skin and a child's black fingers came to mind.

Two months later, we readied ourselves to receive another shipment of specimens at the laboratory. This time, Yamamoto was allowed to stay back with Nomura, Ota and me. We were told the volume would be larger and so two nurses from the Army Medical College were sent to assist us. They stood in the foyer with us, waiting for the delivery. They were only young, no more than twenty or so—too young to be working past midnight, and far too young to be engaged in work such as this. I wondered what they'd been told. Yamamoto tried to engage them in conversation by asking them where they'd studied, but they gave the briefest of answers and hardly met his gaze. I sensed their reticence was due to their knowledge of the nature of our work. I felt stained by my association with the laboratory.

The trucks arrived and the crates were ferried to the basement. Shimada levered them open and we began to move the specimens into the storage room. Most of them were in small jars—hands, feet, heads, hearts and other organs—but one of the crates held a single large metal container filled with formalin and whole bodies. One had gangrenous skin. Another was smooth and showed no signs of malady save for its chest cavity, which had been opened up for dissection. There was the body of a woman, too. She had her arms outstretched as if she were trying to cling on to something.

One of the nurses stepped forward to help move the bodies into the concrete formalin tank in the storage room next to our laboratory, but when she looked inside, she put her hand to her mouth and turned away. It was a strangely polite gesture, as if she were minding her manners for the sake of not offending the corpses. At first I thought it was a bad smell that had made her recoil, but when I looked into the container the cause of her consternation became clear. Among the larger bodies was the body of a child, about two years old. His legs were buckled beneath him. His skin was blackened and covered in blisters. I couldn't see his face, for he was curled up, his forehead resting on his knees and his arms wrapped around them. He appeared to have been sitting in this position when he died.

Everyone stopped.

'I can't,' the nurse whispered. Her eyes filled with tears.

No one wanted to touch the child. Seconds passed. Nobody moved.

'I'll do it.' I reached in and picked up the boy as gently as I could. There was a numbered tag around his neck. His body was light, as if he were hollow.

After we had unloaded all the crates, I went home. It was after midnight when I headed to the bathroom to wash away the day.

Kayoko surprised me in the corridor as I made my way back from the bath. All the lights were out, but she was standing by the sliding doors that led to the kitchen, her face in darkness but the soft light of the moon spilling across her hips.

'Kayoko,' I said, almost colliding with her. She had her hand on her belly, the cloth of her nightdress pulled into her grip. Thinking she was on her way to the bathroom, I stepped aside for her to pass. She didn't move.

'I know why you wash yourself after work,' she said. 'Why you scrub so hard.'

My blood surged. How could she know? Was it the smell of the formalin? Were my clothes soiled with their blood?

'I know what you do,' she continued. 'You think I don't notice, but I do.'

My eyes adjusted to the low light and Kayoko's face emerged from the gloom. I had expected her gaze to be hard, or that she would not be able to look at me at all, like the nurses earlier that night, but her eyes were round and full of pity. As soft as her skin. My wife, my love. She knew, and she didn't hate me. She could still look at me with love. The realisation unhinged me. I felt dizzy with relief.

'Kayoko . . .' I reached out to take her arm, to draw her warmth to me. I wanted to hold her, to hear her tell me it was all right. I wanted her to help shoulder the burden of my pain. But before I touched her, she spoke again.

'I'm not angry, I know you have to do it for work. You have to go to those places, with those *women*—' her face creased '—but you can't do it so much. Not after our baby is born. It wouldn't be fair. Not to me, or the baby.'

The words I had been about to speak caught in my throat. The relief I had felt seconds earlier vanished. Emptiness gnawed at my stomach. To have been on the verge of sharing the pain, and then to have the comfort snatched away! All hope was knocked out of me.

My face must have shown my despair, because Kayoko went on more gently. 'I know how important your work is. When the baby comes, I want it . . . I want us to be more like a family. You've been so distracted lately. When I try to talk to you, it's as if you're not there. You're always at work or out late socialising with your colleagues and geishas. I can't sleep at night because I am so worried. You need to be at home more when our child comes. Can you do that?'

I nodded. I tried to speak, but no words came out. I made a noise in my throat.

'Tomo, are you all right?' She took my hand in hers, and with her other hand she reached up to touch my cheek, wiping away the wetness. I longed to tell her about my work. But I couldn't—I had given Kimura and Shimada my word. Besides, what would Kayoko think of me? What if she couldn't forgive me? It was better to remain silent and never mention it to our families, as Kimura had said.

'What's the matter? It's okay. You haven't done anything wrong. I know it has been hard.' She brought her body closer and slipped her arms under mine. She rested her head on my chest. I felt the warmth of it through my *yukata*, and the warmth of her belly as it pressed against me, our child moving inside.

With Ishii's support, Kimura planned a dissection demonstration at the Army Medical College for staff, students and several key army figures in the new year. He hoped to showcase the work the laboratory had been doing under Ishii's command, and in doing so secure more funding.

Shimada was tasked with delivering the lecture. Everyone in our team had an important role to play, but Shimada asked me to assist with dissection. 'Nomura and Ota are better at analysis than you, but your surgical skills are superior,' he said in his office one afternoon. 'Perhaps it's in your blood. I'd prefer to have you help me on the day.'

I flushed with pride and thanked him for his choice. But as I walked back to the laboratory, my stomach felt heavy. I'd been given another responsibility, just when I hoped to spend more time with Kayoko. I consoled myself with the thought of how proud she'd be to learn Shimada had chosen me.

Snow was falling as I walked home from the station—the first snow of the season. Although I had tried to leave work early, it was nine o'clock by the time I arrived home. I opened our front door and saw two extra pairs of shoes at the entrance. I wondered if we had dinner guests I'd forgotten about. Voices murmured from somewhere down the hall.

'Tomo!' Kayoko's voice was shrill.

A plump woman with silver-threaded hair padded along the hallway towards me. Her skin creased around her eyes and mouth. She looked familiar. I wondered if she was a relative of Kayoko's.

'Dr Ibaraki? I'm Taito, your neighbour. Your wife's unwell, I'm afraid. I heard her crying in the bathroom and came to see if I could help. My husband called a doctor who lives in the neighbourhood.'

I hurried to the bathroom. My legs felt weak. The doctor was crouched in the doorway. He stood up when he heard me, and I saw Kayoko huddled in the corner. She was sitting on the wooden wash stool. Her hair fell in wet, tangled clumps around her face. A blanket cloaked her shoulders. Beneath it, the wet fabric of her nightdress clung to her skin. Blood stained the lower half.

Tightness seized my chest. 'Kayoko, are you all right?' I crouched beside her.

She glared at me. 'Where were you?'

I froze, unable to breathe.

'Where were you?' she repeated, her voice hard.

'I'm sorry, I was at work. I had no idea . . .'

I looked at the doctor. He was only a few years older than me, with hair that was flecked grey at the temples. I noticed that he was still wearing his coat, the sleeves pushed up his forearms, although it was warm inside our house. No one had offered to take it for him. He gazed at me sympathetically. He struck me as the sort of man who was born to do this job: caring for the sick and weak. The sort of man I would never be.

'I'm sorry, but you lost the child,' he said.

I nodded. A lump formed in my throat. I was filled with grief, but my greatest concern was Kayoko. She was slumped against the wall, her expression blank.

'How is she?' I asked.

'She's weak. She's still passing a lot of blood. But she should be okay. The emotional loss will be the most difficult to recover from. It's always hard when it's your first.' He said it so gently that I thought he must have had a similar experience in the past.

'How long has she been like this?'

'I only got here an hour ago, but Mrs Taito has been with her longer. Her husband fetched me. I live only a few streets away.'

I imagined him returning home to his family while there was still light left in the day. He would share stories of the patients he'd treated, and his wife would beam with admiration. I had a sudden urge to ask him about his children, but I suppressed the feeling.

'Should I put her to bed?'

'She said she wants to stay here until it's over. Whatever makes her comfortable—as long as she's not cold. I understand you're a doctor yourself?'

I nodded. 'But I'm now in research.'

'Where?'

'At a new unit attached to Tokyo University. The microbiology department.' I felt bad lying to the doctor, especially since he'd treated Kayoko with such kindness.

'Well, I'm sure she's in capable hands with you. I don't want to intrude . . .' He turned to leave, pushing down his coat sleeves.

'No!' Kayoko cried out. 'Sensei, stay, please stay . . .' Her eyes were wide.

'Kayoko, it's very late,' I said. 'The doctor has to go back to his family—'

'Yes, because that's what good husbands do. They don't stay out drinking when their wife's pregnant.'

I'd never seen Kayoko so angry, so willing to shame anyone—especially not in front of strangers. She was behaving like a different person.

The doctor laughed nervously. 'Of course I can stay, Mrs Ibaraki. It's no trouble.'

I felt as if the air had been sucked out of me. My chin trembled. I tried to blink away tears. Kayoko's rejection pained me more than the loss of our child, I realised, and an even greater sadness came over me. I stepped outside for a moment to compose myself.

Mrs Taito was standing in the corridor, just a few feet away. She smiled. Embarrassed she'd seen my distress, I began to turn away, but she put out her hand. Her face was filled with tenderness. 'It's hard, I know. But she won't be like this for long. Time heals all wounds, you'll see.'

Kayoko's mother travelled from Shonandai to look after her. She arrived the next day with a suitcase in her hand, her hair loose and her face unfamiliar without make-up. I slept on a futon in the living room to allow them the bedroom to themselves. I crept around the house. Whispered conversations floated around me. Sometimes I heard crying. I hovered on the periphery, trying not to make a sound.

I went back to work after a day's absence. I was surprised at how relieved I was to be back at my microscope under the laboratory's bright lights.

Shimada gave his condolences and told me he and his wife had lost two children in similar circumstances. 'Don't worry, she'll have a healthy child in the future, you'll see,' he said. 'At the time, you wonder how any human could go on living after such suffering. And then, years later, you look back and understand.'

Shimada dismissed me early that evening so I could be with Kayoko. The light was off in the hallway when I arrived home. In the living room, I noticed a place set for one person at the table.

The bedroom door slid open and Mrs Sasaki appeared, carefully closing the partition behind her. 'Welcome home. I made dinner. Shall I serve you now?'

She went into the kitchen and reappeared carrying a tray. She set some bowls down on the table. 'Kayoko and I ate earlier,' she said.

'How is she?'

Mrs Sasaki inclined her head and frowned. 'She's still distressed. She didn't want to get out of bed today. Maybe tomorrow.'

'Can I see her?'

Mrs Sasaki's mouth opened a fraction as she drew a breath. 'Maybe not right now . . .'

I started moving towards the bedroom.

'Wait! She doesn't want to see you.' Mrs Sasaki's face was anguished. 'She's still upset.'

'What do you mean?'

'It's not my business, but . . . she's hurt that you didn't come home earlier that night.'

My face felt hot. I was incensed that Kayoko had confided in her mother about our relationship. 'But how could I have known what had happened? What could I have done?'

'Not just that night, but all the other nights, too. A husband needs to provide more than just money to put food on the table. She needed you, and you weren't there for her.'

I stared at Mrs Sasaki's face. Her drawn-on eyebrows. The cheeks that had grown heavy with age. The ugliness of this woman who'd come into my house and presumed to know me. She had no idea of the things I had to do each day, the secrets I had to keep. Neither did Kayoko. She didn't understand the sacrifices I had made to serve our nation—to help ordinary people such as her. A weight that had been teetering inside me finally fell away. Blood rushed to my face.

I said something very foolish. I said it loud enough for my wife to hear through the thin paper walls. 'Very well, then. If that's how Kayoko feels, I won't disturb her tonight. I won't disturb her ever again.' I walked out of the room and left the house. The door shuddered behind me.

I walked around the neighbourhood, stepping through the grey slush of the previous day's snow. I went as far as the river and listened to the burbling black mass whispering its ancient lore.

With fresh air in my lungs, I returned hours later, realising what a fool I'd been. But the bedroom was dark. In any case, the damage was already done.

Kayoko stood in the hallway with her bags at her feet. The fullness of her skin, so smooth and pale yet full of life, released me from the images that haunted me each day. Standing there before me, on the threshold of our house, Kayoko was my only tie to life.

'I shouldn't keep Mother waiting,' she said. Her voice trembled. As she bent to pick up her luggage, her face disappeared in the darkness. The tortoiseshell handles of the bag clicked.

'Kayoko, I wish you'd stay.'

'Please, Tomo. It's settled now. I want to go to my parents'. At least for a little while.'

'I'm sorry for what I said the other day. I didn't mean it. I was frustrated because I hadn't seen you in days. I was worried about you. Please, you haven't given me a chance.'

'Haven't given you a chance?' Kayoko's face contorted. 'How could you say that? All last year you were cold to me. You went out drinking, you stayed back late at work. I tried to get through to you, but you ignored me. Even when you were at home you acted as if you didn't want to be near me. I tried to please you, but it was no use. I thought having the baby would change things, but . . .' Her voice caught. She put her hand to her mouth and began to cry. At that moment, my heart was breaking.

'I don't know what I did to make you stop loving me,' she said. 'Was it the baby? Was that why?'

I ached to hold her, to be close to her again. 'No, no, of course not. It wasn't the baby. It had nothing to do with you.'

'Another woman? Then what? It must be me. Be honest with me, please.'

'No, there's no other woman. There never was. I only went out drinking when I had to. It wasn't you. It's my work—the things I've had to do . . . Don't leave me, Kayoko. I need you. Please . . .' I was overcome with the urge to touch her, to feel her soft skin beneath my fingertips. I longed to breathe in her clean scent. I put out my hand.

'No, don't. It's too late. I've made up my mind. I'm going to my parents'. I'm sorry, Tomo. I need to get away.'

She stooped to pick up the last of her belongings. She slipped on her shoes and stepped outside. For a moment, she was framed in the doorway. A black silhouette against the fallen snow.

The door shut, returning me to darkness.

In the weeks following Kayoko's departure, I moved through life as if in a dream. I ate and went to work, yet the details passed me by. Everything was heavy, drawn out. As much as I tried to move ahead, a current swirled against me, pushing me further downstream.

I spent the new year's holiday by myself. My mother presumed I had gone to Kayoko's parents' house for the celebration, as I hadn't told her about our rift. I suppose I thought that if I didn't put it into words, it might not be true. I also expected Kayoko to return home soon. At midnight, I walked to the local shrine alone. Children in kimonos ran through the *torii* gate, their *geta* clacking on the stone path. Inside the shrine grounds, their parents lifted them up to ring the bell and pray for good luck. When they wished me a happy new year, I looked away.

Snow fell steadily over the next few days, cloaking the landscape in white. I stayed indoors and didn't see or speak to anyone I knew. It was a strange time; sounds were muffled and time moved slowly. My senses were dull, as if a veil had been pulled over them.

I returned to work the following week, catching the crowded train into town. When we rattled across the bridge, I noticed the river had frozen. The surface had turned silent. But the darkness of the icy grooves made me think of the flowing river beneath—the current below the surface, straining for release.

At the laboratory, I tried to keep to myself. When the others discussed their holidays, I turned to my microscope to continue my work. I took my lunch break late so I would be alone in the tearoom. At the end of the day, I left the laboratory without waiting for Yamamoto as I used to. My colleagues must have thought my behaviour strange—perhaps they put it down to the burden of Kayoko's miscarriage. In any case, they had more pressing concerns than wondering about me: the dissection demonstration would take place the following week; many high-ranking officers had been invited, and there was much to be done in preparation. The next few days passed in a blur. I rehearsed the dissection procedure with Shimada, and although I performed to his satisfaction, my mind was elsewhere.

The demonstration was held in an older wing of the Army Medical College, in a low brick building around the corner from the laboratory. On the morning of the event, the branches of the deciduous trees lining the streets nearby were almost bare and the road was scattered with fallen leaves. The scent of pine sweetened the air.

We set up in the frigid first-floor meeting room. At Shimada's request, I brought a dissection table from the laboratory storeroom and assembled a long list of tools. Nomura, Ota and Yamamoto spent the morning going back and forth between the laboratory and the meeting room, pushing trolleys with crates full of specimens.

Shimada paced the area between the chairs and the demonstration table, checking the equipment, adjusting the position of the table, stepping back, moving it again. 'So cold in here. Perhaps this was the wrong location,' he muttered to himself. 'Are you ready?' he asked me more than once.

Guests began to arrive in the afternoon. Major Kimura stood near the door, snapping to attention and saluting the high-ranking military officers who entered the room. Lieutenant General Chikahiko Koizumi, the dean of the Army Medical College, arrived, his bald pate shining. He stopped to survey the room. Our eyes met. Something gripped me, a feeling I couldn't place.

More college personnel, military men and a few outsiders arrived and filled the rows of seats. I tried not to study the audience for fear it would heighten my nerves, and instead busied myself with laying out the equipment.

At three o'clock, Kimura closed the door and addressed the audience. 'You have been invited here today to learn about the latest advances in biological warfare development carried out by the Epidemic Prevention Laboratory. I'd like to welcome special guests Colonel Sato and Lieutenant Colonel Ogawa. Lieutenant Colonel Ishii sends his apologies as he couldn't be here today—he's overseeing a crucial trial in Manchukuo. Today, Professor Shimada, head of operations within the Epidemic Prevention Laboratory, will demonstrate the efficacy of the bubonic plague as a biological weapon. Professor Shimada?'

Shimada cleared his throat. His Adam's apple slid up and down, as often happened when he was anxious. 'Thank you. Until recently, our research focused on developing synthetic forms of the *Yersinia pestis* bacterium, but with the advent of testing overseas, we are now able to analyse and compare the spread of the disease in human subjects across different dosages and methods of infection.'

He signalled to Nomura, Ota and Yamamoto. They removed the blanket from the specimen trolley and opened the metal container beneath. Ota reached in and lifted out a specimen, then placed the body on the dissection table with a soft *thunk*. The corpse was a middle-aged male. The flesh on his neck, arms and hands was swollen and black. Out of the formalin solution, the rest of his skin looked shockingly pale.

'This subject was injected with twenty micrograms of the bacterium and died within two days. Note the necrosis of the extremities, on the nose, fingers and toes, and ecchymosis of the forearms.' Shimada pointed to the bruising on the arms. 'The bubo visible at the groin and armpit also indicate the advanced state of the disease. Ibaraki, make a cut above the inguinal lymph node and remove the bubo.'

Taking a scalpel, I sliced the skin along the top of the groin and carefully peeled it back to expose the swollen node and the cutaneous nerves of the thigh. With several quick cuts I released the node and set it on the table. It was an inch wide.

'Most plague victims would not exhibit such symptoms until the fourth or fifth day of infection; this subject's nodes were swollen to eighty per cent of this size on the first day. Now, if we look at the lenticulae on the abdomen, we notice a similar advanced stage of progression. Ibaraki, could you . . . ?' Shimada hesitated. 'Actually, Nomura, get the infant. It's a better example.'

My breath was hot inside my surgical mask as I watched Nomura reach into the container and remove the corpse. He laid it on the table in front of me, at the feet of the male cadaver. It was the boy I'd unloaded from the crate. His eyes were shut to the world; his head bent as before. His fingers and toes were swollen and grey, progressing to black at the tips. They had a waxy sheen. Black dots like tiny stars covered the boy's protruding belly.

'Make a midline incision to open up the abdominal cavity.'

I heard Shimada say the words, but it was as if they travelled to me under water. I froze. The knuckles of my hand were white.

'Ibaraki? An incision, please.'

I stared at the boy, unable to move. I heard the audience fidget. Someone coughed at the back of the room.

'What's the matter with you?' Shimada hissed near my ear. 'Incise the specimen *now*.'

I felt a gust of cool air as someone moved behind me and took the scalpel from my hand. It was Yamamoto. 'Here, let me,' he said.

In one swift motion, he cut along the child's linea alba, incising the abdominal wall and exposing the organs underneath. As intestines spilled from the cavity, I flinched, suddenly jolted from my daze. Yamamoto stepped back.

I looked up at the audience before me. They were so close I could see the glint on the brass buttons of the military uniforms. Major Kimura and the dean sat in the front row. They were both staring at me.

The following day, I was called to Major Kimura's office as soon as I arrived at work. I knocked on his door, my heart thudding in my chest.

'Yes?' he called.

'You wanted to see me, sir?'

He looked up from a folder open on his desk. 'Ah, Ibaraki. Take a seat.' He gestured to a chair. Although I'd visited his office numerous times, he hadn't invited me to sit there since my initial interview. Dread formed at the pit of my stomach.

The chair sighed as it took my weight. Framed certificates lined the wall behind Kimura's desk, a glass cabinet containing medals and Kimura's porcelain collection stood to my left, and I knew from memory that behind me was a bookcase filled with leather-bound titles in German, English and French. Kimura's desk was neat. A glass lamp, a notepad, a folder, and a desk stand with an ink pad for his seal and two pens were all that graced the broad surface.

He shut the folder with a snap. 'I trust you know why you're here?' He stared at me, his gaze even.

'Yes, sir. If you mean the demonstration yesterday . . .'

'That's right.' He clasped his hands on the desk in front of him. 'How long have you worked for me, Ibaraki? A year? Two years?'

'Almost two years,' I said.

'In that time I've had no cause to complain about you. You are punctual and meticulous. You work hard and have tremendous potential. Shimada has drawn my attention to your achievements on a number of occasions. Even Lieutenant Colonel Ishii approved of you. Until this week, I was going to nominate you to go to Manchukuo to train under him.'

My head felt light.

'Yesterday, however, you showed a different side when you refused to carry out a simple procedure. Your behaviour reflected poorly on our organisation and caused me, personally, a great deal of embarrassment. It would have been even more humiliating if Yamamoto hadn't stepped in to do your job.'

'Please, I was not myself. My wife suffered—'

'Did I say you could speak?' Kimura's eyes blazed. 'Only fools speak when their superior is talking!'

I hung my head. There was a moment of silence before Kimura continued.

'I've been trying to determine whether your recent indiscretion was an isolated incident or whether you might show such insubordination again. We're at a crucial juncture in our research, when we cannot afford to take risks—and you, Ibaraki, are a risk. Now, Shimada has told me of your troubles at home. I understand that work puts a strain on your family. Our families suffer. We all suffer. But a soldier of the

Fatherland fights for His Majesty—regardless of his family, regardless of his personal views. He puts aside his feelings. And so must you.'

He opened the folder on his desk. He picked up a sealed envelope and held it in his hand. 'Here's a letter with the terms of your termination. You'll receive full pay for the next three months. Under the circumstances, it was the best I could do.'

My mouth opened. I felt as if the air in my body had been knocked out of me. If I lost my job, I would have nothing. I wondered who else would hire me. But it was also a matter of pride. A dismissal would affect me for years to come. 'Please . . .' I whispered.

'Is there something you wanted to say?'

'Please, sir, I beg you to give me another chance. I'll never do it again, I promise. I am always discreet. Just that once . . .'

Kimura sighed. 'Try to see it from my position. Our entire unit relies on secrecy. One moment of weakness and we could be exposed. Our honour is at stake. Not just now, but in years to come. If you are truly a man of honour, you'll know to hold your tongue and never speak of the Epidemic Prevention Laboratory again. Take the secret to your grave. Is that clear? To disregard that would bring great shame on you and your family—on all of us. Think of your father: I'm sure he had only the highest hopes for his son. You're still young. You'll be able to find another job in time. You could still do great things.'

He thrust the envelope towards me. 'In a few years' time, we'll be ruling over Greater East Asia, and our suffering will be rewarded. Have faith that that time will come. That will be all, thank you, Mr Ibaraki. Please exit the building in a timely manner.'

Without a job and without Kayoko, there was no need for me to stay in the city. I left the house in Setagaya and returned to my family home.

The weeds in the yard had grown high and the furry heads of the green stalks brushed against the fence. Mother had changed, too. The line of her mouth had softened and her hair had greyed. I'd expected disappointment when I returned to live with her, but she seemed happy to have me back. Nobuhiro was away doing military training in Nagano. Megumi visited with her children twice a week. Hanako, my three-year-old niece, climbed onto my lap whenever she saw me. Megumi tried to teach her the word for 'uncle', *ojisan*, but all she managed was *ji-ji*. Kazuo, my newborn nephew, mostly cried or slept against his mother's breast. Megumi took him to the kitchen while I played with Hanako. I could hear my sister whispering to Mother. I was certain it was about me, but I no longer cared. My life had become one that others whispered about.

I tried to call Kayoko at her parents' home.

'She's convalescing in the country,' her father said, his voice cool. 'Her mother's with her. I don't know when they'll be back.'

And so the days passed. I remember the subtle shift of light in the house at different times of day. The burnt-rice smell of the rice balls I ate. Time seemed to collapse, pulling all meaning into it. The days crawled by and vanished all at once. The weather grew warm, bringing a flourish of green leaves. While my mother and Megumi frequented parks and festivals, I spent the long, hot summer days indoors, too dispirited to go out.

In early autumn, my aunt visited from Osaka, bringing turtle-shaped *manju* and *arare* rice crackers, small and glossy in my hand as I scooped them from the packet. Her husband worked in the shipping industry, and he'd heard of a job at a hospital in Australia, she said. He could make inquiries on my behalf if I was interested.

'Australia—where on earth?' My mother frowned. 'I'm not sure you should bother.'

'We should ask, at least,' I said.

Word came soon afterwards. The job was in Broome, in northwest Australia, thousands of miles away. A very respectable position as the head of a small hospital, but with only moderate pay. A two-year contract, with an option to extend.

'Don't take it,' Mother said. 'Be patient. You'll find a job here soon.'

But the stain of my dismissal meant my prospects in Japan were slim. I wasn't ready to face my friends and former colleagues and tell them about my situation, not yet. Kayoko's silence hung over me, unacknowledged yet ever present. Instead of accepting my loss, I wanted to escape. I yearned to put all the pain behind me and start afresh. The thought of Australia grew more attractive with each passing day.

Broome
1941

I woke early, my back damp with sweat. Although I had shifted my bed to the verandah, I could not escape the humidity. Beyond the pale gauze of the mosquito net, the sky was still dark. Insects trilled around me like the pulse of an ancient heart. From somewhere far away, a bird began its morning call. I decided to take a walk before the sun grew too hot.

The streets were quiet at the start of the wet, the exodus almost complete. President Kanemori had left with his family two months earlier. Only Harada remained, as usual. I planned to celebrate the new year in Broome with him and Minnie, as my friends in Melbourne had returned to Japan earlier in the year. A few luggers were still at sea, making the most of the late start to the wet, so I had decided to keep the hospital open two more weeks.

I listened to the crunch of my feet along the dusty road, the subtle shift when I stepped on a pebble or a twig. The air filled my nostrils and mouth, tasting of metal.

At the hospital, I drew the curtains shut and closed the door against the heat. I sat in the anteroom, updating the log of patients in the light peeking from beneath the curtain. Sister Bernice moved about the ward, unhindered by the gloom. She returned equipment to the cabinet and supplies to their boxes. Doors creaked. Glass clinked. She was going to Geraldton at the end of the week.

'Hello?' a muffled voice called from the entrance. It was one of Ang Pok's laundry boys. Sister Bernice went out to meet him. I heard the hum of their voices.

Minutes later she appeared in the doorway. 'Doctor?'

I looked up. Even in the darkness, I could see her distress. Her brows were knotted. She clutched at her throat. I wondered if there had been an altercation.

'I've just heard some distressing news. Ren Kin just told me Japan bombed Hawaii sometime early this morning. They attacked the US naval fleet, apparently sunk several ships. It's all over the wireless, he said.'

I moved to the corner of the room and switched on the wireless. Sister Bernice stood beside me as we listened to the broadcast.

'. . . In breaking news, earlier today, at seven fifty-five am Honolulu time, Japan launched a surprise attack on the US naval base at Pearl Harbor off the southwest coast of Hawaii, sinking at least two battleships and damaging several others, and destroying hundreds of US aircraft. The National Broadcasting Corporation in Honolulu states that more than one hundred Japanese planes were involved in the attack, which occurred in two waves, forty minutes apart. Heavy US casualties are expected. President Roosevelt has condemned the attacks.'

The broadcaster paused, then repeated the message. After I had listened to it a second time, I lowered the volume. I felt empty. For months, I had feared Japan's entry into the Second World War, knowing the challenges it would present. Now that it had happened, however, I found I didn't feel anything—no fear, regret or even sadness.

Sister Bernice gazed at me. 'Don't you realise what this means? We're at war with Japan now. You mustn't stay here. It isn't safe.' Perhaps mistaking my silence for shock, she continued to speak. 'They'll come for you—they'll put you away. You should have left a long time ago.'

Her face was creased in anguish. I felt a great tenderness towards her at that moment. 'Thank you for your concern, Sister, but you need not worry—I have prepared myself for this outcome.'

'What do you mean?'

'When President Kanemori and the others returned to Japan, I was invited to join them, but I decided to remain. I felt it was my duty as a doctor and as a member of this community to stay and face the inevitable consequences.'

Sister Bernice lowered her hand from her throat. '"The inevitable consequences?" Surely you don't mean that. They'll put you in prison, or worse. What good will you be to this community if you're locked up?' Her cheeks were flushed.

Seeing her agitation, I tried to put an end to the conversation. 'I made my choice, Sister. Whether right or wrong, it is now too late to change. I have to stay here in Broome. I hope I can do so with your blessing.'

She stared at me for several seconds, then lifted her head and drew in a breath. Her mouth formed a tight line. 'Very well, Doctor. As you wish. May I suggest you start gathering your belongings? And we'll need to start making arrangements for the closure of the hospital. There'll be no one to replace you once you're gone.'

She walked out of the room. A moment later I heard her rattling through the medicine cabinet. From the door of the anteroom, I watched as she removed packets and boxes and dumped them on top of the cabinet. Her head shook with the vigour of her movements. She must have noticed me, but she didn't look up.

We barely exchanged another word for the rest of the day. At three o'clock she asked if she could leave early. 'I think it will storm soon. I'd like to return home before it does.'

She had never asked to leave early before. I was aware I'd disappointed her over my decision to stay in Broome, but what else could I do? There was no point in trying to run now. I was an enemy alien. She had to accept that.

'Of course,' I said. 'You know how quiet it has been here. And please don't feel you need to come here in the next few days if you have other things to do. I can manage on my own.'

Darkness crossed her face, but she turned back to the cupboard without saying anything.

Before she left for the day, I made a feeble attempt to put things right between us. 'Thank you for your help, Sister. And for your concern for my wellbeing. I am forever grateful for all you have done. I hope I have not offended you in any way.'

She looked as if she was about to say something, but instead she gave a resolute nod, then opened the door and stepped outside.

Although it was my fourth summer in Broome, it always amazed me how quickly conditions changed. One moment I was sweeping the verandah, the air so heavy it seemed to inhabit me, and the next a cool gust of wind stirred up debris and whipped through the trees. Rain began pelting the roof. Praying it wasn't the start of a cyclone, I hurried to secure all the shutters.

The storm was still raging when I retired to bed. Noise disturbed me throughout the night. Thunder shook the windows and the wind howled outside; the battering of the rain entered my dreams in the form of gunfire.

When I heard a tapping sound I thought it was the wind shaking the shutters. But when the same distinct pattern of tapping occurred again, I got up and went to the door. I opened it and found Sister Bernice standing on my verandah. With no umbrella or raincoat, she was drenched. Her veil had slipped back from her crown, revealing a damp tangle of hair. In her dishevelled state, she seemed a different, much younger person—someone I knew by sight but had little connection with, like the daughters of master pearlers who spent most of the year at school in Perth and returned to Broome for the holidays.

'Sister, what's wrong? Is someone sick?' Thinking one of the other nuns must be ill, I began to turn away from the door to get my things, but instead of answering me, she glanced past me to the hallway and then stepped inside. I offered her a seat but she remained standing. She was breathless, her eyes wide. I had never seen her so flustered.

'I'm sorry for disturbing you—for coming so late. You must think me very strange. But I cannot stop thinking about what you said today. It just does not seem right to me that you expected war to break out with Japan—and yet, knowing this, still you stayed? Wouldn't you have been safer, happier, if you'd returned to Japan?'

I was taken aback. The drumming of the rain on the tin roof grew louder, a roar that filled my ears. I wanted the sound to grow so loud it deafened me. I stared at Sister Bernice. Water beaded on her forehead and trickled towards her eyes. Her gaze was unflinching. I could see she was determined not to leave without an answer. The thought occurred to me that I could tell her. If not about the laboratory, at least about what had happened between Kayoko and me. If there was anyone who could listen without judgment, it would be Bernice. But how to put my pain into words?

'I did not want to go back to Japan. Not yet,' I said finally. 'My family—so much occurred before I left . . . It's hard for you to understand—'

'Why? Because I'm young? Because I'm a nun?' The sharpness of her voice startled me. She glared at me. I blinked. My heart sank as I realised the opportunity was gone. I could not tell her about my past—how I hadn't been there for Kayoko when she'd needed me the most. I certainly couldn't tell Bernice when she was so aggrieved—if I ever could at all.

'No, no. Nothing like that. Something happened in Japan. It is hard for me to say . . .'

I stared at the doorframe behind Bernice. I noticed we were standing in the same arrangement in the hallway as Kayoko and I had been on the day she left. I forced myself to look away. Butter-yellow paint coated the walls. As the rain continued its assault, the space between Sister Bernice and me seemed to stretch apart.

Finally, she spoke again. Her voice was strange. 'All these years we've worked together and I still don't know who you are. I've tried to understand you—the Lord knows how much I've tried. But as soon as you show a part of yourself, almost at once you hide it away. I see you almost every day, and yet I don't know the slightest thing about you. Perhaps I shouldn't care, but I do.'

Unease welled within me, a feeling so strong I had to lean against the wall for support.

'Remember the time I left for Geraldton early? You thought I left because of the way you treated me after I found that thing inside the book. And I was upset—I was angry with you for shouting at me. But that's not why I left. The reason I left was I realised something—a *feeling* was growing within me. For a long time I denied it, but when you reacted so strongly to the wooden tag, all of a sudden I understood: I was jealous. I was jealous of your other life in Japan, the one you never talked about. Maybe I felt like that because you were always so secretive, or maybe it was because of something else, but it made me so ashamed. I wondered why God had burdened me with such feelings. Was He testing my faith? I really did think of giving it up, of throwing it all away because of you. It was a silly idea, of course. You'd never—' She winced and closed her eyes, as if she felt sudden pain. 'I mean, I knew it would come to nothing. I never *wanted* it to come to anything, but I couldn't help thinking . . .'

She shook her head. Droplets spun to the floor, tiny pearls of light. Rain lashed the windows and roof, but everything inside was silent. She remained standing in my hallway with her eyes closed. I was frozen, save for the thumping of my heart. I sensed she was waiting for me to speak, but I couldn't bring myself to say the words. Finally, she opened her eyes.

'Sister, it is very late. Too late to be talking about such things. Let's discuss it in the morning, when the weather is calm and our minds are clear.'

She looked away. The ceiling light reflected in the corner of her eye.

'Stay here until the storm passes,' I said. 'I'll make a bed for you. It's too dangerous to go outside.'

She didn't seem to hear me. She turned and moved towards the entrance.

'Bernice, wait.'

Without pausing, she stepped through the door.

Sister Bernice didn't return to the hospital. For a few days I expected to hear the hospital door creak, the blinds squeal as the rings slid on the metal rods, and then to see her, occupying the doorway to the anteroom, dressed in white. But she never came. I won't lie: her departure saddened me. It was Bernice I thought of as I wiped down the benches and put the last of the medical books into boxes. I imagined her visiting her aunt's family in Geraldton, a clutch of nieces and nephews around her, recounting tales of what they'd done since her last visit. No doubt her disappointment quickly dissipated upon seeing them and our unceremonious parting was soon far from her mind.

Without her, my world shrunk. I continued opening the hospital every day, although there was nothing left to do. Walking through Japtown, I saw the shutters had closed on all the Japanese-run businesses—the Shiosakis' laundry, the Yat Son noodle shop and the Tonan Shokai store, where I'd bought rice, *miso* and other staples. At the hospital, I spent my time going through the medical files. I left the door ajar in case a patient came, although there were very few people left to treat since the arrests had begun.

One day, I heard a voice calling, 'Hello?' into the dim recess of the hospital. When I opened the door, Ang Pok recoiled, his tanned face crinkling in surprise. 'You still here? How come they not take you yet?'

I confessed I didn't know. As Ang Pok listed all the townsfolk who'd been arrested—the Shiosakis, Torimarus, Muramatsus, Tsutsumi and his wife, the Kanegae brothers, Joe Iwata, Johnny Chang—I began to wonder if I hadn't been arrested yet because of my profession. Broome's only other physician, Dr Wallace, was in poor health. If he became too ill to work, the town would have no doctor. What if they didn't take me at all? Perhaps I would remain in Broome under the watchful eye of Inspector Cowie, who was rumoured to have been sent from Perth because of concerns about Broome's large Japanese population. The residents would see me when they had to, and spend the rest of the time talking about me behind my back. The only boon would be a chance to make amends with Sister Bernice. I was sure I had done the right thing—she had her whole life ahead of her and there was no point throwing it away on a silly infatuation with me—but I wished I had been more considerate of her feelings. If only I had her talent for gentle counsel, for soothing people through talk, perhaps things wouldn't have turned out as they had.

That night, I went to Harada's house. Poor Harada, whose body was condensing with age; his spine curved like young bamboo as he shuffled around his home. He'd arrived as a diver during the pre-World War I boom, and had stayed long enough to see the divers come and go and the pearling industry dwindle like an ebbing tide. When President Kanemori had decided to return to Japan in October, he'd urged Harada to join him. 'Return now or you might never be able to go back,' he'd said. But Harada had refused. 'My home is here now, with Minnie. I'll stay, whatever happens.'

But when I visited that night, doubt creased his brow. I sat at his dining table with him and Minnie, drinking tea.

'Did you hear about the crew of *Trixen?*' he asked. 'They were late to shore this season and were arrested by Cowie and his men at the jetty yesterday.' His voice was a whisper. 'I saw them on the road, being led to gaol with nothing but the clothes on their backs. Everyone stopped to watch them as they walked past. The look on their faces—they had no idea what was going on.' He shook his head, a haunted look in his eyes. 'We'll be next, you know.' Minnie's eyes flashed, then she got up and left the room.

Harada leaned closer. 'She's mad at me. She thinks I should've gone back when I had the chance.' He didn't say anything for a few moments. He fingered a button on his jacket. 'We did the right thing, didn't we, by staying here instead of going?' His earnest expression sought my reassurance. But I said I didn't know.

It was a dreadful kind of waiting. Time entered a new dimension—not exactly slow, but a state in which I sensed everything more keenly. I detected the sharp scent of metal in the air, I felt each drop of sweat beneath my shirt, and I observed how the shifting light at dawn and dusk seemed to hide more than it revealed.

I was at the hospital when they came. The cloudy sky cast a sombre light in the thick midday heat. As I sat in the ante-room, the soft grate of men's voices disturbed the air. I was paralysed with trepidation as the murmurs became louder, till I sensed a movement of shadow beneath the front door. Four sharp raps sounded. I jerked into action, suddenly freed from the magnetic pull of my seat. I crossed the floor and flung open the door.

Inspector Cowie smiled, only the corners of his mouth turning upwards. Behind him stood Constable Taylor, the officer who'd replaced Rooney six months earlier when Rooney and his pregnant wife had moved to Perth. Taylor stared straight at me, his eyes like pale beads. The skin around his nose had been scorched by the sun.

Inspector Cowie cleared his throat. 'Dr Ibaraki, good morning. In light of Japan's entry into the war last week, the Australian government has issued an edict for the immediate internment of all Japanese nationals—'

I put up my hand to signal I understood. 'Just let me get my things.'

They followed me inside. Cowie took off his hat and wiped the sheen of sweat from his forehead. Taylor inspected the hospital while I packed up the last of my belongings in the anteroom. I heard footsteps behind me and I spun around to see Taylor, his unblinking gaze bearing down on me. He sniffed and looked away. I closed and locked my suitcases and carried them to the front door.

'One bag only—same as for all the others, right?' Taylor walked up behind me.

'I think we can let this one go, Constable,' Cowie said. 'The doctor's a special case. He needs his equipment if he's to treat anyone.'

'What about these, then?' Taylor held out a pair of handcuffs.

Agitation crossed Cowie's face. 'No, no. They're not necessary. It's just the doctor, after all.' Taylor thrust out his jaw.

I placed my luggage on the ground outside the hospital. Turning around to lock the door, I glanced inside one last time. I remembered how bare it had been when I'd first arrived. Now, even with the mattresses stripped and the equipment packed away, warmth filled the room through the personal touches that had accumulated over time. The assortment of cups and saucers on the shelf above the sink. The floral curtains stitched by Sister Bernice. The ink drawing of her profile done by one of the old Japanese patients who'd been at the hospital for a week with bronchitis. Delighted with it, Sister Bernice had pinned it to the wall, and every day I went to the hospital, the re-created sister gazed into the distance, forever noble, forever serene. I pulled the door shut and turned the key.

We started towards the police station, less than ten minutes walk away. We formed an awkward procession, with Cowie in the lead, holding one of my bags. Taylor and I followed him. I held one suitcase in each hand while Taylor flanked me, gripping my upper arm with one hand and carrying my fourth bag in his other. He was determined to keep hold, no matter how quickly I walked.

Just before we reached the next street, I looked back. White paint flaked from the walls of the hospital, exposing the sun-bleached wood beneath. I noted the patchwork of different-coloured metals on the galvanised-iron roof. A strange feeling came over me. I bit the inside of my cheek and forced myself to look away.

It was done now.

The late-morning sun shone with ferocity, as if it knew its moment of glory would be short. Light reflected on the surface of the muddy puddles and on the glistening leaves of pandanus palms beside the road. I strained to isolate the landmarks I saw every day. The elegant poinciana tree that hugged the curve of Napier Terrace and whose limbs children climbed like a ladder. The rickety sign that pointed to Weld Street. I tried to memorise them, but no matter how hard I tried I knew I wouldn't be able to truly recall them later—they'd be filtered through my memory and warped by time.

'We picked up your friend Harada today; he's in gaol with a few others,' Cowie said.

'Is he all right?' Harada's body had grown weak in the previous few years. He caught simple colds that turned into nasty infections.

'He's a bit frail, but he seems fine. He asked about you.'

The buildings of Japtown rose up ahead: a long line of metal shacks with deep front verandahs that jutted onto the street. Signs such as *T. Weng Tailor, Ang Pok's Laundry* and *Tonan Shokai General Store* sat atop each verandah, as proud as peacocks on display. The first time I'd laid eyes on Japtown, I had been shocked by the state of decay—the dilapidated buildings, rusted signs and dusty lanes well past their prime. *This is my new home?* I had thought. But as the weeks and then months passed I recognised Japtown's dynamic nature, fed by the constant human activity that swelled and waned with the seasons. I liked nothing better than to close the hospital on a Saturday evening in August or September, when it was still light at five-thirty but not too hot or sticky, and stroll along Napier Terrace towards the low-slung roofs of Japtown, surveying the area as the sky turned silver. During my first year, when few people knew me, I strolled unimpeded, observing the men smoking on the verandah of the gambling den, Mrs Yano on the second floor of her boarding house snapping out her sheets, and the children who played hopscotch in the back lanes, their legs coated in dirt.

On the day of my arrest, however, it was clear that the struggle between destruction and renewal, man and nature—whatever one wishes to call it—was drawing to a close. Although a few figures strolled along the main road, without the Japanese population and their businesses, the town was a shadow of its former self. The rusty signs, broken railings and faded curtains in the windows of the restaurants and stores—those elements that had once stood as examples of the town's life force—had become relics of a glorious past. I knew then Broome would never be the same.

We reached the edge of Japtown, and people stopped to stare at us. The sun, so bright and clear, continued to shine. Mr Ong was standing outside his store and saw us. Suddenly self-conscious, I ducked my head. Taylor saw me and smirked. Someone called out my name, and I looked up and saw it was Billy, the Malay who'd got into a fight with the Japanese diver my first year in Broome. He was on the upper verandah of Mrs Yano's boarding house, crouched over a washing pan. He waved and shouted something at me that I couldn't understand. I nodded and smiled, conscious of Taylor's grip on my arm.

We turned onto the dusty expanse of Carnarvon Street, where scattered iron-roofed buildings baked in the sun. There was only a short stretch of road until the police station. On our left was the Japanese Association; the hedge of pink and white oleanders that bordered the verandah was in full bloom. Ahead of me, on the far side of the road, was Ellies' cafe. I remembered when Sister Bernice and I had had our surprise encounter there on the day of the Emperor's birthday. I remembered the rhythmic *thunk* of the fan overhead and the sweet smell of malt. The smoothness of her skin. The way it crinkled around the corners of her mouth. Those memories converged and overwhelmed me, and that is the only explanation I can think of for what I did next. Nostalgia got the better of me, and without thinking I veered off course and started towards the cafe.

I do vaguely remember hearing someone shouting behind me, although for some reason I didn't think it was directed at me. I was in a kind of trance, at the mercy of my desire to go inside one last time—a desire so strong it was almost primal. I suppose I thought if I looked at it again I'd be able to preserve the moment in my mind—a memento of my time with Sister Bernice. I continued across the street at what seemed to me a regular pace, but I was told later I had actually broken free and run from Taylor and Cowie.

I was almost at the shop's verandah, the black, curlicued sign just discernible, when I felt a force on my back. My legs buckled. Pain shot through my left shoulder and dirt invaded my mouth. Someone—Taylor, I found out later—was upon me, cursing in my ear. 'Don't you try to get away from me. Quit moving, you bloody Jap!'

It's possible I suffered a concussion when I hit the ground, for when I lifted my head everything swayed. I recall fragments of images—a man's chin, the surprised eyes of a woman staring down at me, someone's sun-pink hands disturbing the collar of my shirt. There must have been quite a crowd. Then something hard struck the side of my face. Warm metallic liquid flooded my mouth. Time stretched out, like ripples on the surface of a lake. I later learned I was only unconscious for a few seconds, but into the space images floated up, one after another, enough to fill an hour-long reel of film. My mother's grey-streaked hair. Kayoko's ebony comb on her dressing table at home. The rich red sand of Roebuck Bay. Lily-white folds of fabric.

We did the right thing, didn't we? Harada's question came back to me, an echo in that silence.

I don't know. I just don't know.

Loveday
1942

I woke on Saturday to the chatter of men. The walls of the hut creaked and the windows glowed white. Two glorious days without work stretched ahead of me. At the last minute, Hayashi had offered to do my shift on Sunday, the day of the baseball final. 'You deserve it. You've been working harder than anyone else.' I had refused at first, but he'd insisted. 'Wasn't the baseball competition your idea? It wouldn't be right without you there. You can cover one of my shifts another time.' So I thanked him for his generosity and promised to return the favour. During my two days off, I planned to tend the garden near the Buddhist altar. I'd planted some purple-tinged long grasses that I'd picked up on our trip to the river several weeks earlier, and I wondered how they were coping with the frost. I also needed to check on the baseball trophy—I'd asked Sawada and a few of the other craftsmen to make something for the winners.

On the hut doorstep, I stretched my arms. A brisk wind tugged at my jacket and lifted my hair. I looked up. The sky was opaque. It was a strange colour—a shade I'd never seen before. Murky, like the river on an overcast day. I wondered whether a storm was approaching, but there were no discernible clouds in the sky. A haze seemed to hang in the air, making everything appear pale and blurry. Beyond the fence, the trees seemed to quiver in the distance.

I heard a shout from the gate. An army truck trundled into camp, lurching to a stop on the other side of the birdcage gate. Men spilled from the back and fanned out along the fence. Johnny and the others had returned from Melbourne. I was eager to know if their appeal had been successful. They'd want to celebrate, if so. I wondered if Yamada would allow them to have some of the sake hidden beneath the latrines.

The men began filing into our compound. I cut across camp to meet them, weaving between the few remaining rows of tents, the canvas flaps jerking in the wind.

Johnny, Martin and Andy were the last to enter. They trudged along the path, shouldering their rucksacks. I was about to call out to them in greeting, but then saw the expression on their faces. Their mouths were slack, their eyes downcast. Johnny's swagger was gone; his shoulders were slumped. Their appeals must have been rejected, but I couldn't imagine why. Surely at least one of them would have been granted a release?

I caught up to them on the path. 'How was it?'

Johnny didn't look up. Andy frowned. Martin glanced at me, his mouth tight. 'Not now . . .' He shook his head.

'You weren't successful?' I asked.

Johnny's head snapped up. 'What do you think, Doc?' He glared at me.

I opened my mouth, but nothing came out.

'It was a bloody waste of time. Those frocked-up arseholes were against us from the start.' He strode away, each footstep raising a cloud of dust.

'He's been in a foul mood since the decision,' Martin said.

'What happened?'

'We were in there for about fifteen minutes each and they asked us about ten questions. At the end of it, they told us they couldn't deal with our appeal as we were Australian-born and not aliens. They said we had to go to a *different* tribunal— one just for British subjects who are interned. Except there *is* no tribunal like that.' Martin rolled his eyes. 'The usual claptrap. I guess we should've known.'

'No one got a release?'

'Only old Ito.' Martin nodded to one of the other internees. Back bent, he swayed from side to side as he shuffled along the path. I recognised him from the infirmary—he was frequently admitted with various ailments due to his old age. 'Now that it's over, I couldn't give a shit, but Johnny's really taken it to heart.'

Johnny's silhouette skimmed the horizon as he walked back to his hut. Even from a distance, I could see the force of his steps and the way his body angled forward as he walked headlong into the wind.

For the rest of the morning, I stayed in my hut. I wanted to wait for the wind to settle before I ventured to the garden. It showed no signs of abating, however. Now and then, a strong gust blew outside the window, sounding like a muffled shriek. The walls tinkled with the sound of particles pelting the hut's iron exterior. I wondered how Harada and the other TB patients were coping in the rough weather. I took out a piece of paper and a pen to write a letter that was long overdue.

'Dear Mother,' I began. 'Please forgive my silence of the past few months. So much has happened since my telegram informing you of my transfer to Loveday. Winter has set in here at camp. The days are chilly and the nights freezing, but you will be pleased to know there is no snow. *Tsuyu* must be over in Tokyo. How are you coping in the summer heat?

'I received your telegram informing me of brother Nobuhiro's death. I regret I was unable to perform the duties expected of me at the funeral, but every day I pray for Nobuhiro's wellbeing in the afterlife. I hope that Megumi and her family can give you comfort during this difficult time.'

I tried to think of what to write next, but everything I came up with—the names of my friends at camp, the farce of the tribunal—was in danger of being cut by the censors. I thought of Johnny's conduct that morning. I hoped he calmed down before the baseball match—Major Locke would not tolerate such behaviour.

'We started a baseball competition within camp to keep fit and pass the time. I have enjoyed the games, although I'm not the player I once was. The final match is tomorrow, but my team didn't make it that far. Give my regards to Megumi and her family—Hanako must have started school by now.'

After lunch, the wind was still gusting. Dirt stung my eyes as I returned to my hut from the mess hall. Knowing there were only a few more hours left of daylight, I decided to brave the conditions and head to the altar garden. I reasoned it would take only a few minutes to check on the plants. As I made my way between the buildings, an icy wind tore at the collar of my jacket and stirred up eddies of dust. It hadn't rained in months. Leaves cascaded from trees at the edge of the clearing and blew into camp. I wrapped my arms around my body and bent my head as I stepped into the wind.

The altar occupied a space along the outer fence of our compound, about forty feet from the last row of huts. It was in the most isolated area of camp, away from the mess hall and latrines. Its seclusion was the reason it had been chosen for the altar—it was a suitable place for quiet reflection.

I emerged from the shelter of the buildings into the open space of the garden, and was hit by the full force of the wind. I would normally have been able to see the buildings of the duty guard camp beyond the outer fence, but today a rust-coloured pall of dust obscured the landscape. The vegetable garden spread out to my left; to my right was the ornamental garden. As I approached the bamboo thicket that marked the start of the garden, I heard the rustle of dry leaves beneath the howl of the wind. I stepped past the thicket and clucked my tongue at the state of the garden on the other side. It was swamped with loose soil. Although the bamboo shielded the plants from the wind, it also allowed piles of dirt to collect. The purple grasses I'd planted were covered, only their brown tips poking through the earth. Although I knew the weather would worsen, I couldn't help myself. I crouched down, and with my hands started shovelling away the debris. I looked around for some rocks to build a screen around the grasses.

Voices reached me from upwind, too faint to decipher. As I dragged a rock from the other end of the garden, the voices came closer, speaking in low tones. Their words became so clear I realised they must have been standing on the other side of the bamboo thicket, no more than three feet away from me. I recognised the speakers.

'. . . Hayashi thinks he's going to report it soon,' Yamada said. 'The doctor's been in there with a pen and paper, writing everything down. What should we do?'

I crouched by the grasses, hardly breathing.

'Who else saw?' Mori said.

'Nagano and a few others, but I doubt they'd say anything.'

'So it's our word against his,' Mori said. 'Given his recent mental state, I doubt the army will do anything.'

'What if he lodges a complaint with the Red Cross? Dr Morel is due to visit in a few weeks.'

'Dr Morel has to go through the regular army channels. They have better things to worry about than a petty dispute that led to a bruised arm.'

I had had my suspicions, but now I knew it was true: Yamada *had* attacked Stan. I had initially been blinded by the fact that Yamada was kind to me, and because he was a leader of our camp. What else, through my misguided loyalty, had I failed to see?

The wind picked up, whining as it whipped between the bushes. For a moment I thought they had moved away from the garden, as I could no longer hear them. Then I heard Yamada again. His voice reached me in fragments, shredded by the wind. '. . . don't want to be investigated . . . lose my spot on the exchange ship . . . something more permanent?'

A pause. Then I heard Mori, his gruff voice muffled by the rustling of leaves. 'No. Too risky . . . too suspicious.'

Neither of them spoke for a few moments. Then Yamada started speaking again. I could hardly hear what he said, but there was a pleading, desperate quality to his voice I had never heard before. He mentioned Stan several times, and something about the infirmary. Then I heard my own name. I strained to make out what he was saying, but the wind was howling, and I caught only a few words.

'. . . don't think he would say anything . . . can't risk Suzuki telling . . . We need to tell Hayashi . . . without delay . . . No one will ever guess.'

A gust blew sideways, driving dirt into my face. I covered my mouth to keep myself from making a sound. One of them started coughing, and their voices became faint as they moved away from the bamboo thicket.

My chest pounded as I tried to make sense of what I'd heard. Yamada wanted to silence Stan, mistakenly believing that I was writing down the incident in which he was attacked by Yamada so that Stan could report it to the army. What had he said? *Sassoku*, without delay. But as I repeated it in my head, I realised he could have said *sassozai*, rat poison, instead. 'We need to tell Hayashi . . . rat poison . . . no one will ever guess.' Did Yamada intend to poison Stan? My heart skipped a beat as I remembered seeing a packet of rat poison in one of the cupboards in the infirmary kitchen. The authorities must have forgotten about it when they confiscated the other packets in the wake of the New Caledonian's death. I gazed at the grasses before me, still covered in earth, and the measly stone barrier I had started to build. Despite my efforts, everything was in ruins. Why could I never do anything right?

Images crowded my mind. Stan, all alone within the kalei-doscope of sheets. Kayoko in the hallway, her luggage at her feet. It was all so clear to me now: somehow, I always failed the people I cared about. I remembered that Hayashi was working at the infirmary over the next two days. Hayashi, who must have been reporting my every move to Yamada. I had thought he was being kind when he'd insisted on doing my shift. Perhaps he and Yamada had already hatched a plan to hurt Stan. I had to warn Stan before it was too late. I would tell Johnny—he could help. McCubbin trusted him. I had to get to the infirmary. As long as I got to the infirmary in time, everything would be all right.

I hurried back, taking the long route along the perimeter fence so it wouldn't appear as if I'd come from the altar. I didn't want to run into Mori or Yamada. The wind tore at my hair and drove grit into my eyes. I squinted through the haze.

I went straight to Johnny's hut. The building shook as I ran up the stairs. Most of the gang were in the back corner, lounging on their beds. Martin and Andy were playing cards. Charlie read a magazine.

'Johnny, where's Johnny?' I gasped.

Charlie shrugged. 'Dunno. Went somewhere to blow off some steam. I hope he pisses off for good, the way he carried on at lunch. You'd think he'd found out his family had been murdered, not that he had to stay here.'

'I need to talk to him. It's important.'

Martin looked up from his game. 'I'd leave him for a while. You saw how he was this morning.'

'You don't understand. It's urgent. Do you know where he is?'

'Your guess is as good as ours,' Charlie said. 'Could be anywhere.'

'Try the mess hall or the rec hut,' Martin said.

I staggered outside. With one hand over my mouth and my eyes narrowed against the dust, I checked both locations, but couldn't find him. I didn't see Yamada or Mori either. Perhaps Yamada had already gone to talk to Hayashi at the infirmary? I realised I had to act immediately, with or without Johnny's help.

With the collar of my jacket upturned, I stumbled towards the entrance to our compound. In the distance, plumes of dust churned and swallowed the sky. A sentry was usually posted at the gate at all times, but in the thick air I couldn't see anyone standing there.

I clung to the wire. 'Excuse me? Hello? Any guards there?'

I heard the crunch of gravel, and a figure emerged from the haze. He walked with his rifle on his shoulder, cradling the butt in his hand, as if he was on parade. As the guard neared, I realised I had never seen him before. The brim of his cap sat low, hiding most of his face. All I could see was the cleft of his chin and the purple pocks of recent acne.

'Please, I need to go to the infirmary. Could you let me out?'

'Halt!' His voice was cold.

'I need to go to the infirmary in 14B. I'm an orderly. I have to go there now. There's an emergency.'

'State your name.'

'Tomokazu Ibaraki. From hut five.'

'No internees allowed out. Major's orders.' A muscle fluttered along his jaw.

'I just need to go for ten minutes. It's an emergency. I'm a doctor—please.'

'A doctor now, are you?' His lip curled. 'No internees can exit—that's an order.'

'Is Officer McCubbin there? Could I speak to him?'

'Officer McCubbin is on patrol at another camp at the moment. He's not available.'

'Please, this is not a joke. I need to go to the infirmary!' I rattled the gate in frustration.

In one swift move, the guard swung his rifle to his hip and aimed it at me. 'Step back, you bloody Jap! One more move like that and I'll shoot, I swear to God.'

I raised my hands and stepped back. The guard's knuckles were white as they gripped the stock; his finger trembled on the trigger.

I swallowed. 'I am not lying. It really is an emergency . . .'

'Move back from the gate now, or I'll blast you.'

I backed away from the gate, my arms still raised. Then I turned and ran to my hut, my entire body jolting with each step. When I burst in, everyone in the room turned to stare at me.

'Has anyone seen Johnny Chang?'

A few people shook their heads.

'Sensei, are you all right?' Ebina asked.

Without responding, I ran back outside. I searched the compound once more, skirting the perimeter of camp—steering clear of the gate and the hostile guard—checking the ablutions block, the latrines, even the foul-smelling spot beneath the latrines where sake was brewed, and then a few of the huts. But Johnny was nowhere to be found. Feeling helpless, I spent the rest of the afternoon crossing between the mess hall and Johnny's hut, my panic growing with each hour.

Just after five o'clock, we assembled for afternoon headcount in the mess hall, where we always gathered in poor weather. The wind blustered outside, shuddering against the building and rattling the windows. I stood behind my allocated seat, my mind a jumble of thoughts and fears. I spied Mori at his table a few rows away from me.

Yamada sauntered in, talking to Ebina about the baseball match. 'I'm betting on the Borneo team. They've practised more and have good strategy. Of course, as a fellow Japanese from that region, I'm biased.'

As I stared at his broad face, my stomach tightened. I wondered how I had been so deceived by him. I craned my neck, looking for Johnny. His position between Ernie and Martin at the front of the room was empty. If he failed to show up at headcount, he'd be severely penalised. But moments before the officers marched into the hall to start the count, Johnny suddenly appeared at his table. His hair stood in stiff peaks and his shirt was streaked with dirt. Martin whispered something to him, but Johnny didn't respond; he just stared straight ahead.

Major Locke entered the room, wearing a heavy overcoat that dwarfed the rest of his body. Three officers filed in after him and stood to attention in front of the entrance to the kitchen. Lieutenant Perry was first in line, followed by the new interpreter, who'd arrived at camp a few weeks previously. The guard I'd encountered at the gate was the last to enter. He thrust out his lower jaw as his eyes roamed the room. His rifle strap stretched taut across his chest. I ducked my head to avoid his gaze.

Locke rarely came to the afternoon headcount, so his arrival didn't bode well for the next day's baseball match. Perhaps it was the effect of the dust outside, but strain seemed to show in the creases around his eyes.

'Before we start the headcount, I have several important announcements to make. First, I'd like to introduce our new guard, Private Davies, who will be assisting with the patrol of the compound. Until recently he was serving in New Guinea, where I believe many of you are from.' Locke nodded at the private, who pursed his lips. His shoulders were rigid as he continued to scan our faces.

'Second, due to weather conditions, tomorrow's baseball match will not go ahead as planned. The game will be postponed—' Locke raised his voice as cries of discontent rose from those who had understood him '—*the game will be postponed* until further notice. Furthermore, all outdoor activity is banned until the dust storm clears. No walking around the perimeter, no loitering outside, no hanging around the gate. It is for your own safety. Guards have been instructed to enforce this rule. Any internee who disobeys will be *severely* punished. Is that clear? Quiet now. Settle down. I said *quiet!*'

After the interpreter had delivered the message, disbelief spread among the tables of men. The army had recently introduced a rule that no more than six men per hut could be at the latrines at the same time at night, but other than that, we'd always been given a relatively free rein within camp. I wondered why they'd suddenly introduced such harsh restrictions.

A voice growled over the hum of dismay. 'This is bullshit.' It was Johnny.

Locke swivelled his head. 'Mr Chang, another comment like that and you'll be in detention overnight.'

'What? First the tribunal, then you cancel the match, and now we can't even go outside?'

For his sake, I prayed he would stop.

'Chang, I'm warning you . . .' Locke's face was red.

Private Davies stepped forward and aimed his rifle at Johnny. 'Watch your mouth, you filthy Jap.'

Johnny drew himself up tall. 'Yeah? You want to shoot me? Want to claim another Jap?'

'Davies! There's no need for that. Lower your weapon.' Locke pushed the muzzle away. He eyed the private for a moment before turning back to address us. 'As I was saying, aside from walking to your huts or to the latrines or ablutions block, internees are not permitted to linger outside until further notice. Hut leaders, please make sure everyone understands this. There will be serious consequences if anyone breaks this rule.'

After the officers had completed the headcount and filed out of the hall, a rumble of consternation filled the room. 'Why the sudden change? Why now?' I heard someone say.

Instead of joining the conversation, I headed straight to Johnny. He was almost at the door when I caught up to him. I called his name but he didn't turn around.

'Johnny, it's me.' I touched his shoulder.

He spun around. 'Don't you *dare* touch me.'

I sucked in my breath. I'd never seen him so incensed. His eyes bulged. His nostrils flared. A vein at his temple pulsed.

'Are you all right?'

He looked around the room. 'I fucking *hate* this place. I'm so sick of it. All I want to do is get out. I don't care anymore, I don't care what it takes.'

I tried to soothe him. 'Don't worry. You will leave eventually. You will go back to Broome, and everyone there will welcome you with open arms. And in a few years' time, you will think about camp, and the pain will have gone.'

'I feel like I'm going to explode if I stay here any longer.'

Although I felt sorry for him, there was no time for counsel. 'Johnny, I need your help with something. But I can't talk about it here.' I glanced behind me. Yamada was sitting at the table, about to eat dinner. 'Can we go to your hut?'

Johnny shook his head. 'Sorry, Doc. I've got my own problems to deal with.' He turned and started in the direction of his hut.

'Johnny, wait!'

He ignored me, disappearing into the gloom.

I looked behind me again. Yamada brought a spoonful of stew to his mouth, then laughed at something, tipping his head back. His casual cruelty disgusted me; there he was, eating and laughing, when he had just plotted to harm somebody—possibly even murder him. I would not let him hurt Stan.

I returned to my hut alone. Night had descended by the time I stepped outside. The floodlights shone diffusely through the haze. The air churned around me, thicker than before. Particles invaded my mouth and nose. I covered my face and squinted till I could see only a sliver of light. In the howling wind I couldn't even hear my own footsteps. I was careful not to veer towards the fence; Major Locke's warning was fresh in my mind.

The wall of a hut glowed starkly in the strange light. I hugged its side and continued past another hut until I came to mine. I hauled myself up the steps and into the sanctuary inside. I switched on the light. Rows of empty beds stretched away from me. I sighed with relief. Silence, at last.

I paced the hut, walking up and down the rows of beds as I tried to make sense of the situation. Had Yamada talked to Hayashi already, or had he too been stopped at the gate by Davies? If I hadn't been allowed out, it was unlikely Yamada would have been. Could he have sent a message through someone else? I thought of Stan lying in bed, his face turned towards the window, dreaming of Isabelle. Somehow I had to get to the infirmary and arrange for Stan to be moved somewhere safe. His condition had improved noticeably in the past week; perhaps I could recommend he be moved to the ward at headquarters, away from Hayashi.

I heard voices outside. The hut shook as people mounted the steps. The door was flung open, and the first of the men returning from dinner spilled inside. Dirt blew into the room as they stamped their feet, muttering about the weather.

'Sensei, you didn't eat?' one of the men from Borneo said.

I shook my head. 'I'm not feeling well. Just a stomach ache. I'll be fine.'

I sat on my bed to consider my options. I had to face the fact that I had no way of getting to the infirmary and no one to help me; Johnny had refused and McCubbin was in a different part of the camp. There was no other choice: I would have to confront Yamada.

The hut grew noisy as more people returned from dinner. The weather had made everyone boisterous. Each time the door opened, the roar of the wind swelled and more dust blew inside.

Finally, I heard the distinct timbre of Yamada's voice. I turned to see him smiling as he entered the hut. 'It's like a typhoon out there,' he said. His face was flushed.

'Yamada, can I talk to you?' My voice was high and thin. I indicated the corner of the room.

He came over, his face crumpled with concern. 'Sensei, are you all right? I've never seen you so dishevelled before.'

I ran my hand through my hair and took a deep breath. 'It's about Stan Suzuki. I know what you're planning. Have you already spoken to Hayashi?'

He narrowed his eyes. For a second, the facade slipped. Then he smiled and shook his head. 'I don't know what you're talking about.'

'You have to stop him, please. Stan's a good person. He doesn't intend to tell anyone about what happened in the mess hall. He has been talking to me about a girl he has feelings for. I've been writing a letter for him.'

Yamada's smile faded. He gazed at me, the warmth gone from his face. 'Did you eavesdrop on my conversation? How dare you! That was none of your business. You're mistaken in what you heard, anyway. You have no idea what we were talking about.' He turned to leave.

'Wait! Yamada, *please* don't hurt him. I'll tell someone if you do. You think I won't, but I will.'

He stepped towards me. His voice was a whisper. 'But, sensei, you forget that *you* were the one who spurned Stan when he came to see you about his arm. One of the orderlies told me. Isn't that what made him cut his wrist? And then you didn't want to operate on him. Even Johnny knows that. If anything happens to Stan, who do you think everyone will say drove him to it?'

My legs felt weak. Yamada stared at me, looking deep into my soul. A feeling of shame rose up through my body, filling my chest and throat. As much as I wanted to deny it, I knew he was right. My refusal to believe Stan had prompted his deterioration. For that, I couldn't forgive myself.

A siren sounded outside. Starting low, it quickly rose in pitch until it became a constant whine through the roar of the wind.

'What's that?' Yamada turned his head towards the door.

I had never heard the siren before. Thinking someone else must know what it meant, I looked around the room. But everyone in the hut was as bewildered as I was.

'Is it because of the weather?' someone asked.

'Maybe they're warning us it'll get worse.'

'What should we do? Stay inside?'

'We shouldn't go outside unless they come and tell us. Remember what Locke said.'

A thought occurred to me. It took root in my mind and grew until I could no longer ignore it. I started towards the door.

'Where are you going?' Yamada called. 'Sensei, don't be stupid!'

The wind cut through the thin fabric of my shirt. In my haste, I'd forgotten my jacket. But the scream of the siren filled my ears, driving me forward. Grit stung my face. With one hand over my mouth, the other feeling the side of the hut, I staggered along the path until I reached hut two. Dust billowed into the room as I flung open the door. Everyone inside turned to look at me.

'Do you know what the siren's for?' someone asked.

I pushed past the crowd of people gathered near the door and found Charlie and the others at the back of the room. Charlie was on his bed, smoking. Ernie, Ken, Andy, Dale and Martin were seated on two beds, playing cards in hand, midway through a game. They looked up at me, frozen by the siren.

'Where's Johnny?' I asked.

'Haven't seen him,' Ernie said. 'We thought he might be with you. Marty said you two were talking.'

'No. Oh no. This is not good. Johnny was acting strange, but I didn't think—' I caught my breath.

'What? You don't think . . . ?' Charlie stubbed out his cigarette and stood up.

I nodded.

'Shit, shit, shit. That fucking lunatic *would* do something like that.'

'What are you guys talking about?' Andy said.

'The siren, dummy,' Charlie said. 'We think Johnny might have tried to escape.'

'You serious?'

Martin lifted his head. 'He has been acting weird all day. I saw him coming out of the kitchen after lunch, stuffing bread into his pockets. When I asked why, he told me to mind my own business.'

My heart thumped. 'Did you see where he—'

A loud crack cleaved the air. Then another. In the seconds of silence that followed, I couldn't breathe.

'Was that . . . ?' Charlie asked.

I lunged towards the door. Blood surged through my body, giving me strength.

'Doc, wait!'

Dust swirled around me, limiting my visibility to a dozen feet. Stumbling along the path with one hand out in front of me, I headed east, towards the direction of the gunshots. I heard shouts coming from 14B. Fragments of words, like figures in a fog. I ran towards the voices, pushing headlong into the wind. Debris pelted my face. I reached the fence that separated our compound from B compound. I clung to it, straining to hear. The barbed wire pressed against my fingers. The voices sharpened, carried straight to me by the wind.

'He's been shot!' someone cried. 'Get the doctor!'

'Here! I'm here! In 14C!' But my words were torn away from me and carried downwind.

Then a different voice rang out. I didn't recognise it at first. McCubbin's deep voice was so choked with emotion it sounded strange. 'Christ, no. Not him. Jesus fucking Christ, Davies. What have you done?'

I prayed it wasn't Johnny. I prayed he wasn't dead. I contemplated scaling the fence that divided the two compounds, but the coils of barbed wire at the top would shred my skin. So I turned and ran back towards the gate. My legs felt light as I traversed the compound. The wind pummelled my back. I almost collided with the corner of a hut. I tripped on a rock and plunged to the ground, scraping my hands and bruising my knees, but I didn't care. I got up and kept running.

Lieutenant Perry was unlocking the gate to our compound when I approached. I called out to him. He started, and reached for his rifle.

'No, please, it's me—Ibaraki. The doctor.'

'Dr Ibaraki? Thank God you're here! Someone's been shot at the infirmary.'

'Take me there. Quick.'

He let me out and we ran along Broadway, following the line of floodlights that penetrated the haze. I braced myself against the oncoming wind. I wondered why Johnny would be at the infirmary, but there was no time for questions. I would find out soon enough.

We reached the entrance to 14B and one of the guards threw open the gate. Perry led the way, and I followed, staggering into the infirmary grounds. We passed the kitchen, rounded the corner of the infirmary building and emerged into the open space before the fence. I saw McCubbin leaning over someone on the ground. My chest tightened as I took everything in. The victim was slumped on his back, one leg bent beneath him. Hearing us approach, McCubbin looked up. As he shifted his head, I saw the victim's face. The high forehead, the distinct shape of his nose.

It was Stan.

I visited Johnny in detention on Monday, two days after Stan's death. The cell was at headquarters, less than a mile from our camp. It had a single window near the ceiling that was the size of a shoebox. My eyes took a moment to adjust to the gloom. Then I saw him, hunched in the corner. His face was covered in scratches and his hands were bandaged.

He lifted his head. 'How're you going, Doc?'

I felt sorry for him. I had never seen Johnny so weak.

They had found him in the afternoon on Sunday. He was in bushland about four miles from camp on the outskirts of town. With no water and only a pocketful of bread, his ill-prepared escape had ground to a halt. Someone had seen him drinking from a creek and alerted the camp. When he heard an army truck approaching, he raised his hands and walked onto the road.

Now I helped him up from the floor and onto the bed. 'What happened to your hands?'

'Barbed wire on the fences. I went over them with no gloves, no socks, nothing. Stupid idea. Dr Ashton reckons it'll be weeks before I can use them again. You gotta pay for your mistakes, I guess.' He sighed. 'No one saw me when I went over the first fence. It was only the second one—the air must have cleared, and a guard shouted from the tower. I thought he was going to shoot me, but he didn't. Then the siren started up, and I bolted for the trees.'

'How long will you be kept here?'

'Dunno. Perry said they're trying to work out what to do with me. I could be sent to Hay or I could be released back here. But first I'll have to face a military court. It'll be a laugh if it's anything like the one in Melbourne. That was a bloody joke.'

'I spoke to McCubbin yesterday,' I said. 'He told me all the guards were on alert for an escape. Commander Dean was worried there would be an attempt during the dust storm. That is the reason they cancelled the baseball match and said we could not go outside. That is why there were more guards—why Private Davies was on patrol, even though he had not been properly trained.'

Silence fell between us. He didn't comment when I mentioned Davies, so I thought he didn't know about Stan. I took a deep breath. 'Johnny, I have to tell you something. About Stan.' I paused.

'Yeah. I already know. They told me in the truck on the way back to camp. I didn't believe it. I thought they were lying to make me feel bad. But when I got to camp, Perry told me it was true. Christ, poor Stan. What was he doing outside so near the fence?'

'I don't know,' I said. In the confusion of the dust storm and the escape siren, Private Davies had somehow shot Stan. I thought of the time Hayashi and I had seen Stan outside staring at the sky. What had he been thinking?

Johnny bent forward and pressed his palms into his eyes. My nose started to burn. For a moment, I thought I might cry, too. I placed a hand on Johnny's shoulder. It trembled beneath my grip. I almost mentioned Mori and Yamada's conversation about Stan, but it wasn't the right moment. Johnny was already upset, and nothing would bring back our friend. After a minute, he wiped his eyes on his shirt.

'What about the funeral?'

'Stan's mother and sister want to bury him near his home in Sydney. They're collecting his remains this week. But Charlie and I talked about holding a memorial ceremony at camp on Wednesday. Something for all his friends.'

'That sounds like a good idea. Stan would like that. Shame I can't come.' He stared at the floor. 'That bloody trigger-happy bastard, Davies. The way he looked at me at headcount. I should've known. I wish he'd taken a shot at me right there and then. I hope he burns in hell.' He looked up at me. His eyes glistened. 'It should've been me, Doc. It should've been me.'

On Wednesday, I woke to a magpie warbling. It must have been perched on the edge of the roof near the window, but its melody was so clear it sounded as if it was by my ear. I looked outside. The sky was once more a brilliant blue.

The memorial ceremony for Stan was to take place that afternoon in the garden next to the altar. Although it was unusual to hold memorial ceremonies near an altar, we chose it as it was the most picturesque area of the compound. Unfortunately, the dust storm had wrought havoc. Mounds of dirt engulfed the fringe of purple grasses I'd planted. The two summer cypress hedges that had been pruned into spheres were battered out of shape. The eucalyptus sapling we'd carefully nurtured for months had been knocked over, its roots upended. The stone-edged path was hidden beneath swathes of loose earth. Only the bamboo thicket looked the same: the thick green stems stood tall, able to bend in the wind.

Locke had lifted the ban on loitering outside, so we spent the morning sweeping away the debris, replanting the tree and salvaging scattered stones. By lunch, we had almost returned the garden to its previous state.

The ceremony was originally intended for only a small group of Stan's friends—mainly the Australian-born Japanese and me—but that afternoon more than thirty people lined the path that snaked through the garden. For someone so quiet, Stan had many friends. Officer McCubbin stood at the back of the line. He held his hat in his hands, kneading its brim. All the orderlies from the infirmary attended, even Hayashi. I felt a flash of anger when I saw him, but I calmed myself: I didn't know what role he'd played in the plot to hurt Stan. Perhaps he knew nothing.

Sawada and a few of the other craftsmen had made a plaque from a cross-section of red gum sanded back. It was engraved with Stan's name in English and *katakana*, and his dates of birth and death. Sawada and I carried the plaque together down the path through the garden. The air was still. Even the bamboo thicket was hushed, without the usual susurrus of leaves. The sun shone down, warming our faces.

We placed the plaque on a mound between the eucalypts and the cypress brush. We didn't have any incense, so I lit a mosquito coil instead. As I turned to face the waiting crowd, I noticed Johnny's gang at the front so I spoke first in English.

'I only knew Stan a few months, but he left a deep impression on me. He was only twenty-two, but he had the courage to follow his dreams. He joined the army when he was eighteen. He had a pure heart and rarely criticised other people, despite the hardships he suffered. He spoke warmly about his mother, sister and friends. I am sure they will miss him, as will we. Stanley Suzuki, may you rest in peace.'

I swallowed hard. Charlie looked at me, his eyes red.
I repeated the speech in Japanese. Then I placed two offerings
beside the plaque: a bottle of camp-brewed sake one of the hut
leaders had given me, and a cutting of mallee bush. If there
had been a plum tree near camp I would have offered that
in recognition of his pure spirit, but the mallee was a worthy
substitute. Finally, I kneeled, scooped up a handful of dirt
and released it above the plaque.

Charlie was next in line. He placed a folded letter on the
mound and whispered a prayer, then released a handful of dirt.
Ernie followed, saying a few words before placing a packet of
cigarettes. It continued down the line, with the orderlies and
a few from Stan's tent laying offerings to aid his journey, until
finally McCubbin stood in front of the plaque. He turned his
cap in his hands. From my place at the front of the crowd,
I could hear him speak.

'Stan, we didn't get a chance to talk much, but from what
I knew of you, you had a good heart. If only there were more
like you in this world.'

He bent down to take some earth and poured it on top.
Next I sprinkled water above and around the plaque.

As a final gesture of respect, I signalled to everyone to
gather again, and in unison we bowed.

Work outside the camp grounds was temporarily suspended
after Johnny's escape while the army implemented new security
measures. The orderlies, however, were allowed to return to
work at the infirmary, as it was within the camp's perimeter.
Life more or less went back to what it had been before Stan's

death. But there remained a gap that everybody was aware of yet no one ever mentioned.

I visited Stan's old ward when Hayashi wasn't there. The old man in the bed next to Stan's stared at me with his rheumy eyes. The sheets had been taken down from the ceiling. All that was left was his bed, the blanket neatly folded and tucked. The window he'd stared at for so many hours was shut against the midwinter chill. The ward smelled musty. Nothing remained of the person who'd lain there for weeks thinking, sleeping and dreaming of another life.

Yamada gave me a wide berth. He never addressed me directly in the hut or at mealtimes anymore. When we were still friendly, he and several others used to play mahjong near my bed, drinking and laughing till late at night, and I used to join them if I wasn't working at the infirmary the next day. But after Stan's death they moved to the other side of the room. I was also no longer rostered to clean the latrines, a chore I'd been happy to do, and I wondered if it was Yamada's way of appeasing me. We occasionally crossed paths on our way to the mess hall or the latrines, but his gaze skittered away from mine.

I suppose Yamada was afraid. I could have told someone about what he'd done to Stan and what I suspected he'd intended to do, and even if Yamada wasn't found guilty of beating him, the accusation would be enough to force him to resign from his executive position.

I did come very close to telling McCubbin once. He visited me at the infirmary to check that I was aware I had to testify at the upcoming court of inquiry into Stan's death. He paused at the door before he left. 'Did you hear about Mori and Yamada?'

'No. What?'

'They've offered to give Stan's mother the money for the casket. They're paying for it out of the profits of the canteen. It's very kind of them.'

I couldn't help myself. 'Yamada and Mori are *not* good men.'

'What do you mean?' He cocked his head, the scar on his cheek flashing red.

'They seem kind and generous, but they are not. Not when you know them as I do.'

McCubbin's gaze lingered on me, but I said nothing further. I like to think he understood me, but more than likely he thought I was just acting oddly because of Stan's death.

Johnny was released after twelve days in detention. He came back thinner, quieter, more introspective. The threat of doing more time hung over him; his court case would take place in two weeks, at the same time as the inquiry into Stan's death. But more than that, I think he was burdened by the knowledge that his behaviour had indirectly caused Stan's death.

With no outside work allowed, he and the other Australians sat around smoking and playing card games all day when they didn't have chores to do. Unlike the wider Japanese population at camp, many of whom spent their spare time doing crafts and rehearsing for the entertainment group, they had no prior experience—nor much interest—in such things.

When I had a day off from the infirmary, I visited the garden near the altar. Dirt still gathered in mounds, obscuring many of the plants. Old Ohmatsu, one of the camp's keenest gardeners, was trimming the cypress brushes. He'd somehow returned them to their former stepped bonsai shape—two rounded forms among the untamed native shrubs. Stan's plaque looked unsightly, with the earth that had been poured on top and the assortment of bottles, paper, cigarettes and sweets around it. Ohmatsu stopped trimming as I brushed away some of the matter.

'Don't you think his plaque deserves a nicer spot?' he asked.

I looked around. 'Where else would you suggest?'

He surveyed the rest of the garden. 'This place could do with a pond.'

'I suppose we could do that.'

'Only, I'm too old for that kind of work. You'll have to do all the digging. But I can tell you where to dig and what shape it should be.'

I nodded. 'I'll see how much I can get done today. But I won't have another break from the infirmary for four more days.'

Ohmatsu didn't seem to hear me. He gazed at a spot on the ground. 'And it would be good to have a bridge . . .'

Using a shovel made from the lid of a powdered-milk tin, at Ohmatsu's direction I started digging an area at the base of the dirt mound. The sun-baked earth hardly yielded beneath my makeshift shovel. I collected water from the ablutions block and spilled it over the area. I drove a wooden stake into the glistening patch, trying to break up the rock-hard ground. Despite the cool breeze, I became soaked with sweat. By lunchtime, I'd only dug out a depression the size of my head. Blisters had broken the the skin of my palms.

I bumped into Martin on my way to the mess hall. His eyes widened when he saw me. 'You look like you just crawled through a drain,' he said, nodding at the stains on my shirt.

'The garden—I'm trying to build a pond.'

He lifted his brows. 'Yeah? Sounds like a big job.'

In the afternoon I walked back to the garden, hoping the water I'd doused the area with had softened the earth some more. As I turned the corner past the last hut, I saw

Martin, Johnny, Charlie and Ernie standing near the vegetable garden, smiling.

'We thought you could do with some help,' Martin said.

I stepped back. 'Oh, really? But I didn't expect—'

'Just tell us what to do, before we change our minds,' Johnny said.

Ohmatsu smiled when he saw me approaching with the Australians. 'Ah, some strong men to help you. Very good.'

I showed them the stones that traced the outline of the pond. We only had two improvised shovels and a few wooden stakes. Johnny and Charlie started shovelling, while Ernie and I used the stakes to break up the earth. Martin went to collect more water.

By the time the sun was low on the horizon, we'd opened up a three-foot-wide hole. Metallic flecks shimmered in the rust-coloured soil. We still had more digging to do to reach the line of stones, but we'd done most of it in one afternoon. I sat on a rock and mopped my brow with a handkerchief. Johnny leaned on a stake, smoking a cigarette. The tip glowed red like the sun's fading rays.

The court of inquiry took place in one of the administrative buildings at camp headquarters. I waited in the corridor for my name to be called. A small legal team had arrived from Melbourne that morning. Most of the windows in the corridor faced west, so it was bitterly cold inside the building. I breathed mist into the air. Johnny and I had arrived together. He sat next to me, his feet tapping a pattern on the floor. As we waited, he shifted back and forth, his hands clenching and unclenching on his thighs.

After a few minutes, Private Davies entered the building, pausing in the doorway when he saw us. He had been suspended immediately after the shooting, so I hadn't seen him for several weeks. He seemed a different man to the soldier I remembered. Shadows pooled beneath his eyes and cheekbones. His neatly pressed uniform hung loosely on his frame. He looked away from us. Johnny sat up and stared at him. I was certain he would say something, and I was about to warn him not to, but after a few moments he looked down at his thighs and unclenched his fists. Less than a minute later, the door opened and Johnny's name was called.

Davies slunk to an empty seat. The fingers of his right hand worried the clasp of his watch. He threaded the leather band in and out of the loop. In the wake of Stan's death, I'd had many dark thoughts about Davies. But seeing him so wretched changed my mind. He couldn't meet my gaze, and I realised even he was filled with regret.

Lieutenant Perry and another guard arrived, a portly man in his forties or fifties. I later learned he had manned the eastern watchtower at the time of the shooting. Although visibility was very poor the night of the dust storm, he had seen more than anyone else. He had spotted Johnny clambering over the outer perimeter fence near the southern guard tower, an incident that somehow the guard in that tower had missed. He immediately alerted the guardroom, triggering the siren. Then he noticed Stan standing next to the fence around the grounds of the infirmary, so close it looked as if he was going to climb it. He was about to shout to Stan to get back, but a dust cloud rolled in and engulfed him. Then he heard the two gunshots.

Johnny was in the inquiry room for half an hour. When he emerged he ran a hand through his hair.

'How was it?' I asked.

'Okay. I only told them the truth.' He eyed Davies. 'I'm going to go outside for a smoke. Back in a sec.'

Davies had been called into the room by the time Johnny returned. He collapsed into the seat next to me, reeking of bitter smoke, and tipped his head back till it touched the wall. He folded his hands over his abdomen and settled in to wait until I had given evidence so that we could return to camp together.

When Davies emerged, more than forty minutes later, he headed straight outside without looking at us.

Perry was called next and I sighed, compelled to wait another half an hour. Johnny appeared to be asleep, exhaling long, noisy breaths. I went over my statement in my head. Stan had been depressed but his condition had improved considerably in the week before his death. He was no longer suicidal. His decision to write to Isabelle was evidence of that.

What had he been thinking about as he stared at the sky? A better life with Isabelle? He had such a naïve, pure love. I'd had that feeling once. But now too much had happened to return to that.

After some time, the door opened and Perry walked out. Soon afterwards, the other guard was called into the room. Minutes passed; he was in there for a long time. I grew agitated, wondering whether I would ever be summoned. Finally the guard exited and I heard my name.

Inside the room, four men sat behind desks arranged in a horseshoe shape. Two were in uniform and the other two were in civilian clothing. A large black typewriter sat on the desk to my immediate right. The clerk gestured for me to take the seat at the front that faced the bowl of the horseshoe.

The military man to my left clasped his hands over a folder. Silver flecked his hair. 'Tomokazu Ibaraki, I understand you speak English—is that correct?' I said it was. 'Good. I am Major Donnelly. I am the chairman at today's proceedings. This is the military lawyer Captain Gibson, to his left is his assistant Mr Quigley, and at the end is Mr Stott, who's transcribing today's proceedings. You're one of the last people we're questioning today. We'll continue with proceedings tomorrow, before delivering our verdict.'

Captain Gibson cleared his throat and sat up straight. His eyes were a pale brown, like the colour of dried buckwheat. 'Please state your name, date of birth and profession.'

'Tomokazu Ibaraki. March the twentieth, 1908. I am a medical physician.'

'Do you promise to tell the truth to the best of your abilities?'
'I do.'

'I'd like to start with what you saw or heard on the night of the shooting. Lieutenant Perry told us earlier today that he came to the compound to get you, is that correct?'

'Yes. It was a few minutes after the gunshots. I went outside after I heard them. I could hear a lot of men shouting, then I heard Lieutenant Perry calling for a doctor from Broadway. He let me out of the compound and we ran to the infirmary.'

'And what did you see at the infirmary?'

'I saw someone on the ground, face up, a few feet from the perimeter fence. I realised it was Stan.' My voice quavered.

'Stan—you mean Stanley Suzuki?' Captain Gibson asked.

'Yes. There was blood on the front of his shirt. His body was still warm, but there were no vital signs. We rolled him onto his side and saw a wound on his back, behind his heart. The bullet must have entered his heart and—'

'We already have a coroner's report, Dr Ibaraki,' Captain Gibson said. 'Please just state what you saw.'

'We placed him back down the way we found him. I noticed that his face and the front of his clothes were coated in dust, as if he had been standing outside for a long time. I waited beside the body until the ambulance came. It took about fifteen minutes. The blood flow had stopped by the time it arrived.'

'Thank you, Dr Ibaraki. Could you tell me why Suzuki was in the infirmary?'

'He had cut his wrist three weeks earlier. It was a deep cut, so it was taking a while to heal.'

'Cut his wrist? How?'

'With a piece of glass.'

'So he did it himself?'

'Yes.'

'So it was a suicide attempt—he tried to kill himself?'

I shifted in my seat and glanced at the clerk, his fingers pounding the keys. 'Yes.'

'In your medical opinion, was he suffering from melancholy?'

'When he cut his wrist, yes. But his disposition had improved recently. The depression was only because of the bullying.'

'The bullying?' Captain Gibson's voice was sharp.

'Yes. He came to me in the infirmary about a week before he cut his wrist. He had an injured arm, and said some men had forced him out of the mess hall.'

'What did you do?'

'I bandaged his arm.'

'Did you tell anyone about the bullying?'

My throat was tight. 'No, I didn't think it was my place. I'm only a doctor—I try to stay away from camp disputes.'

'But after he tried to commit suicide, surely you told someone then?'

Everyone stared at me.

'He was in the infirmary by then. I didn't think it would happen again. I thought he was safe.'

Captain Gibson whispered something in Mr Quigley's ear. The assistant made a note.

'Private Davies told the court he fired at Suzuki because he was climbing the fence. He thought he was trying to escape. Captain Christie said he saw Suzuki on or near the fence. Did Suzuki ever talk of escaping, or wanting to get out?'

'He wanted to get out—but many people here do. He had a female friend he wanted to see. But he never talked about escaping. It sounds strange, but the night he was shot, I think he was looking at the sky. He was fascinated by it. I'm not sure why. I once saw him staring at the sky on a windy day, standing very close to the place where he was shot.'

'But why would he be outside in such conditions unless he was contemplating escape?'

'He—he was just looking at the sky.'

Captain Gibson tilted his head. My chest felt hollow. 'Dr Ibaraki, do you think Stanley *wanted* to die on the night he was shot?'

'I—I don't know.'

The captain paused. He seemed to sniff the air. 'I am asking you this because various people—both internees and officers—have named you as the closest person to Suzuki at camp. Is that a fair judgment?'

I said it probably was.

'How would you describe his relationship to you, Dr Ibaraki? A friend—is that an appropriate word?'

'Yes, he was a friend.'

'Well, if he was a friend, why didn't you know how he was feeling the night he died?'

I looked aside. My nose burned. I put a hand up to my mouth to try to suppress the feeling rising from within, but it was no use. I began to cry. Tears escaped and rolled down my cheeks. I took short whimpering breaths. It was as much a shock to myself as to anyone else in the room. No one said anything for a few moments.

'Goodness, do you need a handkerchief?' the chairman asked.

I shook my head. I fumbled in my pocket and found mine. I pressed it to my eyes as the tears continued to flow. 'I'm sorry. I'm so sorry,' I said. I covered my face with my hands.

Finally, the chairman spoke. 'Captain, if it's all right with you, perhaps we can resume tomorrow?'

'That sounds like the best option.'

I nodded. 'Thank you. I'm very sorry. I don't know what's wrong with me.'

With a guiding arm on my elbow, the clerk led me to the door. Still holding the handkerchief to my face, I made my way down the corridor as quickly as possible.

Johnny sat up. 'You okay?'

I moved past him, past the guard waiting in the seat and the guard at the door, and stumbled outside. I turned the corner. The sun was shining. I leaned my cheek against the building and felt the warmth of the sun-baked bricks. I closed my eyes as I heard footsteps approaching.

'What's the matter?' Johnny said. 'Fuck, you're a mess.'

I drew a long, shuddering breath. 'I could have helped him. I could have done something more. Not just for him. For all of them. Why didn't I?'

'It's not your fault, Doc. That bastard Davies got him. There was nothing you could've done to save Stan.'

'No, no, you don't understand. Not just Stan—all the others. I could've done something. I could've helped them, but I didn't.' I covered my face with my hands. My fingertips were hot and wet.

I felt a hand on my shoulder. 'Shhh,' Johnny said. 'It's not your fault. You did all you could. It's not your fault.'

I'm not sure how long we stood like that, the two of us beside the administrative building in the sun. We stayed there until my tears were dry and my breath became even once more. Johnny fetched the guard. Then, with his palm against my back, Johnny led me back to camp.

The court found that Stan had been shot while attempting to escape, but that Private Davies had failed to issue the appropriate warning, failed to notify other guards and used excessive force to deter Stan, leading to Stan's death. There was no mention of Stan's mental state. Private Davies was suspended without pay indefinitely. I was glad they found Davies guilty of negligence, even though his sentence seemed light, considering he took a man's life. They were mistaken in their judgment of Stan, though. I knew in my heart he hadn't tried to escape.

Johnny was given fourteen days' detention for escaping. As he had already served twelve of those, he only had to spend another two days in the cell. On the second day, the guards let him out before the evening meal.

At headcount on Monday morning, Locke told us he'd be returning to camp later that day to make an announcement. My thoughts immediately turned to the prisoner exchange program. Whispers broke out among the lines of men.

'Silence!' Locke shouted, slapping his crop against his thigh. 'All your questions will be answered this afternoon.' But the murmurs persisted.

During breakfast, the mess hall was abuzz with chatter about the possibility of returning to Japan.

'I dream of eating *manju* and seeing the peak of Mount Fuji again,' said Watanabe, who sat opposite me.

'What about your wife?' Ebina said.

'No—she can wait,' Watanabe replied, and broke into laughter.

'Sensei, what about you? What do you miss most about Japan?'

'Oh, I'm not sure,' I said.

'Come on, there must be something,' Watanabe pressed.

And then I remembered. 'The sea. I miss the sea in Japan. The beaches of my boyhood. They're so familiar to me.'

All the orderlies were concerned about missing the announcement while we were on our shift, so we asked the guard at the gate to fetch us when he saw Locke approaching. The day dragged on. Although I tried to put the idea of exchange out of my mind, I couldn't help but dwell on it. Thoughts of the future filled me with fear. Where would I work? Who would employ me after my dismissal from the laboratory?

The sky darkened and the first stars glimmered. Still we heard nothing.

'Maybe it's not happening today,' Matsuda said as we packed up at the end of our shift.

We trudged back to our compound. Dinner had finished an hour earlier, but hundreds of men were still in the mess hall, talking.

'No Major Locke yet?' I asked.

'Not yet,' Ebina said. 'We don't think he'll come till tomorrow.'

Someone shouted from the direction of the gate. We fell silent, straining to hear.

'Locke!' the voice cried. 'He's coming!'

The hall exploded with activity. People dashed to their huts to tell their friends. I jumped up to take my place at the other side of the table, sending a chair clattering.

Major Locke and his retinue marched into the mess hall as internees were still arriving from their huts. He carried a leather satchel bulging with paper.

'Everyone stand on the south side of the room,' he said, indicating the wall behind me. 'Just find a place as best you can.' He repeated the directive as more and more internees entered the room.

There were far too many of us to line up neatly in the narrow corridor along the wall; we bunched around the tables and chairs and fanned out between the rows.

'Quiet, please. Do it *quietly*,' Locke said in response to the chatter that erupted.

Locke unfastened the clasp on the satchel and removed a roll of paper. The hut was so quiet I could hear the rustle of the pages.

'According to an arrangement with the International Red Cross, it has been decided that some internees and prisoners of Japan and the Allied countries will be exchanged at the neutral port of Lourenço Marques in Portuguese East Africa,' Locke said. 'Only those internees whose names I am about to call out will be allowed to return home on the next exchange boat.' He paused to allow the interpreter to speak. A hum of excitement rose from the crowd.

'When you hear your name, move to the opposite side of the room,' he said. 'Hiroyuki Ikebata.'

A man of about my age pushed his way through the crowd and crossed to the other side of the room. He was beaming.

'Kariya Masaru,' Locke said. The next man let out a cry of delight as he joined his friend.

Locke continued reading out names. The numbers facing us swelled. I noticed many standing before me were from Borneo, Surabaya and Java in the Dutch East Indies. My feet tingled.

'Ichiro Mori.'

Whispers broke out as the mayor made his way to the other side of the room. A new mayor would have to be elected. My palms felt wet. Thirty or forty more names were called, and then Yamada's name was called out, too. Those around me whispered their congratulations as he stepped forward. When he reached the other side of the room and turned to face us, his expression was full of glee. My shoulders sagged. Despite my own mixed feelings about returning to Japan, it didn't seem fair that Mori and Yamada were lucky enough to be chosen.

Space had opened up between the people on our side of the room. I shifted from foot to foot. The air felt heavy, as if it were about to storm. Locke turned the page. There was only one more piece of paper. As he read out more names, I took comfort in the prospect of life at camp without Yamada or Mori.

'Tomokazu Ibaraki.'

My head snapped up.

'Congratulations, sensei,' someone said. I felt a hand on my shoulder, urging me forward.

My head felt light as I made my way across the floor. Was I really going back to Japan? I wondered if my ties to the laboratory had anything to do with my name being chosen.

Locke read out a dozen more names, then said, 'That's all, I'm afraid.'

Two-thirds of the camp population remained on the other side of the hall. But as I looked across at them, they seemed like the minority. Some hung their heads, as if they had done something wrong. Others tried to smile, but I could see the disappointment in their tight mouths. I felt ashamed to be included on the list—I didn't deserve it, not after how misguided I'd been at camp.

In the weeks following the announcement of the prisoner exchange program, the atmosphere at camp was tense. Those who hadn't been chosen to return to Japan brooded over their continued confinement. Small matters, such as rearranging the beds and creating a new chore roster, threatened to erupt into disputes. A divide opened between those who were leaving and those who had to stay. As I was one of the lucky ones, I did my best to tiptoe around the others. At mealtimes, I avoided conversations about the exchange, and only packed my bags when no one else was around.

Yet sometimes the issue was impossible to evade. Soon after the announcement, Ebina approached me in the hut. 'Sensei, not you, too?' Our hut had a large number of people who'd been chosen to return. When I nodded, tears sprang to Ebina's eyes. Seeing him before me, his face drawn and his shoulders hunched, I realised how troubled he felt. Not only would he lose some of his closest friends at camp, he would also remain separated from his wife and children, whom he missed dearly.

At the infirmary one afternoon, Dr Ashton pulled me aside and asked me how the news of the prisoner exchange had been taken at camp.

'Most are coping well, but some are experiencing prolonged distress.' A few men in my hut seemed unable to recover from their melancholy. They sat on their beds for most of the day, complaining about their misfortune, and refused to return to work. Some openly wept.

'Do me a favour and keep an eye on them, would you?' Dr Ashton said. 'More suicide attempts are the last thing we need.'

Although I knew I was lucky to be leaving, the thought of returning to Japan filled me with dread. I slept fitfully at night, my mind consumed with what lay ahead.

In a welcome reversal of fortune, only Johnny and his friends were happy to learn that they would remain in Australia. While rumours of the internee exchange had swirled, they had been worried they would be sent to Japan against their wishes, even though they were British subjects. 'They locked us up in here, didn't they?' Johnny had said. 'Who knows what they'll do to us next?'

When the gang discovered none of them were on the prisoner exchange list, they celebrated. After Locke and the other officers left the mess hall, Ernie brought out a bottle of rum he'd bought from one of the guards and started passing it around. They continued drinking after lights-out in their hut, becoming so rowdy their hut leader threatened to kick them out.

One evening a few weeks later, Johnny approached me after dinner in the mess hall. He told me that he, Charlie,

Ernie, Martin and Dale had applied to transfer to Woolenook woodcutting camp, several miles away on the banks of the Murray River. It was a much smaller camp, with only two hundred internees. 'McCubbin said there are a few Aussies there like us, so hopefully we won't get as much grief.' The weak electric lights threw shadows on his face, making him appear drawn. I would miss him, I knew. With the gang soon leaving, there was nothing left for me at camp. Yet a part of me wanted to stay.

The day before my departure, I visited the infirmary one last time. My heart was heavy as I entered the dim corridor, knowing I would never again see the familiar faces of the staff and patients, nor hear the building's creaking floorboards. I bent my head and hurried past the room where Stan's bed had been. In the tuberculosis ward, sunlight streamed through the windows, forming patterns on the floor. Harada was asleep. I touched his shoulder and his eyelids fluttered open.

'Come to say goodbye?'

I nodded. 'I'm leaving tomorrow morning.'

'That's too bad. I'll miss you, old friend. You're like a brother to me. I feel like I've know you a lifetime.'

I squeezed his hand. Harada had regained some strength in the previous month, and his appetite had increased. His face appeared fuller in the morning light.

'You make it sound as if we'll never be in contact again. I promise you, I'll write.'

He shook his head. 'No use. I'm going to die in here.'

My smile faded. 'Nonsense. You're not going to die here. Why would you say something like that? Just last week you put on two pounds, and your breathing has improved.'

But he didn't seem to hear me. 'I'm going to die, I know it. And I'll never see Minnie again. I can't even contact her—she's with her family somewhere.'

I grew troubled as my thoughts turned to Kayoko. I hadn't heard from her in years and wondered whether our silence would continue after my return.

We gathered along the fence to say our last goodbyes. A bitter wind buffeted my face and brought tears to my eyes. A collection of suitcases and sacks were at my feet. My luggage had swelled in the six months I'd been at camp. Sawada had made me a puzzle box as a farewell present, its different-coloured panels sliding in a series of movements to reveal the internal cavity. Ebina and the rest of the baseball team had given me a notebook filled with their memories of our time together. I also had a number of letters and wooden keepsakes from many left at camp who'd asked me to forward them to their families in Japan.

A line of trucks waited on the other side of the birdcage gate, ready to transport us to Barmera station. From there, we would board a train bound for Melbourne, then we'd begin the long voyage home.

Mori stepped forward, his glasses flashing white as they reflected the overcast sky. He gave a short speech, thanking everyone for their support and welcoming the new mayor, Abe Denkichi from Borneo. 'Against all odds, we've been able to make a happy life here. I trust this will continue under Mayor Abe's leadership.' I curled my lip at his affectation. I had to endure several more weeks with him and Yamada on the voyage. I consoled myself with the knowledge that they wouldn't be able to harm anyone else at camp.

As I waited at the fence, Johnny came up to me and extended his hand. He no longer wore bandages, as his cuts had finally healed. Wearing a knitted jumper, his hair wet and falling over his eyes, he looked like the young man I had known in Broome.

'Look at you, you lucky bugger. You can finally go home. You're one of the few who really deserves it. Can't say the same about some of the others.'

'Johnny, I will miss you. You have become a good friend. I only wish we had become friends sooner—not only at camp, but also in Broome. I should have trusted you earlier.'

He nodded and looked away. His eyes glistened.

'Start filing out, one at a time!' the guard called from the gate.

Charlie, Ernie, Martin, Andy, Ken and Dale wished me luck and patted my back. I bowed to Ebina, Sawada, Ohmatsu and the other men from my hut one last time. As I fell into line, a feeling of panic gripped me. I looked back at the hundreds of men waving goodbye. *Let me stay!* I wanted to cry.

The guard marked my name off a list and I stepped onto Broadway for the last time. As we walked along the wide street, our friends in 14C followed us inside the fence. 'Goodbye!' they yelled. 'Don't forget us!' Tears were streaming down Ebina's face.

We reached the junction at the middle of camp and I looked back. The blur of my friends pressed against the fence. The sweep of ochre dirt. The rows of galvanised-iron huts. The guard tower rising up beyond the fence. It was bleak, but it was home. A place where I belonged.

On the other side of Broadway, the Germans in 14D and Italians in 14A had gathered along the inside fence to see us off. '*Lebewohl!*' they called '*Addio!*' I heard music and thought it was a record playing in one of the compounds, but as we walked past the Italian compound I realised it was a live band. A four-piece on guitar, mandolin, accordion and tambourine played us a parting song. Men clapped and sang around them, cheering as we went by.

We reached the birdcage gate and passed through it for the last time. McCubbin waited on the other side. His cap was pushed back off his face. He grinned, and a crease formed along the scar on his cheek.

'Glad I didn't miss you. I just wanted to say goodbye. It's been a pleasure. I've got your address in Japan. Let's keep in touch. You're one of the good ones—I hope you know that.' He held out his hand. It almost swallowed mine. He brought his other hand on top.

'Thank you for everything. I won't forget—' My voice faltered.

'Hey, cheer up. No need for that. Aren't you happy you're going home?' But his own eyes were wet.

We dragged our luggage to the line of waiting trucks and loaded it inside. I stepped into the back and sat on the bench. The engine coughed into life. The truck jerked forward and a cry escaped from my throat. I craned my neck to watch the scenery shrinking away through the canvas opening at the back. The long stretch of barbed-wire fence. The squat buildings of the duty guard camp. The guard towers, shining silver in the bleak light. Clouds of dust billowed across the track. Then we turned a corner, and it was gone.

SS City of Canterbury *and* Kamakura Maru
1942

We boarded the train at Barmera and travelled through the night, reaching the outskirts of Melbourne the next morning. Through the carriage window, I saw heads of wheat swaying in the dawn light. Beyond them, the sun spread on the horizon. My heart ached. I would miss the sunrises and sunsets in Australia—the vivid wash of light.

We disembarked at Port Melbourne a few hours later. A line of ships spread out before us. Among them was the *City of Canterbury*, the British naval ship that would take us halfway home. The long grey vessel huddled at the water's edge, ready to slip towards Lourenço Marques, where the prisoner exchange would take place.

On the train, the atmosphere had been lively; we'd played card games and whispered through the night. But once we stepped outside, blinking against the sudden brightness, we fell silent. The guards marched beside us as we walked towards the foreshore. I was struck by the paradox: although I'd been released from camp, I'd never felt my enemy status so keenly till now. Ahead of us, a small crowd of onlookers was gathered at the top of the stairs. From a distance, they looked like a typical group of sightseers there to admire the ships, a handful of children among them. But as we neared, their mouths set hard. We were nearly on the gangway when one of the men shouted, 'You should kill them!' 'Yeah, shoot the bastards!' a woman cried. My chest felt tight. I thought back to the train journey to Loveday, when I'd seen the woman with the little girl on the platform—the expression on her face.

Before leaving the port, we were joined by more Japanese internees and officials, including the Japanese ambassador to Australia and the consul-general. Soon we numbered more than eight hundred. The diplomats and officials would travel in the first-class cabins on the upper deck and eat in a separate dining room staffed by the crew, while the remaining internees were to sleep on hammocks on the lower deck and cook for themselves from the ship's supplies. About seventy women and children also boarded the ship, and it was a relief to hear women's voices and see children again. I had been living among men for far too long.

We finally left Melbourne, launching from the port with a single shrill of the whistle. We stopped at Fremantle to pick up more passengers and supplies before embarking on the long journey across the Indian Ocean. I stayed at the stern as we slipped through the sapphire waters, watching the land shrinking behind us. When we had travelled half a day, I noticed a difference in the quality of light—the sky seemed thinner, the colours less bright. I realised we had finally left Australia, and something broke within me and drifted away.

I had been embarrassed to discover I was one of the few people assigned to cabins on the lower deck, along with Mori, Yamada and several businessmen. At pains to free myself of their association, I spent my days wandering the deck and mixing with the rest of the internees. Mori and Yamada didn't seem to notice my frequent absences as they cooked with and conversed among their privileged coterie.

The days passed without incident. Surrounded by the ocean again, I regained a measure of calmness after the turbulence of the previous few months. I spent many hours wandering the decks and looking through portholes. Sometimes I saw whales in the distance, their backs like oil slicks on the surface. Despite the cramped quarters and the freezing night-time temperatures, the atmosphere was genial. I became friendly with a group of men from the Dutch East Indies who'd been held at Hay camp, and shared many meals with them.

Over stew one night, as we sat in a circle with blankets around our shoulders, talk turned to the diplomats on board the ship.

'I heard Ambassador Kawai's a strange sort,' one of the men said. 'Have you met him, sensei?'

'Briefly, yes.' I had treated one of the other diplomats for seasickness, and was introduced to the ambassador while I was there. 'Kawai didn't strike me as strange, exactly—more circumspect, I'd say.' I leaned forward. 'Apparently, Kawai has four white boxes in his cabin containing the ashes of the naval officers who died in Sydney Harbour. The Australian government gave them to him to return to the families in Japan.'

The men around me exclaimed in disbelief. At camp, we'd read about the midget-submarine attack in one of the newspapers smuggled from the guards' barracks. The submarines had only hit a depot ship before they sank, but I was astonished they'd gone so far down the east coast. Mori had organised a big celebration at camp, with camp-brewed sake at each table. When I later learned that the Australian authorities had given the Japanese officers a funeral with full naval honours, I was shocked. They seemed to treat their enemies with more respect than their own people, I thought, with Johnny in mind.

As we sat on the ship's deck, scraping out the last of the stew from the saucepan, the discussion turned to the dead men.

'To think, those men went into the water knowing they'd never return alive,' someone said. 'I couldn't do such a thing.'

Goto, a rubber planter from Borneo, put up his hand to signal he wanted to speak. His voice was a whisper. 'To give one's life to one's country, for the greater good of all—it's the greatest sacrifice. They're true heroes,' he said, shaking his head. Everyone around me nodded.

But as I thought of the men in their metal coffin, their final breath escaping from their lungs, I imagined them at peace with themselves, knowing what they had done. It is much harder to descend to the depths of suffering and then find a way to keep living. I know, because that is what I have done.

A memory comes back to me from my time at the laboratory. It was from those final traumatic weeks when our baby had died and Kayoko had left me.

Shimada had called me into his office to discuss the schedule for the dissection demonstration, which was to be held in two days' time. Soon after I had reported to his office, an officer appeared at the door and told Shimada that Kimura wanted to talk to him. He excused himself, promising to return soon. There was a manila folder on his desk. Thinking it was related to the dissection demonstration, I picked it up and flipped it open. The title read: 'Hydrogen cyanide toxicity by inhalation'. I began reading the report. 'Subject A: Female 26 years. Subject B: Infant 22 months. Experiment began with 1000 mg of HCN released into 5 cubic-metre enclosure. At 50 seconds, "B" showed signs of disturbed breathing, despite attempts by "A" to cover respiratory tract. Convulsions in "B" began at 1 minute 40 seconds. "A" collapsed at 4 minutes. Lay on top of "B" to little effect. Convulsions began thereafter. "A" displayed signs of flushing on face and neck and foaming at the mouth. Convulsions continued sporadically until 17 minutes. At 21 minutes, respiratory signs ceased. Experiment was terminated at 30 minutes. Both subjects were pronounced dead.' I closed the file, my hands trembling.

A few days later, after Kimura dismissed me, I had less than an hour to say goodbye to my colleagues and gather my belongings. Before I left, I slipped into the storage room one last time. I frantically searched for the specimen, praying it hadn't been incinerated yet. At last I found it. The boy's corpse had been returned to one of the jars and stored on a shelf. Guts spilled from the stomach cavity, but the face was untouched. Eyes closed, his expression was serene. I removed the lid and reached in to slip the wooden tag from around his neck.

After weeks of sailing across the Indian Ocean, a blur had finally emerged: a rolling lip of green that opened into the wide bay of Lourenço Marques. The bustling port of the neutral African nation glittered in the golden light.

The next day, we marched across the dock to board the waiting *Kamakura Maru*, while Allied prisoners boarded the *City of Canterbury* in our place. From there, we cut across the Indian Ocean once more, until we reached Singapore, our journey across the world and back almost complete. The air was milky with warmth. Charred shells of buildings lined the shore—reminders of the Japanese conquest seven months earlier. As I gazed at the crumbling edifices and the blackened dwellings, I realised the battle had been fierce. Before the last leg home, we made a brief stop in Hong Kong where the Japanese flag was raised on Victoria Peak.

On the final day of our voyage to Japan, I stood on the deck of the *Kamakura Maru*, staring out to sea. My fingertips pressed against the cracked paint of the railing. Spray buffeted my face. A few times during the previous weeks, the skies had darkened and the atmosphere had condensed into a squall, rocking our ship across waves as if it was something small. But now the sea was calm, like a sheet of glass. I wiped spray from my brow, and the sour scent of metal filled my nose. I looked up. Black smoke from the ship's funnel stained the sky. Seabirds hovered above me, slipping and shifting on the air currents. They appeared each morning, stark against the blue, before disappearing to an unknown place at night.

I heard a creak behind me.

'Sensei, still out here?'

Torimaru, the young assistant diplomat from the ambassador's office, smiled. We'd become friendly in the past few weeks as we shared a cabin on the *Kamakura Maru*. He was returning to his family home in Tokyo after several years in Australia. We often talked late into the night.

I dipped my head sheepishly, conscious of Torimaru's gaze. 'Just for a few minutes,' I said. In fact, I had been on the deck for most of the day. It would be the last time I had the opportunity to gaze at the endless stretch of sea: the next day, we would dock at Tateyama, two hours south of Tokyo, to go through quarantine and immigration before continuing to our final stop, Yokohama.

'Thinking about tomorrow?' Torimaru raised a hand to shield his eyes.

I nodded. 'I don't know what it will be like.'

Torimaru joined me at the railing. The world spread out in blue monotony. No land or reef or rocky outcrop blemished the horizon. He drew a deep breath. 'You know, I'm sure your wife will be glad to see you after all this time.' He was trying to be kind; I had hinted of our estrangement. 'She'll see that things have changed. Think of it as a second chance, an opportunity to start afresh.'

I smiled weakly. 'You may be right.'

For a few moments, we admired the water and the chalky colour of the sky. Then Torimaru stepped back from the railing. 'Well, I won't disturb you any longer. I'll see you at dinner—the ambassador has promised a special feast.'

I watched him walk away. I sensed he had wanted to continue our conversation from the previous night, and I felt bad for not inviting him to stay. As I stared at the glassy surface, I realised there was truth in what he'd said. I, more than most, knew how quickly things could change.

I felt calm with the blue all around me and warm spray on my face. My homeland was a day's journey away. I was safe in the ocean's wet embrace. The silence was not a suppressant, but the opportunity to renew. As Torimaru had said, it was an opportunity to start afresh. I would regrow from the embers of my former life, like a mallee tree destroyed by bushfire. I would make myself anew. I promised I would never look back.

Tokyo
1942

After our ship docked in Yokohama, I returned to my family home in western Tokyo, where the streets were narrow and electricity wires crowded the sky. The area was dirtier than I remembered, as if the ashes of war had settled upon the buildings. But perhaps it was just because I was accustomed to the view in Australia, where each day my surroundings had been rinsed by the vivid light.

Mother came towards me from a dark corner of the house, a pained expression on her face. 'Tomo, you've come home.' She wrapped her arms around me, something she hadn't done since I was a boy. For several seconds she didn't let go. My chin brushed the crown of her head. The smell of smoke mingled with the oily scent of her hair. I felt the frailness of her body through her *yukata*—my mother, who had always been so strong. When she stepped back, she looked drawn. I realised how much she must have suffered over Nobu's death. Consumed by my own grief, I hadn't stopped to consider how she must feel. Her letters hadn't expressed the hardship that her physical presence revealed.

The world seemed crowded during those first shaky weeks back in Japan, when I felt for the edges of my existence. The sun blazed outside but I kept to the darkness of my home. It was a new kind of confinement. Sometimes I walked to the market stalls near the station. The neighbours who recognised me smiled and welcomed me home. No one mentioned my time at the camp in Australia or my dismissal from my job in Japan, but when they hovered nearby even after I had bid them a good day I sensed they wanted to know more about my past.

Several months passed before I contacted Kayoko. I waited until I had found employment at a hospital on the outskirts of the city. Even though the possibility of being sent to the frontlines as a doctor hung over me, I wanted her to know I was doing my best to build a future with her in Japan, if that was what she wanted.

She sounded tired on the telephone, her voice stretched thin. *Tomo, is that you? I'm glad you returned safely. Really, I am.*

We arranged to meet the following week at a coffee shop in Ginza. I arrived early and sat at a table in the corner, facing the doorway. As I waited, I studied the sky through the window. The blanket of clouds held the promise of first snow. Snow had covered the ground the last time I had seen Kayoko, almost five years earlier. It had formed a backdrop of glittering white.

In the coffee shop, a dark figure came towards me. My heart fluttered when I realised it was Kayoko. She wore navy *monpe* trousers knotted above her waist and a matching coat. In the unfamiliar clothes, I hardly recognised my wife. Grey threaded her hair. Her cheeks had lost their fullness and her mouth was tight. We sat together, the hum of conversation surrounding us as we shared fragments of our pasts. She smiled when I told her about releasing the lanterns in Broome and the baseball competition at camp. She described the friends she had made at the factory where she worked, assembling munitions parts.

'Most of the other women's husbands are away at war. Some of them have already died. It made me realise how lucky I am that you're still alive.'

I sensed an opportunity to raise the possibility of our reunion. 'Kayoko, all the years I was in Australia, I never stopped thinking about you. When you didn't respond to my letters, I almost gave up hope. But now that I'm here with you . . .' Outside, the air had turned opaque. Figures walked by the window as if in a haze. I drew in a deep breath to steady myself. 'Now that I am back, it would make me happy if you returned to live with me.'

Her eyes were fixed on the spoon she held between her fingers. For a while, I thought she would not reply. When she did, her words came haltingly.

'I want to return to you. The baby, when you weren't there . . .' She hesitated.

I realised I had to tell her before the moment was gone. I would tell her then or forever hold my tongue. 'There's something you should know—I should have told you long ago. The work I did at the laboratory, it wasn't what you thought—'

'No, just listen to me, Tomo. I know it was not your fault. You had your commitments. I can see that now. What I'm trying to say is, I want to return to you, I do. But I can't. I'm not ready. Not yet.'

I felt as if I would collapse. I longed to put my arms around her as I used to when we were still together, or at least take her hand. But instead I only nodded. 'If you need more time, I understand. I will wait.'

The cold of that winter seemed to chill me to my bones. The days crawled by. To keep my mind from dwelling on Kayoko, I dedicated myself to my work. The hospital was understaffed because of the war and there was always plenty to do. Because of the shortage, I began to assist during surgeries, even though I hadn't received proper training as a surgeon. I became first assistant to the chief surgeon, and I was often asked to lead other operations. I performed only minor surgeries at first, but as my skills and confidence grew I began to undertake more complicated procedures.

The months passed, but there was still no word from Kayoko. I did receive a letter from Ebina, who was still interned at Loveday. He told me Harada had died a few months after I left. Although I wasn't surprised by the news, in the loneliness of that first year back in Tokyo, his death deeply affected me. Late the following year, Tokyo became the target of American attacks. Lying in bed at night, I heard the wail of the siren, warning of another raid. Mother and I crouched beneath the kitchen bench as the walls shook around us and the sky lit up with flames. The hospital was filled with burns victims and the stench of their scorched flesh. The smell inhabited me, seeping into my skin and clothes. It was a smell I never grew accustomed to. When the patients arrived, either wheeled in on stretchers or walking, they screamed for me to help them. I disinfected their wounds and applied moist bandages, but there was little else I could do. I couldn't even give them anaesthetic to relieve them from their terrible agony; it was in such short supply that we were only allowed to use it for operations. The most severe cases—the ones who would surely die—were put into the ward furthest from the entrance. Nurses staffed the ward but no doctors were assigned. I visited the patients from time to time. Their blackened and blistered bodies were unsettlingly indistinct, stripped of gender or any distinguishing features. If I closed my eyes I saw the people I had dissected years earlier, their bodies ravaged by disease. I noticed that the closer the patients came to death, the quieter they became. Their screams, which had been so insistent when they were first admitted, soon turned into low moans. In their final hours, I heard only the sigh of their breath as they struggled for air. That sound, so weak and insignificant, was their last tie to life.

One evening, after a particularly long and gruelling day at the hospital treating victims of the latest air raid, I returned home to find Mother waiting for me. She stood up when I walked into the living room. Her eyes were swollen and she clutched a white handkerchief to her chest.

'Oh, Tomo,' she said. 'Mrs Hattori came to see me today. You remember, Kayoko's aunt?'

Unease bloomed within me and spread throughout my body. Mrs Hattori and her husband had occasionally accompanied the Sasakis and our family on outings to the beach when I was young. She was a jolly, round-faced woman who had stayed late at our wedding. I liked her, and was sorry I had not had the chance to get to know her better.

'She came to give us some terrible news. Last night, in the air raid—'

I reached out to grip the edge of the sliding door. My fingers punctured the rice paper.

Before she spoke the words, I knew: Kayoko, my wife, was dead.

Tokyo
1989

I open my eyes. Sunshine glows beneath the blinds in a line
of light. My cheek is warm against the pillow. Perspiration
prickles the back of my neck. I pull the sheet from my body
and wince at the pain the movement brings. My joints are not
what they once were. I allow myself to linger in bed a little
longer, shutting my eyes to try to return to sleep. Although
it is still early and my apartment is on the fifth floor, I can
hear the sounds of the neighbourhood outside. The persistent
beeping as a truck reverses. The distant blare of a horn. From
somewhere within my building, a television drones, alternately
clear and faint as if carried to me on a breeze. Above me, the
ceiling creaks in the gathering heat. I persist with the charade
of slumber for a few minutes more, then give up. I am wary of
idling in bed for too long—a danger when one is retired and
living alone.

I get dressed and open the blinds. In the kitchen, I spoon
ground coffee into the filter and fill the machine with water.
As it gurgles and hisses behind me, I shuffle to the front door.
I open it just as Mrs Ono descends the stairs to my landing,

plump arms swinging. There's an elevator just a few metres away, but she always takes the stairs. *For exercise*, she says. But she's not in her usual walking gear of sun visor, polo shirt and slacks. Instead she's wearing a straw hat over her perm, a skirt and a short-sleeved top that rolls at her neck.

'Good morning, sensei,' she says.

'Good morning, Mrs Ono. Going somewhere special today?'

She walks past the window, over the rectangle of sunlight projected onto the tiles, and marches across the landing towards me. Before I have a chance to bend down, she scoops up the newspaper at my feet.

'Isn't it terrible,' she tuts at something on the front page, before handing it to me.

I glance down to see what she's referring to. My smile fades. I stare at a small headline at the bottom of the page: 'Shinjuku bones not suspicious, police say'. The article is accompanied by a photograph of an excavation site. There is an inset picture of two skulls shining through the earth. Memories disturb my subconscious, like the beating wings of a dove.

Mrs Ono shakes her head. 'I hate to think what happened to them. Those poor souls deserve a proper funeral, don't you think?'

I blink and stare at her face. Foundation mottles her skin. Painted blood-red lips.

'Going somewhere special today?' I repeat, like a simpleton, tucking the newspaper under my arm. I try to make my voice sound bright. Surprise transforms Mrs Ono's features. It's the sort of reaction I dread as I grow older. The subtle missteps one makes.

'The summer festival is on today. Didn't you know?'

Ah—I forgot. I remembered last night, when the radio began to announce today's activities. But since waking I forgot all about the festival, the most important day of the year in our neighbourhood. A purification ceremony at the local shrine will take place in the morning. After that, *mikoshi* carried by teams of men will be paraded in the street to chanting and the beating of drums. The area will be flooded with people. I am relieved I don't have any plans to leave the apartment.

'Yes, of course. My memory . . .' My hand flutters at my brow. 'The ceremony at the shrine—is that where you're going?'

'I never miss it.' She inclines her head as she studies my face. 'You won't attend?'

'No, I don't think so. The weather—it's difficult for me . . .' I smile, hoping to send her on her way, but she doesn't move.

'You don't get out much, do you? Socially, I mean.'

I bristle at her comment, so characteristically misinformed. I regularly see my old hospital acquaintances, and I play *go* in Kanda with a group of friends every weekend, although I doubt she'd approve of the hours we spend staring at the board, arguing and drinking tea. I visit my sister's family every other week. The weeks when I don't visit, I always call Megumi to hear her news. She tells me what she did that day—*ikebana* at the cultural centre or a visit to her daughter, Hanako—before passing the phone to my great-nieces so I can say goodnight. I take daily walks in our neighbourhood park. I pride myself on remaining active—even though I'm now retired, I have to practise what I once preached.

Perhaps my irritation shows, because Mrs Ono doesn't wait for my response. 'I'm sorry. I shouldn't say such things. Only . . .' Her eyes wander to the inside of my apartment. 'In my experience, I've found it helps to go to these events.

It's something I've had to learn since my husband passed away.'
Mrs Ono straightens up. Her smile snaps back into place.
'Anyway, a bit of fresh air and sunlight in the morning is vital
for a healthy body, wouldn't you agree? If you decide to come
to the ceremony, look out for me near the front.'

She excuses herself and walks down the stairs, straw hat
bobbing. My heart thumps as I close the door. I walk towards
the study, annoyed. The way Mrs Ono talked, as if she was an
expert on my personal life. In the corridor, the dusty photo
of Kayoko catches my eye. Leaning against a tree beside the
Kamo River, she smiles uncertainly, her hair pinned in soft
waves around her face.

I enter the dim recess of the study and sit at my desk,
touching the cool tips of my fingers to my eyelids. When my
head clears, I switch on the lamp. It throws a circle of light onto
the newspaper before me. I take a deep breath and start to read.

'The investigator appointed by Shinjuku police to examine
the bones of more than thirty-five people discovered beneath the
former National Institute of Health building found no evidence
of violent crime. Eguchi Kenichi says the remains belong to
men and women who died at least twenty years ago. Based
on his findings, a criminal investigation will not take place.
However, some historians believe the bones are connected to
Unit 731—the military unit responsible for biological warfare
development during World War II—although no evidence
has been found to prove this link. Shinjuku ward officials
are pressing the Ministry for Health and Welfare to conduct
further tests on the remains, after their initial request was
denied last week.'

I pass a hand across my brow. The strain of the morning
has condensed into a faint pulse behind one eye. The heartbeat

of a long-buried memory. After all these years, for it to come back now.

In Broome, it was always there, like a shroud across the surface, the edges drawn tight. When I froze before the operation on the young Malay. Even in my dealings with Sister Bernice—her innocent attempts to learn more about me brought painful recollections to the fore. At camp, I strove to further distance myself from my past and assimilate better than I had in Broome. But just when I thought the worst was behind me, Stan's death had brought it back into sharp relief.

For years, I thought I would never be able to forget. But over time, the memories faded. The long hours I worked meant I was too busy to stop and reflect. Only once, in 1959, did the past threaten to overwhelm me. Mother was still alive then, and one morning she showed me a notice. 'Didn't you used to work for him?' It was an obituary for Ishii Shiro. According to the article, the 'former army general and gifted medical pioneer' died a peaceful death at home, surrounded by his family. He was sixty-nine. I snatched the paper from her and demanded to know why she had showed it to me. 'Because you knew him,' Mother said. 'I don't understand—why are you so upset?'

In the years after the war, I often thought of Sister Bernice. Once, on my way back from visiting Kayoko's grave, I saw a group of Catholic missionaries, the nuns' long black habits flapping in the March wind. I searched their faces for any resemblance to the pale oval countenance I remembered so well. Years later, when foreign businessmen and their wives became common in the city, seeing a particular sort of dark-haired Occidental woman would inspire nostalgia in me. By then, I was working at a hospital in Tsukiji, where many of the nurses were trainees, performing tasks with a fraction of Sister Bernice's assurance and much less of her grace. Bernice sometimes used to appear in my dreams, her white habit stirring as she approached. She never judged me in those dreams. Her face, turned towards me, was always full of light.

From the bottom drawer of my desk, I take out an envelope. In thick, calligraphic script it is addressed to 'Dr Tomokazu Ibaraki, Harvey Camp, Western Australia', but this has been crossed out and the address of my family home in Japan written next to it in pen. I reach in and remove the letter, now yellow and stiff with age. It crackles as I unfold it. Although it is dated January 1942, I received it in 1948, many years after I'd left the camps and returned to Japan. It must have been held by the censors and then forwarded to Loveday after my release. I will never know how it reached me, but the uncertainty of those thin, shaky lines, the writer's hand pausing over the unfamiliar arrangement of letters, makes me think that perhaps Officer McCubbin received it and forwarded it to me.

It was the only letter Sister Bernice ever wrote to me. When I first read it, I wept with regret. But in 1948, when I received the letter, I was still reeling from the shock of Kayoko's death. Although I longed to reach out to Bernice, I decided not to, for fear of the memories it would release. Some things are best left in the past.

And so the letter became a forgotten thing, like all the other mementos from that era—the wooden tag from the boy's neck and my rusted surgical tools. For years, they gathered dust in a box among my files. It wasn't until Emperor Showa's death earlier this year that I thought of them again. On the day of his funeral, I watched the televised procession. Seeing the self-defence personnel lining the wet streets, saluting the hearse as it passed, stirred something within me. I spent several hours searching for the box. When I finally found Bernice's letter, I pored over the small, cursive script for hours. Reading and rereading, until I had committed it to memory.

17th January 1942

Dear Dr Ibaraki,

First and foremost, I would like to apologise for my behaviour the other week. It was wrong of me to accost you at your home and question you. During my time at the hospital, you were kind to me in so many ways, so when I had the chance to return the kindness, I was disappointed you wouldn't allow me to. My emotions got the better of me, and when I finally realised my error, you were already gone. I am truly sorry we never had the chance to say goodbye.

There are so many things I would have liked to say to you. When we stood on the beach watching the lanterns and you told me about how you made them as a boy, I saw a part of you I'd never seen before. I was also grateful for all the books you lent me.

Whenever I felt we were growing closer, you seemed to step away. I recall your irritation when I found the tag inside the book. We all have our secrets, and I did not wish to know yours, but I longed to be able to relieve you of your burden. I wish you had shared a little more of yourself.

I would have liked to have said such things and more to you in person. Not doing so is my greatest regret. 'When I kept silence, my bones waxed old through my roaring all the day long.' (Psalms 32:3)

I pray for your wellbeing, Tomokazu, and for all that has been left unsaid.

Yours truly,

Bernice

I look up and the brightness of the lamp momentarily blinds me. Finally, Sister Bernice's words open up to me. I'd clung to the ideal of discretion, when it was courage—and forgiveness—I'd needed all along. My silence had been weak.

I shift in my seat. Hunger gnaws my stomach, but there is no time to eat. I reach for my writing pad and turn to a new page. The paper, at first glance crisp and white, on closer inspection bears the indentations of my pen pressing onto the page before it—ghostly lines, the almost imperceptible grooves of the past.

I imagine Mrs Ono's shock when she reads the paper next week. She might miss her morning walk in her hurry to call her friends. No doubt I'll be the subject of gossip for weeks. My *go* friends, my former hospital colleagues—everyone will be surprised to learn that mild-mannered Ibaraki did something such as this. My heart flutters when I think of my sister's family. Her grandchildren are of college age and might be taunted by their friends. But I will explain why I had to do it. In time, it will be worth the shame. I hope they understand.

I pick up my pen and begin to write. At first, the words come slowly, as I hesitate over every phrase. But soon the sentences start to flow.

'Dear Editor, My name is Ibaraki Tomokazu. I used to work at the Epidemic Prevention Laboratory within the Army Medical College in Tokyo. General Ishii Shiro was the head of our organisation. I am writing to you in the hope that you will publish my letter, because there is something the Japanese people should know.'

Acknowledgements

I would like to thank Annette Barlow, Christa Munns and the rest of the team at Allen & Unwin for their expertise and enthusiasm in bringing my novel to fruition. My thanks also go to my mentors Debra Adelaide and Delia Falconer for their guidance and faith in my work.

I gratefully acknowledge the assistance of the following organisations: the University of Technology, Sydney; the Japan Foundation Japanese-Language Institute, Kansai; the Ragdale Foundation (and the family of Alice Hayes); Virginia Center for the Creative Arts; Varuna, the Writers' House; Bundanon Trust; the Copyright Agency; and the Department of Industry, Innovation, Science, Research and Tertiary Education.

I would like to thank those who shared their time and wisdom to assist my research: Yuriko Nagata, Yasushi Torii, Shigeo Nasu, Norio Minami, Kazuyuki Kawamura, Masashi Hojo, Mary and Peter Jarzabkowski, Evelyn Suzuki, Maurice Shiosaki, Mutsumi Tsuda, Pearl Hamaguchi, Rosemary Gower, Max Scholz and the late James Sullivan. Also: Pam Oliver, Noreen Jones, Trevor Reed, Marie-José Michel, Mayu Kanamori, Robert Cross, Robert Rechner and family, Mary Rosewarner, Ken and Heather Wilkinson, Dorothy Wise, the Broome Historical Museum, the Adelaide Migration Museum, Tatura Museum,

Bill Ballantyne, Malcolm Thompson at the National Railway Museum and the staff at the National Archives of Australia.

I am indebted to friends, family and colleagues who provided feedback on the first draft: Carlos Mora, Aditi Gouvernel, Elizabeth Cowell and my parents. Others who gave input along the way include Kevin Maruno, Kim Jacobson, Jo Quach, Bill Woods, Marina Gold, Patrick Boyle, Kevin O'Brien and the fiction feedback group, Samantha Chang and the Iowa Writers' Workshop summer class of 2011.

Most of all, I am grateful for the support of my family. My mother deserves a special mention for her tireless translation work. My father and sister gave much-needed encouragement and advice. Evelyn, Don and Michelle have been enthusiastic champions of my writing. My heartfelt thanks go to my partner, Kris, who gave feedback at all stages and endured my frequent absences, and returned it with patience and love. I hope it was worth the wait.

To write the scenes set at Loveday internment camp, I consulted military records held by the National Archives of Australia and the Australian War Memorial, Yuriko Nagata's *Unwanted Aliens*, Susumu Shiobara's memoir in the *Journal of the Pacific Society*, and the internment diary of Miyakatsu Koike. Interviews I conducted with former internees and their relatives also shed light on living conditions and the emotional experience of internment. Rosemary Hemphill's *The Master Pearler's Daughter* provided valuable insight into life in prewar Broome. For the scenes set in Japan, I referred to books and articles by witnesses and historians such as Yoko Gunji, Sheldon Harris, Hal Gold and others.